# COLD PURSUIT

# Peril in the Park Series

Avalanche
Dangerous Ground
Wildfire
Cold Pursuit

# COLD PURSUIT

Book Four of Peril in the Park

By
## Gayla K. Hiss

To the Fountain of Living Water, Jesus Christ,
who makes all things new.

Why spend money on what is not bread,
and your labor on what does not satisfy?

Isaiah 55:2

# CHAPTER ONE

FAITH CHANDLER STARED AT THE MAN walking in the distance. She couldn't get a good look at his face, but something about him reminded her of Jake Mitchell. When he disappeared behind the lodge where she would be staying, she decided it must be her mind playing tricks on her. After all, what would Jake be doing in Moose Run, Montana on a Sunday night in mid-December?

Something pelted her on the back of the head. Spinning around, she glared at her friend, Shelly Dickerson, who was making another snowball.

Shelly laughed. "Just checking to make sure you hadn't frozen in place. What were you staring at anyway?"

Faith bent to pack a snowball in her gloved hands. "The ghost of Christmas past." She raised her arm and aimed. The sudden ring of her phone caused her to miss, and the snowball landed at Shelly's feet.

Eying her, Shelly put a hand on her hip. "I thought we agreed to turn off our phones when we got here."

Faith shrugged as she pulled hers from her pocket. "Old habits—maybe it's about a job."

A spark of skepticism flared in Shelly's brown eyes. "Who are you kidding? You're addicted to that thing, and you know it."

"Shh." Faith checked the caller ID. No name, and a number she didn't recognize. "Hello?"

"Faith, it's Tad."

Despite the December cold, the sound of Tad's voice stoked an angry fire. "Goodbye—"

"Wait! It's about Monica."

Faith scoffed. "Let me guess. You two are engaged."

"Engaged? No." After a brief pause, his voice became oddly somber. "Monica is…missing. I was hoping maybe you'd heard from her."

The phone slipped through Faith's fingers to the blanket of snow on the ground.

"What is it?" Shelly asked.

Faith managed a reassuring look. "Nothing. I'm fine."

Tad's voice summoned Faith through the phone at her feet. "Faith, are you still there?"

She hesitated to pick it up. Was this for real or a sick ploy of Tad's to get her to talk to him? He wouldn't dare call her now, unless it were life or death. Then again, this was the same guy who'd dumped her for Monica, in addition to beating Faith out of a promotion—while she got a pink slip.

When Shelly had invited her on the free trip to Yellowstone National Park, Faith jumped at the chance to get away from Tad and her problems at home. However, now that she'd arrived at the lodge, her problems seemed to be following her. Maybe she should have powered off her phone, but she needed to find a job and hoped to hear from the companies she'd sent résumés and applications to.

Tad's voice called to her again. "Faith? Faith, if you're there, please answer."

Finally, she reached for the phone, wiped it down, and forced it to her ear. "Yeah, I'm here."

"You had me worried for a minute."

"How long has Monica been missing?"

A brief pause. "Four days. It's been on the news. I'm surprised you didn't know."

Despite her falling out with Monica, Faith hoped she was all right.

"Hey, are you at home? I was hoping I could stop by. You and Monica were friends and—"

"That friendship ended, thanks to you. Unless you have more news about Monica, do not contact me again." She ended the call and punched the off button.

With a disgusted expression, Shelly shook her head. "That was Tad-the-cad, wasn't it?"

Faith was still steaming. "He must have a new number.

Otherwise, I wouldn't have answered."

"After everything he's put you through, he's got a lot of nerve calling you now."

Faith's heavy sigh emitted a vapor in the cold air. "He told me that Monica is missing."

Shelly flinched. "What?"

"He thought I might have heard from her and wanted to come over."

Her friend crossed her arms and gave Faith a pointed look. "You'd better watch out. I wouldn't put it past that guy to try to worm his way back into your life."

Faith stashed her phone in her pocket. "Don't worry, I'm wise to him now. Besides, he's in Texas and we're in Montana. He won't bother me way out here."

"Let's hope not." Shaking her finger, Shelly scolded, "Maybe that will teach you to keep your phone off for the rest of this trip."

Jake Mitchell waved the tour group roster in the face of his older cousin and employer, Chip Reynolds. "Tell me this isn't who I think it is."

Seated at his desk, Chip shrugged. "Okay, it's not who you think it is—who are we talking about anyway?"

"Faith Chandler. What is she doing in my tour group?"

"Oh, that." Chip leaned back in his chair.

"Yeah, that. So what's up?"

"That's what we do for a living, Jake. People pay to go on a tour of Yellowstone. I assign them to a tour group. You lead the tour group…"

"But you assigned her to *my* tour group."

"You had openings. Besides, it's been ages since you two broke up. Aren't you the least bit curious to see her again?"

"No. That ship sank a long time ago."

"Good. Then there shouldn't be any problem with her being in your group, right?" A smirk escaped Chip's serious expression.

Jake clenched his fists, resisting the urge to give his cousin a fat lip. "You did this on purpose."

A knock at the door interrupted them, followed by the soft footsteps of a person entering the office. "Excuse me. I wonder if you could help us."

The familiar woman's voice stopped Jake cold. He didn't bother turning around. He didn't need to.

"We're here for the Yellowstone Christmas Tour. Do you know where the orientation is?"

Chip jumped from his chair and came around the desk. "Well, well, well, look who's here."

Jake kept his back to her, glimpsing Chip from the corner of his eye.

"Chip?" the woman said. "Is it really you?"

He rubbed his thinning short hair. "Minus a few hair follicles."

"Wow, it's great to see you. What a nice surprise."

"You too. Life must be treating you well, Faith. You haven't changed a bit."

She laughed. "I don't know about that. You always did exaggerate. But it is good to see you again."

Jake slowly rotated his body. He couldn't put the inevitable off any longer.

Faith had finished giving Chip a hug. When she glanced at Jake, she froze.

For the first time since his freshman year in college, he stood face-to-face with the only woman who had ever stolen his heart and broken it. He regarded her now as he would a jagged fragment of stained glass—captivating, yet dangerous to the touch. From the anxious way she fidgeted with a long lock of brown hair, she was equally ill-at-ease.

Chip was wrong. She had changed. Her eyes appeared even bluer than Jake remembered—and she was like a stranger to him now.

She broke the ice with a tentative smile. "Hello, Jake."

He kept his distance. "Hello."

When she approached, he drew back.

Chip put a firm hand on his shoulder, blocking his retreat. "Jake's going to be your tour guide."

"Oh." Her eyes widened with surprise—and possibly horror—as the color drained from her face.

Jake took solace from her reaction. After all, why should he be the only miserable one on this tour?

She cleared her throat and gestured to the shorter, dark-haired woman with her. "This is my friend, Shelly."

Extending his hand, Jake greeted her with the graciousness he'd withheld from Faith. "Welcome aboard, Shelly."

She grinned excitedly. "Thanks. I couldn't believe it when Chip called and told me I won the contest for a free tour."

Jake shifted his gaze to Chip. "A free tour?"

He shrugged. "It's a new promotion. I was going to tell you about it."

After aiming a quick glare at his employer, Jake addressed Shelly again. "Well, congratulations. It appears your friend isn't quite as excited as you are."

Faith spoke up, her tone indignant. "On the contrary, Jake, I'm happy to be here."

He glanced her way. "Really. If this is you happy, I'd hate to see you ecstatic."

Shelly slanted her head. "So how do you two know each other?"

Chip slipped in between Jake and Faith, putting his arms around them. "We're all from the same hometown in Colorado." He eyed Jake. "It's like old times, isn't it?"

Amusement flickered in Shelly's eyes. "Small world, huh?"

"Yeah," Jake said. *That and Chip giving away free tours when he can't afford it.* As his cousin returned to his desk, Jake noticed Faith's tense expression.

She glanced down, twisting her hair around her index finger, a habit from her youth whenever she was anxious or disturbed.

Why was she upset? She was the one who broke it off with him, and that was seven years ago.

When she lifted her gaze, the color of her eyes had

darkened to a deep shade of indigo.

Concern broke through Jake's hardened shell. "What's wrong?"

Stiffening, she looked away. "Nothing."

Shelly filled in the awkward silence. "She just learned that her friend is missing."

He rubbed his face. "Oh…sorry."

Crossing her arms, Faith stared at the floor. "She's not my friend. It came as a shock, that's all."

Jake cleared his throat uncomfortably. "It's really none of my business." Not that she would care what he thought anyway. She'd made it clear when she walked out of his life that she wanted nothing more to do with him.

Chip nudged Jake, interrupting his thoughts. "The orientation will start pretty soon. We should be going." His cousin turned and addressed the women. "Let me get my jacket, then Jake and I will walk with you next door to the lodge."

Jake followed him into the back room and closed the door so the women couldn't hear. Alone with Chip, he spoke in a low growl. "This isn't going to work. You need to move them to a different tour group."

"Relax. It isn't going to kill you to be nice to her for a few days. Besides, the other groups are full."

"What's this about a contest and a free tour? Since when do we give tours away?"

"It's all part of my new marketing campaign. If Faith and Shelly have a great time, maybe they'll give us a testimonial for our website and some of our ads. We need the publicity."

Jake scoffed. "So now you're giving away free vacations?"

"I'll admit it was a bit of a gamble, but you can make it pay off. You're the best guide I have."

"I wouldn't bet on Faith for an endorsement. I doubt spending a week with me is her idea of a dream vacation, even if it is free. You could have at least given me a heads-up that she was coming."

"I didn't know myself until Shelly sent me an email last

week that said Faith would be accompanying her on the tour. To tell you the truth, I thought it must be someone else with Faith's name." Chip used his most persuasive tone. "You know, there was a time when you two wouldn't have minded being together for a whole week. Maybe you can recreate a little of that magic now."

Jake rolled his eyes. "You're dreaming, Chip. We're not kids anymore. Why don't you swap the two of them with a couple in a different group?"

Chip shook his head. "It's too late. The rosters have already been printed along with the other handouts, and they've all been delivered to the lodge for the orientation." He glanced at his watch. "We'd better hurry. I want to get there a little early."

Jake crossed his arms, not budging.

After a brief pause, Chip sighed. "All you have to do is treat her like you would any customer. If you won't do it for me, do it for Beth and the girls. Money's tight and Christmas is coming. They've had to make sacrifices for this business too, and they deserve a better Christmas than I can afford this year."

At the mention of Chip's wife and kids, Jake eased up.

"By the way, Leslie Turner and her cameraman will also be in your tour group."

"The reporter from the cable news channel? Did she win a free tour too?"

"Not exactly. I invited her to do a special feature about Yellowstone in winter. It's all part of my—"

"Marketing campaign," Jake finished for him. "What other surprises do you have in store for me on this tour?"

Chip held up his hands. "That's it. Honest. So what do you say? Are you in?"

Jake scratched his head. He almost regretted that he'd let his cousin talk him into working for him as a guide two years ago, though he had always paid him on time even when money was tight, plus the tips were good. "Do I have a choice?"

"I knew I could count on you." Chip gave him a hearty pat on the back and turned toward the door to the main office.

Though Jake wasn't happy about the arrangement, he decided he would make the best of things. After all, he was a professional. Faith, on the other hand, was the wild card.

He strode ahead of Chip and blocked the door with his hand. "I'll lead the tour, but if this publicity stunt of yours backfires, it won't be my fault. Faith is the one you should be worried about. The way things are going, she won't last a day, much less a week."

# CHAPTER TWO

Walking beside Shelly, Faith followed the men to the Moose Run Lodge for the orientation. Though it was only a short distance away, the crunching of their footsteps in the snow seemed to amplify the awkwardness she felt from Jake's frosty reception.

This wasn't a vacation. It was a nightmare. First, the news about Monica. And now Faith would have to spend an entire week with the man she'd spent years trying to forget. Maybe she should have done more research before accepting Shelly's invitation to join her on this tour. Impulsively, Faith had agreed, eager for any excuse to get away. In retrospect, a tropical island might have been a better choice. *Oh, Lord, help me make it through this tour with Jake—and please let Monica be all right.*

Chip stopped at the main entrance to the lodge. "Here we are."

Jake politely opened the door to the lobby. "After you, ladies." Despite his cordial tone, a spark flared in his eyes when Faith approached.

Fixing her gaze forward, she brushed past him and strode inside the rustic lodge.

When Shelly joined her in the entrance hall, Faith waited for Chip to show them where to go next.

He gestured to a corridor. "The orientation is in the meeting room at the end of the hall."

Faith and Shelly let him lead, while Jake lagged behind.

Proceeding through the hallway, they passed a laundromat and exercise room before Chip stopped at another door and opened it for them. "Here we are." He glanced at his watch. "The orientation will begin in about ten minutes. Help yourselves to the complimentary beverages and snacks."

Going inside with Shelly, Faith found a group of about thirty people milling around, chatting excitedly about the tour.

The friendly, cheerful atmosphere brought welcome relief from the tension with Jake.

Shelly stopped at a table near the door to browse park and tour brochures, while Jake and Chip began mingling with the other people in the room.

Thirsty, Faith spotted a pitcher of water at the far end of the brochure table where the refreshments had been set out. She went there and poured herself a glass.

Casually sipping her drink, she observed Jake from a distance. The last time she'd seen him he was only nineteen. Still a boy, really. His hair was shorter now and a shade darker than the golden sun-streaks of his youth, but his pensive blue eyes and boyish dimples hadn't changed.

While he talked to other guests, he removed his jacket and laid it on a chair. Faith's eyes gravitated to his broad shoulders and athletic body, accentuated by his dark gray sweater and blue jeans. Though time had chiseled away some of his appealing youthful features, his new rugged masculinity was even more attractive.

As if he'd heard her thoughts, he glanced in her direction.

Embarrassed to be caught staring, she quickly turned and shifted her focus to Chip. Watching her old friend shake hands and schmooze with his guests was a pleasant diversion from Jake's perceptive gaze. Other than Chip prematurely losing his hair, he was still the same born salesman Faith remembered. No one could beat him when it came to fundraising. Jake, on the other hand, had always been more into sports and academics.

Shelly walked up to her and grabbed a cookie from a tray. "Mmm. These look good."

Faith took one also. "I hope the orientation doesn't take very long. We still need to unpack and eat dinner."

She was still munching on the cookie when a tall young woman with straight blonde hair approached. "Hello, ladies, where are you from?"

"Dallas, Texas," Shelly replied.

Jake came over and smiled at the statuesque woman to his

left. "Hello, Jillian. I see you've met Faith and Shelly."

Finishing her snack, Faith noted Jake's amiable tone with Jillian, a sharp contrast to how he'd greeted her.

He turned to her and Shelly. "Jillian works at the lodge and is helping us out with the orientation tonight."

His attractive assistant zeroed in on Faith. "Which tour group are you in?"

"Jake's," Faith said, hoping Jillian might want to switch her to a different one.

"Lucky you." Tossing him a doting glance, the woman's shoulder-length hair swished like fringe. When she looked at Faith again, her cool gaze belied her practiced smile. "He's in high demand."

Jake winced slightly and crossed his arms, appearing uncomfortable with the woman's praise.

Faith couldn't help noticing his bare ring finger. Had he really remained single all these years?

Jillian eyed her, then clutched his arm and gazed at him. "We're a team. If there's anything we can do to assist you, don't hesitate to let us know."

*Uh, how about booking me on the next flight to Dallas?* Faith cleared her throat. "There is something…"

Jillian pried her eyes away from Jake. "Yes?"

Faith gestured to the three circles of folding chairs. "Where should we sit?"

Jake pointed to the far one. "My group will be in the very back."

Eager to get away, Faith left him and his admirer and strode across the room. When she reached the last circle, she grabbed the first empty chair that faced away from the couple. After plopping down in her seat, she took off her jacket and inhaled a deep breath. This could be the longest week of her life.

In a span of only a few days, she'd not only lost her job, but her laptop had been stolen, her one-time friend had gone missing, and now she was in a winter wilderness about to begin a tour with a man who couldn't stand her. The practical, responsible side of her said she should be searching for another job instead of squandering precious time on this boondoggle of a trip, even if the tour was free.

Two men who looked like they could be brothers wandered over and sat to her left. The man farthest away was talking about the weather. "The thermometer outside says it's twenty-eight degrees. I'm surprised it's this warm."

The one sitting next to her responded. "It won't last long. The forecast is calling for an arctic blast later this week."

Packing for the trip, Faith had been so consumed with other things she hadn't paid much attention to the weather reports for Yellowstone, though she knew it would be colder than Dallas. Now she wondered if she'd brought enough wool socks and thermal underwear. At least she'd splurged on a new parka and snow boots for the trip, though she couldn't really afford them right now.

She spoke to the man beside her. "Excuse me for interrupting. How cold is it supposed to get?"

When he turned his head, he paused and smiled at her. "In the single digits." He shifted his body in her direction. "By the way, my name is Alec Underwood." After shaking her hand, he gestured to the man next to him. "And he's Rick Morrison."

Faith introduced herself and made light of the forecast. "Temperatures that cold might be a shock to my system since I'm from Texas."

The men chuckled. "We're from Atlanta," Alec said. The hint of gray peppering his wavy, dark hair made her think he was at least five years older than his friend, who she guessed was about thirty. Though Rick's hair was also dark and wavy, he didn't have the older man's sophisticated looks, but his longer and narrower face gave the impression he might be the more intelligent of the two.

As Alec scooted his chair closer to Faith, she detected a spark of interest in his eye. Under different circumstances she might have been attracted to him. Still recovering from Tad's betrayal and having Jake to contend with, all she wanted right now was a fun, relaxing vacation without complications.

Shelly took the empty seat to her right. "Why didn't you wait for me?"

Deflecting the question, Faith introduced her to the two men. "We were just talking about the arctic blast forecasted for later this week."

Shelly gamely waved it off. "What's a little cold weather? That's why we brought warm clothes, right?"

Faith smiled at her friend's positive attitude. Athletic and outdoorsy, Shelly would probably relish the cold weather ahead. She was always ready for any sort of adventure. Faith admired that about her, and how she took life in stride. She didn't even pack a hair dryer for this trip. Her short, low maintenance hair fell neatly into place without it. Faith, on the other hand, had packed a hair dryer and curling iron among the many necessities in her luggage. Her long, wavy hair had a will of its own, and she'd spent a good part of her life trying to tame it.

Despite the forbidding forecast, Faith had to admit she would still rather be in Yellowstone than at home alone, searching through job listings. Glancing over her shoulder, her lighter mood dipped when she saw Jake walking toward them. Touching a lock of her hair, she twirled it around her finger.

Shelly elbowed her in the ribs. "What's the story behind you and Jake?"

Hoping to diffuse her friend's curiosity, Faith acted casual. "I knew him a long time ago. We sort of grew up together."

"He's not your old flame, is he?" Shelly's naturally loud voice amplified with interest.

Before Faith could reply, Alec inquired in her other ear. "Old flame?"

Surprised that he had been listening, she glanced his way. "A long time ago." Her gaze found Jake again. He had stopped to talk to Chip, who handed him a small stack of paper.

While they were conversing, Jillian strutted over with a hot beverage and offered it to Jake. The way she carried on, touching his arm and batting her eyes, it was obvious she was making a play for him. Jake's feelings toward her were less clear. Though he didn't reciprocate her overt touching and flirting, he didn't rebuff her either. Maybe he was only tolerating her to be polite—or maybe he liked her attention but was keeping things professional for the public.

Faith vaguely heard Alec respond to her earlier comment that she and Jake were history.

"Good, that keeps things simple."

His words didn't quite register as Faith was more interested in the goings-on between Jake and Jillian. What *things* was Alec talking about?

Rick's snarky tone interjected. "If you'd stayed at home, Alec, maybe *I* would have more time for relationships."

*Relationships?* Faith realized she'd better forget about Jake and Jillian and pay closer attention to her conversation with the two men beside her.

With a dismissive wave, Alec brushed off his friend. "Ignore Rick. He's mad because I decided to accompany him on this tour."

"This was supposed to be a vacation from work," Rick said. "With you here, I'll never get a moment's peace."

Faith interrupted their bickering. "You two work together?"

Rick rolled his eyes. "He's my boss."

Ignoring his disgruntled employee, Alec grinned at Faith. "And now that I've had the pleasure of meeting you, I'm glad I tagged along."

Shelly whispered in Faith's other ear. "Whoa, he's laying it on thick."

Catching her friend smirking, Faith gave her a dry look.

By now, others had joined the group, filling in the circle. All the seats were taken except three, one directly across from Faith and two next to Shelly.

A husky female voice spoke from behind them. "So where are you girls from?"

Faith twisted around in her chair.

A woman with perfectly coifed, stiff-looking, bright red hair waited for an answer.

"Dallas, Texas," Shelly said.

The redhead texted into her phone as if taking notes. "And your names?"

Bothered by the woman's questions, Faith interrupted. "Excuse me, but who are you?"

The nosy female appeared indignant. "I'm Leslie Turner—with News First Network." She waited a moment, as if expecting Faith and Shelly to recognize her.

Shelly finally responded. "You mean the cable news channel?"

"That's right. I'm doing a special feature on Yellowstone. Smile for the camera, girls." Leslie grinned, exposing perfect white teeth as she waved to a person behind them. "Meet Phil. He's my cameraman."

Shelly and Faith slowly rotated their heads until they spotted the jean-clad young man with curly brown hair, holding a large video camera. They exchanged surprised looks.

"You're only filming the orientation, right?" Faith asked in a hopeful voice.

The redhead took a seat on the other side of Shelly. "No, we're here for the entire tour. And since we're going to be in the same group, I'm looking forward to getting to know all about you."

Faith cringed. This was supposed to be a vacation, not a reality TV show.

Meanwhile, Jake took the empty chair across from Faith and began the session. "Hello, everyone. My name is Jake Mitchell, and I'll be your tour guide this week. Our group will be known as the Elk group. The others are Bison and Grizzly."

"I can't wait to learn more about *him*," Leslie said to Shelly in a loud whisper.

Overhearing, Faith's eyes darted to Leslie. The thought of Jake with either the brash woman or Jillian churned her stomach.

He continued the orientation. "Since we'll be together for the next few days, why don't we start off by introducing ourselves? I'll go first. I'm originally from Colorado. I also spent some time in Alaska before moving to Montana. I've been a guide in Yellowstone for the past two years. My favorite hobbies are cross-country skiing, hiking, and photography."

"Are you married or single?" Leslie called out.

He paused and chuckled softly, scratching his face. "Single."

His gaze wandered to Faith and stopped there long enough to light her cheeks on fire.

Thankfully, he looked away and changed the subject. "Before we go on, I should introduce our special guests, Leslie Turner and her cameraman Phil Wagner, with News First Network. They are doing a special feature on Yellowstone."

The group buzzed with excitement.

"I hope that won't be a problem for any of you. If it is, please let me know."

Faith wasn't crazy about the idea but didn't want to spoil everyone else's fifteen minutes of fame.

When no one objected, Jake picked up a small stack of paper on the floor and began passing it around. "These are release forms, giving NFN permission to film you on our tour."

Shelly gave Faith an eager smile. "Maybe it'll go viral, and we'll be famous."

Faith sighed. *A private island would definitely have been a better choice for a vacation.*

After the forms were distributed, Jake spoke again. "Now that everyone knows who I am—and my marital status," he paused while the group chuckled, "let's resume the introductions. Leslie, why don't you tell us more about yourself?"

The reporter beamed as she began talking. After she went over her education, how many places she'd worked, and the many awards she'd received, she finally seemed to be wrapping up. "...and most recently, I've been at News First Network for six years—and I live in the Big Apple." Once she'd concluded, she flashed Jake a bold smile.

He gave her a polite nod and kept the introductions going, moving on to Shelly.

She waved to the group. "Hi, I'm Shelly Dickerson. I'm a

flight attendant from Dallas, Texas."

"Thanks, Shelly," Jake said. "Faith?"

Faith quickly told them her full name and said she was also from Dallas.

When she'd finished, Leslie prompted her. "You forgot to tell us your occupation."

Annoyed that Leslie wouldn't let her off the hook, Faith hesitated. "Well, I was an accountant for Syngexas Enterprises until a couple of weeks ago. I'm currently unemployed." She lowered her gaze, unable to face the curious stares of the group. It was bad enough to be laid off after she'd worked so hard and invested so much time in the company, but Syngexas had let her go right before Christmas. The only reason she'd been given was that the company was downsizing.

Leslie responded in a shrewd voice. "If you worked for Syngexas, then you must have heard about the CEO resigning today. There's talk of a scandal and a shakeup going on there."

Stunned by the news, Faith was at a loss for words.

Jake mercifully spoke up. "Alec, you're next."

The man gestured to himself and his employee. "I'm Alec and this is Rick. We're both from Atlanta and work for my family's consulting firm, Underwood-Stanley."

Following the two businessmen, Norman and Ruth Bauer introduced themselves. They were from Idaho. Faith guessed they were in their mid-seventies. In their sporty fleece jogging togs, they appeared better suited for a round of golf on the Senior Tour than braving the elements. She wondered how they would fare in the bitter cold.

Ruth spent the next few minutes talking about their many children, grandchildren, and great grandchildren until Jake finally had to interrupt. "Thank you, Ruth. Do you have anything else to add, Norman?"

The patient man shook his head. "No, I think she's done enough talking for the both of us."

That drew a chuckle from the circle. Then the group heard from the last two—Mary, a sweet middle-aged woman from Portland, Oregon, and Donna, from Seattle, Washington, who appeared to be about ten years older than Faith. Neither mentioned a significant other, so Faith assumed they were both single.

With the exception of the nosy reporter, and Jake's cold shoulder, the group seemed pleasant enough.

The introductions over, Jake told them what to expect for the week, how to dress and what to bring each day on the tour. "By the way," he said, "cell service isn't reliable in most of the places we'll be going, and the subfreezing temps can disable your phone. If that happens, bring it inside. It should work again once it warms up."

Shelly shot Faith a teasing grin. "Maybe that will keep you off your phone this week."

Faith rolled her eyes, though she had to admit the idea of going so long without her phone made her antsy.

Jake continued. "Our tour officially begins tomorrow morning at nine a.m. We'll meet in front of the lodge and ride into the park for our first stop, Mammoth Hot Springs." He went over the daily schedule, handed out more forms for the group to fill out, and answered their remaining questions.

When the orientation ended, Shelly peered at Faith. "Before we bring our luggage to our room, why don't we take a walk? The woman at the front desk mentioned there's an outdoor skating rink on the other side of the woods behind the lodge. I want to check it out."

Faith wasn't as keen on the idea as Shelly. "I don't know. First, I need to find a paper or watch the news to see what's going on with Syngexas."

Shelly shook her head. "Oh, no, you don't. Whatever is going on there isn't your concern anymore."

It took a moment for Faith to realize her friend was right. Even so, it was hard for her to let it go and stop caring about the company she had worked for. However, like her history with Jake, that part of her life was over. It was time to move on. She straightened with resolve. "So where is this ice rink?"

"Atta-girl." Shelly patted her lightly on the shoulder.

After they put on their coats, they stepped outside and

followed the shoveled pathway lit by strings of white Christmas lights. It led them through the woods to a frozen pond where a dozen skaters glided across the icy surface by lamplight. Near the rink, sweet scents of cocoa and apple cider wafted from the steaming mugs of spectators who chatted casually near the warmth of a bonfire.

The scene took Faith back to her youth when she, Jake, and his younger brother, Joey, skated on their neighborhood pond. She hadn't thought about that in years. The two boys were her closest neighbors and friends growing up. Joey always kept her laughing and entertained. It was Jake, however, who captured her heart.

Shelly's voice interrupted her thoughts. "Faith? I asked if you want to go skating."

Tired and hungry from the long day, she still didn't want to disappoint her energetic friend. "Maybe tomorrow. It's getting late, and we need to eat and unload your car, remember?"

Releasing a long sigh, Shelly nodded. "Let's take care of our luggage first. Then we'll grab dinner."

As they started to leave, Shelly stopped and jerked her head a couple of times toward the rink. "Don't look now, but I think we're being watched."

Faith spotted Leslie staring at them from the other side of the ice.

"Call me paranoid, but there's something about that woman I don't trust." Shelly's words echoed Faith's thoughts. "I'd like to knock that smug expression off her face with a well-aimed snowball."

That caused Faith to laugh. "Don't worry. As soon as she realizes there's nothing interesting about us worth reporting, she'll get bored and leave us alone."

Shelly sniffed the air. "Mmm, that cider smells too good to pass up. Wait here. I'm going to buy us a couple to go."

While Shelly walked to the line at the small concessions stand, Leslie's mention of the strange developments at Syngexas reentered Faith's mind, along with Tad's news about Monica's disappearance. If anyone knew what was going on inside her former company, it would be Tad, but she'd rather remain in the dark than call him. At least she didn't have to see him in the office anymore. She only had Jake to deal with now—but that might be the biggest test of all.

While she waited near the bonfire, she noticed Leslie was gone. Maybe she'd found someone else to spy on.

A boy of about seven approached and handed Faith a blank envelope.

"What's this?" she asked.

He shrugged. "Someone told me to give it to you."

Amused and curious, Faith bent to the child's level. "Who was it?"

His face scrunched in a serious frown. "I promised not to tell. It's a secret."

"Oh, I see. Well, thank you."

Faith smiled as the boy ran off and disappeared into the small crowd of people near the pond. Curious, she opened the envelope and removed the slip of paper inside. As she read the printed words, an arctic chill invaded her jacket and shot up her spine.

*I'm watching you and keeping track of your every move, so you'd better keep things under wraps—or you'll get worse than a lump of coal this Christmas!*

She stared at the ominous note, mystified. Was it a sick joke, or a serious threat? Her name wasn't on the envelope so maybe it was meant for someone else. Scanning the area, she searched for any suspicious-looking characters, but without more clues, it would be impossible to identify the one responsible.

The boy! He knew what the person looked like. Faith searched the area around the rink, asking the people there if they'd seen a kid matching his description. No one had, and he was nowhere to be found.

Realizing he'd probably left by now, she reluctantly halted her search and returned to the bonfire. Reading the note again, she examined it more closely. What did it mean to *keep things under wraps*? Though she didn't fully understand it, the threatening intent of the message was clear. If she failed to meet the sender's cryptic demand, there would be consequences. But what kind of consequences?

# CHAPTER THREE

Faith couldn't shake the uneasy feeling of being watched. It had followed her from the skating rink to the parking lot of the lodge, where she and Shelly had retrieved their things from Shelly's SUV and loaded them onto the luggage cart.

Earlier, when Shelly had returned with the cider, Faith didn't tell her about the note. She didn't want to worry her needlessly. Faith still hoped it was only a prank or delivered to her by mistake. She considered reporting it to the police, but what if the author of the note found out? Would he or she make good on the threat? She banished the thought from her mind. No need to overreact. It was probably only a joke, and she didn't want to cry wolf and waste the police's valuable time. Better to wait until she could find out more or something else happened.

Shelly closed the back of her SUV and locked it, then the two guided the full, heavy cart to the lodge entrance. While Shelly held the door open, Faith pushed the cart into the lobby.

Stopping for a quick break, Faith's growling stomach reminded her that they hadn't eaten a full meal since noon, and it was almost eight. "One of us should go to the front desk and ask for a recommendation for dinner."

"I will," Shelly replied and went to speak to an attendant.

Waiting for her to return, Faith eyed Shelly's two small bags and backpack resting on top of the mountain of luggage she had brought. How on earth had her friend packed everything she needed in them?

Lifting her gaze, Faith scanned the old, frontier-style lobby. Its rustic log walls, vaulted timber-beam ceiling, and hardwood floors provided a warm and inviting refuge from the cold, complete with a cozy fire in the stone fireplace.

A giant Christmas tree, dressed in red and gold ornaments,

stood as the centerpiece in the entrance hall. It was complemented by evergreen swags and wreaths hung over the fireplace and on the walls.

The festive lodge couldn't exude more Christmas cheer if it were at the North Pole—yet the holidays always filled Faith with mixed emotions. On one hand, this time of year reminded her of the miracle of Jesus's birth. On the other, it brought back painful memories from her past that she wanted to put behind her. Seeing Jake again had caused those to resurface. Since her breakup with him right before Christmas seven years ago, winters had become drearier, and the holidays, a time of loneliness and regret.

Adjacent to the lobby was a small gift shop. It probably had a newspaper stand. Rather than turn on her phone, she could scan the headlines to see if there were any stories about Syngexas.

Since Shelly was still busy at the front desk, Faith quietly left the luggage cart and slipped into the store. The newsstand was close to the entrance, and she found a business paper right away. She was in the middle of reading the front-page story when Shelly's voice startled her. "Aha! I knew it. I can't leave you alone for a second."

Ignoring her friend's rebuke, Faith pointed to the headline. "Look, here's an article about Syngexas. It says they're being investigated by the Feds."

Shelly's eyes darted to the page. "That's odd. You didn't get wind of anything fishy going on when you worked there, did you?"

"Nothing that would warrant a Federal investigation. However, I worked in the accounting department for a small subsidiary, not corporate…" A possible connection entered Faith's mind.

"What is it?"

"Monica worked in corporate accounting. I wonder if she knew about any of this."

"Don't go there. Maybe she needed a vacation and didn't want anyone to know where she was going." Shelly gave Faith an encouraging smile. "Let's switch to a more pleasant topic, like deciding where to eat."

Still bothered by the nagging questions on top of the suspicious note, Faith did her best to ignore them while she and Shelly made dinner plans. A nice relaxing meal was exactly what she needed to take her mind off of her worries for the rest of the evening.

The Bison Grill was busy, even for a Sunday night in December. Jake sat at his favorite booth near the warm fireplace as Gene Autry's classic rendition of Rudolph the Red-Nosed Reindeer played in the background.

Stirring his piping-hot cup of cocoa, topped with whipped cream, Jake took solace from the aftermath of seeing Faith again. Chip owed him big time for this. Maybe a special bonus for pain and suffering.

A woman's voice interrupted his solitude. "Well, hello."

Jake peered up.

Jillian gestured to his hot beverage. "I think I'll have one of those too." She joined him, uninvited, sliding down the opposite bench. "Looks like you could use a little cheering up."

He whisked his spoon in his drink. The last thing he wanted right now was company. "Actually, I'm good."

That didn't stop her. She raised her hands in dramatic fashion. "Behold, I bring you tidings of great joy."

He placed his spoon down and rested his hand on the table. "Okay, what's up, Jillian?"

A spark lit in her eyes. "Rumor has it that Ned Watson plans to retire in a couple of years."

"I heard."

"So the park service is advertising a position for his apprentice. Whoever lands the job will eventually take over Ned's responsibilities as the land resources manager for Yellowstone. I think you should apply."

"I already have a job."

She frowned at his response. "Jake, this is a shot at a real career with a future. I know Chip is your cousin and everything, but let's face it, your job is going nowhere. Your talents are being wasted as a guide. In this new position, you could make a real difference in Yellowstone. Instead of just educating people about the park, you'd have the power and influence to protect its natural resources."

He decided not to let on that he'd already applied for the position. Ned had told him last week he would be retiring and encouraged Jake to go for it. Working for Chip had been good, but Jillian was right—it was time to move on. The truth was, he'd been considering making a change for months. "Thanks for the tip."

She lectured in a stern voice. "Jake, this kind of opportunity doesn't come knocking every day." Her lips curled in a cunning grin. "You know my dad is good friends with Ned's boss. All he has to do is put in a good word and the job will be yours."

If it wasn't so ridiculous, Jake would have been offended by her meddling. "Your father wouldn't give me the time of day much less a job reference. Besides, I'd want to get the job on my own merits."

"Don't be so noble. Let me help you. I'm sure I can convince Daddy to overlook those minor transgressions you reported to the park officials—as long as you don't make a habit of it."

Jake wasn't amused or impressed. "Jillian, I have no doubt of your influence over your father, but that's not how I operate. You told me about the job. Leave the rest to me." He didn't want to be rude. However, this wasn't up for debate.

She sighed and rolled her eyes. "Eventually, you'll come around and see that I only want what's best for you, but since this is obviously a touchy subject, let's talk about Christmas instead." She fluttered her eyelashes. "I'd like you to spend the holiday with my parents and me at their cabin."

He bristled at the idea. "Given how your father feels about me, I don't think that's a good idea."

She tilted her head to one side. "I told you, I can take care of that. Don't you want to come?"

Hesitating, he searched for a polite way to decline. "I wouldn't want to intrude on your family's holiday."

She patted his hand. "You wouldn't be intruding. It'll be a great opportunity for my parents to get to know you better, and you and Daddy can mend fences."

Since politeness didn't work, he tried a different tack. "There's also my job. Chip is short-handed, and I told him I'd help out with the end-of-year accounting."

Her expression soured. "After all the hours you've been working, Chip owes you a little time off. I can speak to him if you won't."

Actually, Jake wanted the extra hours to stay busy. It was the first Christmas since his mother passed away, and he wasn't really in a festive mood. Shifting his focus, he spotted Faith and her friend at another table.

Jillian interrogated him. "Who is she?"

He stared at his tablemate. "Faith Chandler. I introduced you to her, remember?"

"I don't mean what's her name? I mean who is she to you?"

Dropping his gaze to his mug, he lifted his spoon to stir his drink again. "Just someone I knew a long time ago."

"An old girlfriend?"

The jealous edge in Jillian's voice took him by surprise. It suddenly dawned on him that she thought—or wanted to think—things were much more serious between the two of them than they were. Because Jillian worked for the lodge, she helped host the tour orientations held there. That's how they'd met. From his point of view, they were merely work friends, who hung out once in a while when they happened to bump into each other. "Look, Jillian, I appreciate your invitation for Christmas, but I'll have to pass."

She huffed at him as if he'd poured his drink in her face. "Well, at least I know where I stand." She slid across her bench to get up.

"Jillian, wait. I think there's been a misunderstanding—"

"I don't want to discuss this now, Jake. You need time to come to your senses, that's all."

After she stormed out of the restaurant, Jake sipped his lukewarm cocoa, relieved that she was gone.

As he set his cup down, Faith's girlish laughter tickled his ears like an old familiar melody. At first, he thought she'd overheard the drama with Jillian, then realized she and her friend were sharing a joke.

Too annoyed and distracted to enjoy his solitude, he quickly downed the rest of his drink, dropped some money on the table, then grabbed his coat to leave. When he came to Faith and Shelly's table on his way out, he stopped to be hospitable. "What do you think of this place?"

Faith peered up at him, surprised. "You mean the restaurant? It's good… Actually, my dinner was great. I'm glad the grill was still open. All the other restaurants close early on Sundays."

"You should try the carrot cake for dessert." As he slowly stepped away, her voice kept him from leaving.

"What a funny coincidence that I should be in your group this week."

*Coincidence and Chip's marketing campaign.*

A wistful smile touched her rosy lips. "I know it's a little awkward, but it is good to see you again. Yellowstone even reminds me a little of Colorado. Remember the frozen pond where we used to skate when we were kids?"

It annoyed him that her smile could still touch something deep inside after all these years. "I remember you falling in."

She gave a rueful nod. "If you hadn't rescued me, I might not be here today."

Since she'd become a stranger to him, he couldn't join her on the trip down memory lane. "The way you beat feet out of town, I'm surprised you kept any memories at all."

She winced, the pink in her cheeks matching her lips.

After saying goodnight to Shelly, he strode toward the door.

Once outside, a harsh wind slapped his face.

He figured he probably deserved it due to his snarky remark, but the fact that Faith could still get under his skin bothered him worse than his stinging cheek.

The cold gust of air Jake had let in on his way out of the restaurant gave Faith a shiver, though it was nothing compared to his chilly rebuke—not that he wasn't justified. Even so, she couldn't change the past, as much as she would like to.

From across the table, Shelly stared at her with a perceptive glint. "I take it things didn't end well between you two."

Faith stopped twisting a lock of hair. "Really? How could you tell?"

Her sharp retort didn't stop her friend's prying. "So what happened?"

"It's ancient history," Faith replied, not wanting to discuss it.

"Maybe for you, obviously not for him."

Realizing that Shelly wasn't going to drop it, Faith finally gave in and told her. "I was young and didn't have the courage to break up with him in person, so I sent him a text and left town right away."

Shelly grimaced. "Ouch…poor Jake. He's the reason you left the college in Colorado and transferred to the University of Texas, isn't he? I never believed your story about wanting to switch to a better accounting program."

Rather than dredge up more of her painful past, Faith shifted her gaze and saw Alec and Rick seated at the bar. Alec had noticed her as well. "It appears we're not the only members of the Elk group having a late dinner."

Shelly turned her head. "Let's invite them over."

When she started to wave, Faith grabbed her wrist. "No, let's don't."

Her friend lowered her hand. "Why not? We can have dessert and get to know them better. I'm dying to try that carrot cake."

"Maybe another night. It's late and we still need to

unpack." Faith gestured for their server to come over.

"Are you ready for dessert?" the waitress asked.

"Actually, we'd like the check, please."

"Oh, it's already been taken care of."

Surprised, Faith tilted her head. "By whom?"

"That man at the bar."

Faith looked at Alec again, and he tipped his glass in her direction. Though she didn't feel comfortable with a man she barely knew buying her dinner, she sent him a polite nod. Tad's betrayal had taught her to guard her heart and not be swept away by flattering words and deep pockets.

Shelly's voice interrupted her thoughts. "Nice of Alec to do that."

Faith shrugged. "I guess, as long as he doesn't want anything in return."

Her friend chuckled softly, then gave her a sympathetic smile. "Look, I know you're jaded because of Tad, but you're on vacation and it's almost Christmas. How about a little peace on earth, good will toward men? It's only dinner."

Shelly's point was well taken, and since Faith didn't want to spoil their holiday by being a wet blanket, she decided to give Alec the benefit of the doubt. While she was at it, she tried to convince herself that the anonymous note was only an idle threat. After all, what was the worst that could happen on a guided tour of Yellowstone?

CHAPTER FOUR

Back in their room at the lodge, Faith and Shelly finished unpacking their luggage. Faith was glad that Alec and Rick hadn't invited themselves to their table or tried to accompany them after they left the grill. It was late, and she was still dealing with the emotional toll of seeing Jake again and reading the disturbing note.

When Shelly finished filling her drawer, she closed it. "Well, I'm done. The rest of the dresser is yours."

Faith paused from her task. "I don't know how you brought everything you needed in those two small bags."

Her friend simply shrugged. "I'm a flight attendant. I'm used to traveling light. You could benefit from a few lessons in that department."

"Maybe I should become a flight attendant like you. Can you get me into a training program?"

Shelly cast her a sideways look. "I don't think that's such a good idea. Remember, you don't like to fly."

Conceding her point, Faith laughed. "I guess that would be a problem." She wished she could so easily dismiss her job predicament. "I only have enough in my savings to keep my condo and car for a few more months. Hopefully, I'll find a suitable job before I have to give them up."

Shelly sat on one of the two beds in the room. "Instead of a *suitable* job, how about doing something you enjoy?"

"Who said I didn't enjoy my old job?"

"No one had to. It was obvious. You never took a vacation, and you worked those crazy hours. Then there were the headaches and stomach aches, remember? You were constantly sick with something."

Faith thought it over. "You're right. Maybe now that I'm not working for Syngexas, I'll at least be healthier."

After she'd stowed all of her clothes away, Faith grabbed

her robe and headed to the bathroom to take a shower. When she pulled back the shower curtain and saw the ancient cast iron tub with claw-shaped feet, she couldn't believe her eyes. She poked her head out the door. "There's no shower in here."

Lying on her bed, Shelly casually glanced up from the book she was reading. "There isn't?"

"No, there's only an old-fashioned bathtub. There must be another room with a shower they could move us to."

"I'll call the front desk."

Still in her clothes, Faith left the bathroom and sat on the other bed while Shelly dialed.

"Well?" Faith asked when Shelly hung up.

Shelly flicked her hand casually. "There are rooms down the hall with a private shower, but no bathtub. However, the place is booked, and we can't switch. There's a shared women's shower across the hall from us. That's our best bet."

"A public shower?"

Shelly shrugged. "Pretend you're back in the college dorm."

"Great. My entire life is reverting back to my college days. I guess I can't complain though. It is a free vacation." Faith studied Shelly's book. "What are you reading?"

"It's a guide to surviving in the wilderness." She handed it to Faith. "Feel free to borrow it. You never know when a few survival skills might come in handy around here."

Faith flipped through the book and snorted. "Surviving the wilderness is easy compared to surviving a tour with an ex-boyfriend. Do you have a guide for that?"

Faith found the women's bathroom across the hall. At least it had plenty of room and was warm and toasty from the radiator heat. She quickly closed and locked the door behind her. Then she set her tote bag on the wooden bench beside the shower and retrieved her phone.

Holding it in her hand, she paused. Maybe Shelly was right about her being addicted. The recent theft of her laptop had caused her to become even more dependent on it. Thankfully, her phone was with her at work the day her car was broken into or she'd have no means of communication with the outside world except the landline in the lodge.

Finding no responses to the job applications and résumés she'd sent out before leaving Dallas, she checked her junk folder, in case any landed there. An email from a sender she didn't recognize caught her attention. The subject line said, *New Job Opportunity*. It could still be junk, but she decided to open it anyway in case it was in response to her job queries. When she started reading, she discovered the content wasn't at all what she'd hoped or expected.

*Faith,*

*I hope for both our sakes you won't ignore this. You're the only person I can trust now. I'm in big trouble and need your help. Please call me right away, and whatever you do, don't mention to anyone that I contacted you.*

*Monica*

Stunned, Faith stared at the message. The serious nature of it compelled her to overlook the fact that Monica had tricked her into reading it with the misleading subject. It was dated a week ago, only a few days before Tad said Monica had gone missing. Faith tagged the message as not junk, then found Monica's phone number and called it.

After three rings, a recording of a female voice answered and said the number was no longer in service.

Strange. Monica must have changed her number as well as her email address.

Faith typed a quick reply to Monica's message. When she sent it, a notice immediately appeared that her reply to the sender was undeliverable. Without a way to contact Monica, Faith didn't know what else to do. *If she was in trouble, why would she reach out to me, of all people? Had Tad double-crossed her as well?*

Despite being angry with Monica, Faith never wanted anything bad to happen to her, so she looked up and prayed. "Lord, I know I haven't spent much time with You lately, and I haven't gone to church like I should… Okay, I don't go to church at all. With my job, I never had enough time…" She paused, realizing she was only making excuses. "No, the truth is, I put other things ahead of You. I'm sorry for that. Help me to do better from now on."

She took a deep breath before she continued. "Also, Lord, help me to forgive Monica for how she hurt me with Tad and have her contact me since I can't get through."

The ring of Faith's phone surprised her. Was that Monica now? "Hello?"

"It's me again."

Recognizing Tad's voice, Faith held the phone away and poised her finger to end the call.

"Please, Faith, don't hang up."

She gritted her teeth and pressed the phone back to her ear. "Tad, I told you never to call me again, unless it's news about Monica."

"Actually, it is about her. I'm worried. I need someone to talk to. Would you mind if I stopped by tonight?"

Faith recalled Monica's warning not to mention her email to anyone. "That's not a good idea. I have to go."

"Wait—"

She hung up on him, then powered off her phone before stowing it in her tote bag. Peering up, she finished her prayer. "I'm sorry, God. That's one person I don't think I can forgive."

# CHAPTER FIVE

LOUD FOOTSTEPS FROM THE ROOM ABOVE, combined with disturbing thoughts about Monica and Tad, kept Faith awake most of the night. When she woke the next morning, she noticed Shelly wasn't in her bed or in the bathroom. She must have gone downstairs to the lobby.

Since her roommate wasn't around, Faith jumped out of bed and bee-lined it for her bag where she'd stashed her phone. She hesitated as Shelly's voice, lecturing her about her cell phone obsession, echoed in her mind.

Ignoring the voice, she powered up the device and searched her new messages. Nothing from Tad, thankfully. Nothing new on the job front either. Her eyes gravitated to Monica's email, though she didn't want to read it again. It had bothered her enough the first time.

Hearing a knock at the door, she hid the phone in the pocket of her parka hanging on the bed post. A moment later, she opened the door to find Shelly standing in the hall, holding two steaming cups in her hands. Staring at Faith's flannel pajamas, she arched a brow. "You're just now getting out of bed?"

Faith shrugged. "I'm on vacation."

The doubtful look on Shelly's face faded as she entered the room. "Well, I hope you enjoyed your beauty sleep because tomorrow we'll have to get up at the crack of dawn."

Faith groaned and took one of the coffees from Shelly. "Sounds like boot camp."

After changing into her wool tunic sweater, black leggings, and boots, Faith grabbed her parka and descended the stairs with Shelly to the lobby. On their way to the main doors, they passed the registration and concierge desk.

Faith felt a strange vibe. Remembering the threatening note, she paused and cautiously glanced around.

Jillian was at the concierge desk—watching her. The blonde's surly frown quickly morphed into a professional smile. "Good morning."

Shelly also stopped and pivoted to Jillian. "Hi. Where's a good place for breakfast with fast service. We're running late."

"The nicest restaurant is a couple of blocks north on Main Street, but the Wonderland Diner is less expensive and has faster service. It's only a block south of here. Enjoy your day."

Despite Jillian's chipper reply, Faith couldn't forget the suspicious look on her face. Had Jake told her about the two of them?

"Come on, Faith," Shelly said. "We need to hurry."

A few minutes later, they were seated at a table in the diner next to a window decorated in Christmas lights and artificial frost sprayed on the panes. While waiting for their server, Faith examined the interesting collection of old-fashioned snowshoes and skis mounted on the wall for local color, alongside festive boughs of holly.

Their waitress soon appeared carrying two waters and a couple of plates with warm biscuits for them to enjoy while they scanned their menus.

As soon as Faith had decided what to order, a commotion at the door caused her to glance over her shoulder.

Leslie harangued the poor hostess in a loud voice for all to hear. "What do you mean there are no tables? I demand to be seated right away. I can't be late." She looked around and spotted Faith and Shelly. "Never mind. I'll sit over there. Please send a waitress to my table immediately." In her designer leather boots, she promptly marched across the floor to their table and claimed the empty chair beside Faith. "Hello, girls."

Faith and Shelly exchanged incredulous looks at the unwelcome intrusion. So much for a peaceful breakfast.

Still angry, Leslie ignored their awkward silence. "They told me it would take ten minutes to seat me. Unbelievable! I'd go someplace else if I could, but I don't have time."

Faith watched the busy waitress a few tables away. "I think they're short on staff."

"Then they should hire more people."

When the waitress appeared at their table, Leslie stopped her rant to order. Once the waitress had left, and the reporter had nibbled on a biscuit, she seemed more agreeable. "Ready to hit the snow, girls?"

"Where's Phil?" Shelly asked.

"I don't know. He didn't answer his phone this morning." Leslie scanned the dining room. "I thought he might be here."

Faith glanced around at the breakfast crowd. "I don't see him."

"I'm sure he'll show up before we leave for Mammoth Hot Springs."

After the waitress returned with their food, Leslie gazed out the window. "This place is scenic, but it's about as exciting as a used car. The only thing interesting around here is our tour guide." She arched a brow at Faith and Shelly. "There's definitely more going on with him than meets the eye, and I'm going to find out what it is."

Her remark needled Faith. "Why do you say that?"

"Because he's too attractive and intelligent to be whiling away here in the hinterlands. My instincts tell me there's a story behind him, and my instincts are always right." The reporter cast Faith a pointed look. "By the way, I did a little research online last night and discovered that you and Jake are from the same town in Colorado. You even attended the same high school. That's an interesting coincidence, don't you think?"

"I'll say." Shelly had polished off her eggs and came to Faith's rescue. "I actually won this tour in a contest and invited Faith to come with me. Neither of us knew that Jake would be our tour guide until we showed up for the orientation yesterday. It was quite a surprise."

"Yes, I would imagine." Leslie continued to scrutinize Faith. "And what exactly was your relationship with Jake in high school?"

Faith shrugged. She didn't want to divulge anything Leslie

could use for her feature. "We were friends, though I haven't seen him in years. We haven't kept in touch. I think Alec Underwood would make a more exciting story."

Leslie sniffed and ran a hand over her sprayed hair. "I've met a million Alecs. However, I don't come across too many Jakes. There's something different about him that intrigues me. I wish I could have found out more about him online. He must not be very active on social media."

Faith didn't respond. She put her energy into finishing her pancakes instead.

When the door chimed behind them, the reporter turned her head. "Well, look who just walked in."

Faith twisted around. At seeing Jake heading toward their table a slight flutter touched her heart.

He stopped to talk to them. "Good morning, ladies. We'll be boarding in about thirty minutes. I'm on my way to get the van."

His gaze settled on Faith, increasing her heartrate. "I need to speak to you at the lodge before we leave this morning."

She hid her curiosity. "Okay, I'll be there in a few minutes." After he left with a coffee and pastry to go, she took a nonchalant sip of her water.

Leslie eyed her with a smug expression. "Just old friends, eh?"

Having finished breakfast, Faith walked with Shelly back to the lodge. The sensation of being watched plagued Faith again, making her nervous. She couldn't get the anonymous note out of her mind either. As she glanced behind her, she remembered Jillian staring at her in the lobby that morning. Faith hardly knew the woman and couldn't imagine why she would have sent the note, but she did work at the lodge.

"Why do you keep looking around?" Shelly asked.

"I know it sounds strange, but I think someone's watching us."

Shelly stopped and glanced at the road and sidewalk. "I

don't see anyone." When she turned to Faith, concern reflected in her eyes. "You've been under a lot of stress lately. Maybe it's getting to you."

Faith flinched at her remark. "There's nothing wrong with me, and it's not my imagination."

"Sorry, that's not what I meant. It's just that you've been acting a little weird since Tad's phone call. I don't want this business with Monica and Syngexas to ruin your vacation."

Faith considered telling Shelly about the anonymous note and Monica's email, but decided to put it off. She and Shelly were already running late, and Faith didn't want to worry her friend or waste any more time thinking about the two disturbing messages.

When they reached the lodge, Faith opened the door to the lobby.

Shelly caught her arm. "Where are you going?"

"Up to our room. I need to get my snacks and water bottle."

"There isn't time. I've got extra snacks and water you can use. And we'll be eating lunch in Mammoth Hot Springs. Besides, Jake said he wants to talk to you, remember?"

Faith hadn't forgotten, but she wasn't eager to hear what he had to say. "I wonder if he's moving us to a different group, or maybe only me." It surprised her to realize she actually hoped that wasn't the case. As uncomfortable as it was to be around him, he would be a good guide, and she felt more secure having someone she trusted guiding her in the wilderness than a person she didn't know, especially if someone was spying on her.

Waiting for the van, Faith read the large thermometer on the post of the portico she was standing under. Thirty degrees. She could handle that, as long as it didn't get much colder. In fact, it was a brilliant winter morning with blue skies and a fresh layer of snow that sparkled in the sunlight like a dusting of tiny diamonds. Anticipation rose inside her at the prospect of her first excursion in the famous national park.

Alec walked toward her and smiled. "Good morning."

She returned his greeting and thanked him for paying for dinner last night. While she was talking to him, Jake drove up in a blue passenger van with traction tires and the Wild Adventures' bison logo painted on the side. After parking on the circular drive, he got out and came around to the passenger side.

Eagerly rubbing his hands together, he addressed the Elk group. "Good morning, everyone. I hope you are all rested and raring to go. We have a fun day ahead in Mammoth Hot Springs, so let's get started." He opened the sliding door for the people to board. "Watch your step climbing in."

Faith hung back. She wondered what he wanted to speak to her about. She'd done her best to extend an olive branch last night at the restaurant, but if he wanted her in a different group, there wasn't much she could do about it.

Alec had stayed behind with her and spoke in a low voice. "If you'd like to get away from your ex-boyfriend, we can play hooky and rent some snowmobiles."

She tossed him a polite smile. "That won't be necessary. Why don't you go ahead? I need to talk to Jake for a moment."

Alec hesitated before moving past her to climb in the van.

When the other passengers had all boarded, Faith met Jake at the sliding door. "You said you wanted to speak to me?"

He nodded and stuffed his hands in his coat pockets. "I want to apologize for what I said last night at the grill."

Thrown by his apology, she wasn't sure what to say. "It's okay. This isn't easy for either of us."

His wry grin affirmed what she'd said. "At least it's only for a week."

"Right." Somehow that didn't make her feel any better.

Stepping aside, he waited for her to enter the van.

Shelly had saved her a spot on the front row behind the driver's seat. Faith settled there beside her friend, in front of Alec who was on the second row with Donna and Phil.

"Buckle up everyone," Jake said before he hit the button to shut the door.

As soon as it closed, Shelly nudged Faith. "So what did he

want?"

Lowering her voice, Faith filled her in. "He apologized for his remark last night."

Shelly's mouth fell open in surprise. "That's big of him. Maybe he's ready to forgive and forget your breakup."

Doubtful, Faith squinted at her friend. "I wouldn't go that far."

Twenty minutes later, they had passed through the entrance for the national park, and Jake pulled the van into the lot across from the Mammoth Hot Springs Hotel.

Anxious to leave the cramped vehicle, Faith waited for the people in the back to exit first. Once everyone was out, Jake led them on a short walk to the hot springs.

Faith lagged behind with Shelly, hoping to lose Alec, but he stuck to her like gum on her shoe. His friend Rick hung around also. While Alec told her about his life in Atlanta and his clients at his family's consulting firm, she concentrated on crossing the slick boardwalk to the springs without slipping.

After taking a picture with her camera, Shelly skillfully wedged herself between the two of them and spoke to Alec. "Aren't you going to take any pictures? This is a great photo op."

He paused and studied the landscape. "You're right. I should snap a few while we're here. You two go ahead. I'll catch up."

Rick stayed behind with him.

"Thank you for running interference for me," Faith said to Shelly as they increased their pace toward the hot springs without the men. "But you didn't seem to mind him buying us dinner last night. What happened to peace on earth, good will toward men?"

"I've changed my mind. I don't like the way he's glommed onto you, and he's too smooth and cocky. I don't think you should get too chummy with him. As your best friend, it's my duty to protect you from wolves on the prowl this week."

"I appreciate that, but thanks to Tad, I'm wise to womanizing men," Faith said, giving Shelly a sly wink.

The threatening note from last night popped into Faith's mind again, and she scanned the cluster of people in the area. Could a wolf in sheep's clothing be among them?

Glancing ahead, she saw steam rising off a huge, limestone waterfall. Drawing closer for a better view, she marveled at its terraced steps, streaked in red, orange, green and brown like paint splashed on a giant canvas. The intriguing terrestrial beauty of the springs captivated her and took her mind off of the suspicious note.

Her reverie was broken by the high-pitched ring of her phone. She grimaced at Shelly's arched-brow reaction, wishing she'd remembered to power it off after she'd checked her messages earlier.

"Like I said, you're addicted to that thing," Shelly remarked.

Faith stopped walking and retrieved the phone from her coat pocket. She stared at the unfamiliar number as it rang again. "I'm surprised there's any cell coverage here."

A man spoke from behind her. "There's a tower in Mammoth Hot Springs and at Old Faithful, but not in the more remote areas of the park."

Turning, she saw that it was Rick. He and Alec had caught up to them.

Shelly clasped her arm. "Be strong. Don't answer it."

"It might be about a job." Faith accepted the call and put the phone to her ear. "Hello?"

"Faith Chandler?"

Not recognizing the serious bass voice, she slowly responded. "Yes?"

"I'm Special Agent Gordon Baxter with the FBI. I understand you know Monica Wallace. Do you mind if I ask you a few questions?"

*Why on earth would the FBI want to ask me about Monica?* "Hold a minute, please." Faith muted her phone to address the others. "Excuse me, I have to take this. I'll catch up with you in a minute."

She stepped away and took her phone off mute. "Okay,

I'm back. Is Monica all right?"

"We don't know. We believe her life is in danger, and she may be on the run. I understand you worked with her at Syngexas."

"Actually, we worked in different departments. However, I was laid off recently."

"Yes, I know. I also know she tried to contact you before she disappeared. We traced her computer and phone records."

His words elicited a shiver, despite Faith's warm, winter parka. "I didn't realize she'd sent me an email until last night. I found it in my junk folder. There was a problem with her email address and phone number so I couldn't call her back."

"So you haven't spoken or met with her recently?"

"No. In fact, I'm on vacation in Yellowstone right now. I didn't even know she was missing until someone called and told me."

"Who was that?"

She hesitated to answer. "A former coworker."

"Monica's boyfriend, Tad Winters?"

Had the agent tapped her phone, or was it a lucky guess? "Yes."

"When did he call you?"

"Yesterday."

"Did he tell you anything else that might be pertinent to the case?"

"*Case?* What case? I don't understand."

"Sorry to disturb you on your vacation, Ms. Chandler. If you think of anything else that might help us find Monica or if she tries to contact you again, please notify me at once."

After he provided his contact information and hung up, Faith removed the phone from her ear and hit the off button. A strange buzzing filled her head as the agent's words sank in. Monica's disappearance was under FBI investigation—it must be connected to the scandal at Syngexas.

CHAPTER SIX

By the time Faith returned to her group, they were all busy taking pictures and videos of the colorful hot springs. She found Shelly talking to Ruth and Norman, not far from where Alec and Rick were standing. The older couple from Idaho waved to Faith as they moved on to a different area to take more pictures.

Shelly pivoted and her eyes met Faith's. "Who was that on the phone?" she asked.

After a brief hesitation, Faith responded in a low voice. "The FBI."

"The FBI," Shelly repeated several decibels louder than her normal voice. "Last time I checked, it was mid-December, not April Fools' Day."

Faith didn't smile.

After giving her a double-take, Shelly paused. "Seriously?"

Closing her eyes, Faith nodded. When she looked at her friend again, she continued speaking in a quiet voice. "It was a special agent who wanted to know if I'd heard from Monica."

"Why?"

"He thinks she may be in danger because of the Syngexas scandal."

Shelly's brows shot up. "Whoa."

"I hope she's okay." Remembering Monica's email asking for her help, Faith wished she had read it sooner. If she had, Monica might not be missing or in danger right now.

"Look, I know you're upset," Shelly said in a softer, consoling tone, "but I can't help wondering if Monica might have brought this on herself."

Faith slanted her head. "What do you mean?"

"Well, she wasn't the most trustworthy person—don't forget she stole your boyfriend—and she always acted like she thought she was better than everyone else. Maybe it's a good thing you two fell out and you lost your job. Otherwise, she might have put you in danger too."

Faith wanted to tell Shelly about Monica's email, but because of the FBI investigation, she thought she should keep it to herself, for Shelly's sake as well as Monica's.

The fact that the special agent already knew about the email bothered Faith. It also made her wonder what else he knew and where all of this was going. She was glad she didn't know much of anything that would help his investigation. Hopefully, she wouldn't hear from him again.

The sound of Leslie's distinctive voice turned Faith's attention to the spectacle going on in front of the terraced springs.

The reporter had staked out a prime viewing spot and was narrating into a microphone, while Phil recorded her on his camera.

Faith nudged Shelly. "Let's go someplace else."

Her friend nodded and left with her.

Distancing themselves from the reporter, Faith could hear Jake talking from the other side of the viewing area. He was sharing the history of the hot springs and how it had been formed from calcium deposits in the superheated water that flowed underground. Faith and Shelly stopped to listen.

His contagious enthusiasm for Yellowstone held Faith's interest as much as his impressive knowledge of the park. It reminded her of the boy she grew up with, who loved the outdoors and adventure.

Jake and Joey would often include her on their hikes and outings in the Rockies, and she was happy for the escape from her bleak home life. She'd moved in with her great aunt at the age of eight, after her parents died in a car crash. Aunt Gertrude was a strict, no-nonsense woman who didn't have much money or much of anything good to say, especially when it came to Faith.

No matter how hard she worked to please her, the woman could always find fault. The only time Faith was free to be herself and have fun was when she was with Jake and Joey.

They were the brothers she never had, and their parents, Helen and Donald, provided the positive parental influence she desperately needed.

After the Elk group left the hot springs, Jake led them on a walking tour around the old military buildings of historic Fort Yellowstone. He told them how the fort was once used by the U.S. Army when it was in charge of the park, before the administration duties were transferred to the National Park Service in 1918.

From Fort Yellowstone, the group went inside the visitor center and explored the various exhibits about the park and its wildlife. When they'd finished, Jake led them to the Mammoth Hot Springs Hotel for a quick stop before lunch.

While Faith and Shelly admired the stateliness of the historic hotel, Jake shared with the group its interesting background. It fascinated Faith to think that tourists like herself had been coming there since the 1930's.

By the time Jake led the Elk group out of the hotel through the main doors of the lobby, it was almost noon and Faith was hungry. They crossed the road to a separate building where the hotel dining hall was located and went inside.

Faith and Shelly found an open table near a window, took off their coats, and sat down. A waitress came and offered them hot tea and coffee before she took their orders.

While waiting for their food, Faith sipped her tea and gazed out the huge windows at the snowy landscape.

"May we join you?"

Turning her head, Faith saw Alec accompanied by Rick. She hoped Shelly might find a polite way to say no.

Instead, her friend merely shrugged, lobbing it back into Faith's court after she'd told Shelly she could handle things with Alec.

"Yes, of course," Faith said to the men, catching Shelly's pointed stare.

When the men quickly removed their coats to sit down, Alec's expensive maroon wool sweater and Rolex watch immediately caught Faith's notice as he sat next to her. The man obviously had swank. She too appreciated fancy things, though she'd learned that could also be a pitfall. It was Tad's extravagant and ambitious lifestyle that had first attracted her to him. The fact that Alec reminded her even a little of him made her a bit more wary, though it still didn't qualify him as the wolf Shelly suspected him to be.

Once the men had ordered, Shelly struck up a conversation with Rick, who was sitting next to her and across from Alec. "I'm curious, how did you find out about this tour?"

"I saw an ad on a travel blog."

Alec gestured to Rick. "He talked me into coming at the last minute. I usually go skiing this time of year."

That drew a derisive snort from his employee. "No, you invited yourself."

Remembering Rick's earlier remarks about Alec tagging along and spoiling his vacation, Faith broke in. "Sounds like Chip's marketing campaign was very effective."

Shifting his gaze to her, Rick lifted his brow. "Did you see the same ad?"

Faith grinned. "No. Shelly won the tour in a contest Chip sponsored."

"Congratulations," he said to Shelly. "How do you like your prize so far?"

"When you win a free trip, what's not to like?"

"And you?" Alec asked Faith.

She stirred her tea. "At first, I wasn't sure I'd like vacationing in Yellowstone this time of year, but I've been amazed at how beautiful and interesting it is. What do you think of the park?"

"The park is all right. It's the lodging that's a bit too rustic for my taste."

After their food was served, Alec continued his conversation with Faith while they ate. "Do you like to cross-country ski?"

"Having grown up in Colorado, I prefer downhill. It's also a lot less work."

He acknowledged that with a slight chuckle. "I didn't

realize you lived in Colorado. I go to Denver now and then on business."

"Actually, I'm from Rockville. It's a small mountain community."

"Is it near Vail or Aspen?"

"It's closer to Rocky Mountain National Park. Rockville used to be a mining town during the Gold Rush. Now it's mostly a rock quarry."

"No wonder you moved to Dallas," he dryly remarked. "You mentioned earlier you were hoping someone was calling you about a job."

"Yes, I applied for a few positions before I came on this trip."

"Too bad you were let go. However, you're probably better off."

She slanted her head. "Why do you say that?"

Alec leaned toward her, as if sharing insider information. "Syngexas is in serious trouble. They're being investigated by the FBI. I saw in the business section of the paper this morning that the CEO and a number of other executives have already resigned. If you ask me, the company is going under."

Faith stared at him as the news brought back the uneasy feeling from her conversation with the FBI agent about his investigation and Monica's disappearance. "It's so hard for me to believe. I guess you were right about me being better off not working there."

"If you'd like, I'd be happy to take a look at your résumé. We might have a position for you at my office in Atlanta." He opened his wallet and took out a small business card. "This has my contact information."

She took the card and scanned it. "Thanks."

Shelly conspicuously cleared her throat. "So, Rick, at the orientation last night I heard you say that you work for Alec's firm. What do you do there?"

Rick washed down his last bite of steak with a drink of water. "I run the IT department for the firm."

Faith smiled. "It's funny, when I first met the two of you, I thought you were related. You could be brothers."

Rick wiped his mouth with his napkin. "If we were, I'd be a partner in the firm. Instead, I'm only a lowly IT director."

"Who's very well-compensated," Alec added.

The warmth of the dining room after being in the cold made Faith a little drowsy, and she stifled a yawn.

Alec chuckled. "I get bored when Rick talks about his job too."

Embarrassed, she quickly explained. "It's not Rick. Last night, the people on the floor above us sounded like gorillas pacing the floor, and I didn't get much sleep."

"It was probably the snowmobilers next door to us," Rick said. "They were pretty rowdy."

Alec sighed and shook his head. "I complained to the front desk twice, before they finally quieted down. The walls in that old lodge are thinner than paper. You can hear everything. It's so ancient it's a wonder they have running water."

Faith lifted her tea mug and took a sip. "I take it you don't have a shower in your room either."

An incredulous look crossed Alec's face. "Of course we do. Don't you?"

She glanced at Shelly and put her cup down. "Uh—no. We have a real cool bathtub though. It's the charming, old-fashioned kind—you know, made of iron, with feet and everything." She appealed to them with a humorous expression. "Wanna trade?"

Both Alec and Rick shook their heads.

"I didn't think so."

An electronic ring interrupted their conversation.

Alec pulled his phone from his pocket and glanced at the caller. "Excuse me. I need to answer this. By the way, lunch is on me." He pulled out his wallet and tossed it to Rick. "Take care of it."

Talking into his phone, Alec left before Faith could refuse.

She turned to Rick. "I'd rather pay for my own meal."

"Too late," he said, rising from his chair. "Besides, it's no big deal to Alec. He likes to throw his money around, especially when it comes to women.”

Faith sighed as she watched Rick walk to the register with Alec’s wallet to pay for their lunch. “Alec sure puts a lot of trust in his IT director… Speaking of Rick, he reminds me of someone, but I can’t think who.”

“Probably his boss since they resemble each other. Alec reminds me of Tad.” Shelly was staring at her with a furrowed brow. “You’re not really going to apply for a job with his firm, are you?”

“I’m not sure. I realize Alec is coming on pretty strong, but it’s the first real lead I’ve had.”

“All I’m saying is think hard about what you really want and where you want to live before accepting an offer. You don’t want to do anything you might regret later.”

After lunch, the Elk group gathered outside the hotel, where they waited for a snowcoach to pick them up and take them on a wildlife tour. Soon a modified van, rigged with front skis and rear tracks instead of wheels, drove up.

Chip jumped out of the driver’s seat of the contraption to address the group. “Who’s ready to see some wildlife?”

Amused by his arrival in the funny-looking vehicle, Faith grinned and showed her support. “I am.” She approached the snowcoach and formed the line to board, followed by Shelly.

Chip opened the side door and gallantly gestured to the passenger seats. “Your carriage awaits. Watch your step going in.”

Faith laughed as she climbed inside and squeezed through the narrow aisle to the last row.

Shelly joined her there.

Then Phil, Leslie’s cameraman, followed and sat beside Shelly.

When almost everyone had boarded, Alec appeared and settled on the front row with Leslie and Rick, which suited Faith fine. She appreciated Alec’s offer to look at her résumé but didn’t want to spend all of her time with him.

Once everyone was seated, Jake got in the front passenger seat across from Chip, who was behind the wheel. As the snowcoach pulled out of the drive and onto the main road, Faith and Shelly struck up an enjoyable conversation with Phil. It turned out he was originally from Austin, Texas, and they all attended the University of Texas, which gave them plenty to talk about, being fellow Longhorn fans.

Time passed quickly as they chatted and checked out their surroundings whenever Jake announced points of interest on his microphone in the front.

At the junction of the Madison and Firehole Rivers, Chip made a right and followed the road that paralleled the Madison River. A few minutes later, they slowed to a complete stop.

Jake pointed out a moose in the woods on the right, and everyone readied their cameras and binoculars to get a rare view of the enormous but shy creature. It eventually tramped away. Then Jake pointed to the opposite side of the snowcoach. "Looks like we have company."

Faith stared out her window and was stunned to see a herd of bison slowly approaching. She watched with a mixture of delight and trepidation as they surrounded the snowcoach.

"Everyone stay inside," Jake said. "They won't bother us as long as we're in here and leave them alone."

His words gave her pause. She thought of the note from the ice rink. Hopefully, whoever wrote it wouldn't bother her either since she still didn't know what it meant to keep things under wraps.

"You don't think the bison will stampede, do you?" Shelly said in her ear.

Studying the huge, docile animals, Faith felt like she'd stepped into the Old West, when buffalo freely roamed the plains. "They appear pretty calm right now."

The creatures puffed large vapor clouds from their frosty snouts as they wandered past the snowcoach, the younger ones sticking close to their mothers.

Faith felt sorry for them, having to endure the bitter cold, yet this was their natural habitat, and their snow-crusted fur appeared thick enough to keep them warm.

After the herd eventually left, Chip drove a little farther down the road until Jake pointed out a fox. Faith saw it right before it scampered into the woods. The snowcoach proceeded on, and she spotted two bald eagles high above in the bare tree branches.

Chip parked by the river for a few minutes to let the group view the goldeneye ducks and trumpeter swans before he turned the rig around and drove them back toward Mammoth Hot Springs.

Faith stared out the window, watching for more wildlife on the way. The close encounter with the bison had piqued her interest and curiosity about the creatures that lived in the park.

By the time the group returned to Mammoth Hot Springs and exited the snowcoach near the hotel, it was late afternoon. Jake told them they had about thirty minutes to visit the gift shop and visitor center one last time before he would pick them up in the van to take them back to their lodge in Moose Run.

The Elk group quickly dispersed and headed in different directions, some to the hot springs for one more picture, and others to the visitor center. Shelly wanted to buy a fleece jacket at the gift shop as well as a few other souvenirs.

Without a job, Faith didn't want the temptation of buying keepsakes she couldn't afford, so she stayed outside, hoping to see more wildlife. Spotting a lone bull bison in the distance, she cautiously walked in that direction for a little closer look.

As she waited on the curb for a pickup truck to pass before she crossed the snow-plowed street, she noticed there were no other tourists around. The realization pricked the hairs on her skin.

At that moment, a sudden hard push from behind thrust her into the road in front of the truck.

Screaming, she landed on her hands and knees, only a few feet from the oncoming vehicle.

The driver's face twisted in horror as he slammed on the brakes, triggering his truck to slide toward her on the slick surface.

Sucking in a sharp breath, she immediately rolled out of the way—only seconds before the truck shot over the place she had fallen.

It took a moment for Faith to gather her wits. From the corner of her eye, she caught sight of a fleeing cross-country skier in a hooded black jacket, before he disappeared in the woods.

A strong arm took hold of hers and gently helped her up. "Are you okay?"

She lifted her head toward the familiar male voice.

Deep concern flickered in Jake's eyes as he assisted her to her feet. "What happened?"

"I-I'm not sure. I was waiting to cross the road… I think someone pushed me in front of that pickup." She scanned the area. The truck had driven away.

Once she was steady on her feet, Jake let go. "Did you see who it was?"

She stared at the icy road and shook her head. Still a bit dazed, she tried to make sense of what had happened. "I saw a skier go that way," she said, pointing, "only from the back though."

"We'll be leaving in a few minutes. Why don't you wait in the hotel? I'll walk with you."

"No, Shelly is in the gift shop. She'll be worried if I'm not around."

"Okay, we'll head in that direction."

Faith carefully looked both ways before crossing the road again. Having Jake at her side helped to calm her frazzled nerves. He'd always had that effect on her. His quiet strength had been a rock she could lean on when she was younger. Now she was once again drawing on that same strength and support.

Shelly appeared from the visitor center carrying a shopping bag. She met them on the cleared walkway. When she saw Faith, a frown darkened her expression. "What happened?"

Faith didn't want to talk about it, so Jake filled Shelly in. "She had a close call with an oncoming vehicle."

Shelly gasped and put a hand on Faith's shoulder. "Are you

okay?"

"It was a shock, but I'm all right now."

Jake spoke to her in a tender voice. "Now that you're in good hands, I'll go get the van. I'm sure you'll feel better once you're out of the cold and back at the lodge."

Faith watched him as he hurried toward the hotel.

"He's right," Shelly said in a cheerful tone as they began following his footprints in the snow.

Faith thought about the close call. Now that her nerves had settled down, she silently thanked God that she was all right. She would have liked to dismiss the whole matter as a freak accident—except for the fact that she was pushed.

She recalled the threatening note saying there would be consequences if she didn't keep things under wraps. The skier dressed in black flashed in her mind again. Was this one of the consequences? If so, what would be next?

# CHAPTER SEVEN

AFTER THEY ARRIVED AT THE LODGE in Moose Run around five that evening, Faith and Shelly headed upstairs. The strong smell of fresh paint permeated the hallway, and Faith noticed the walls were a brighter shade of beige than when she'd left the building for breakfast that morning. She wished the management had upgraded their room with a new shower too.

Seeing there was no one else in the corridor on the way to their room, Faith finally divulged to her friend that she was pushed into the road.

Shelly halted, her mouth gaping.

Faith knew it sounded crazy. While she was confiding all of this, she decided to go ahead and tell her about the threatening note and her suspicions that the fleeing skier and the note were linked. As she filled Shelly in, Faith wondered if her assailant somehow knew about her phone call with the FBI agent and had misconstrued it as her not keeping things under wraps. It would help if she knew what things the note was referring to.

When they reached their room, Faith retrieved the key card from her pocket and held it out—the lock was damaged! She exchanged disturbed glances with Shelly, then slowly opened the door.

Faith gasped. The place looked like a tornado had ripped through it. Dresser drawers pulled out. Clothing strewn everywhere. Open suitcases lying on the bed and floor.

Clasping Shelly's hand for support, she fought a spinning sensation as they crossed the floor, inspecting the mess.

"It's been ransacked!" Shelly exclaimed.

"This can't be happening." Faith reached down to pick up her clothes.

"Wait!" Shelly said. "This is a crime scene. We shouldn't touch anything, not until we report it to the police. I'm calling the front desk." She went to the phone and dialed.

Leaving her clothes alone, Faith studied the chaos. It appeared mostly her things were disturbed, not Shelly's.

Faith stepped into the bathroom to look around. When she faced the mirror on the wall, she froze.

Written in lipstick were the words, *I warned you*!

A moment later, Shelly entered the bathroom. "Faith? Are you all right?"

She pointed to the mirror. "This was no random break-in. Someone's sending me a message."

Shelly turned and stared wide-eyed at the words. After the initial shock, she put a comforting arm around Faith. "Let's not jump to conclusions. The police are on their way. They'll help us sort it all out. The manager of the lodge is coming as well." She coaxed Faith out of the bathroom and pointed to the glowing light on the base unit of the phone. "Look, someone must have called while I was talking to the front desk."

Faith twisted a lock of hair while Shelly listened to the recording.

After her friend hung up, she addressed Faith. "That was Chip's wife. She invited us to their home for dinner tonight. Said she'd like to meet us."

As the initial shock of the mess in the room and the words on the mirror began to subside, Faith considered the invitation. "I don't think I'd be very good company after this."

"We still have to eat, and maybe spending an evening with them will cheer you up and take your mind off of things. You ought to do it while we're still in Moose Run. Later this week we'll move to the lodge at Old Faithful."

Faith did want to meet Chip's family. "Okay—as long as you come with me."

"Of course," Shelly replied.

When Faith returned the call, she spoke to Chip's wife, Beth, and thanked her for the dinner invitation. "We're running a little late. Is that all right?"

"That's fine," Beth said in an understanding voice. "We'll hold dinner until you get here. Chip has told me so much about you, I can't wait to finally meet you in person." While Beth gave directions to her house, Faith jotted them down on the notepad by the phone.

As soon as she hung up, there was a knock at the door. Answering it, she saw two police officers, a man and a woman. Another man in plain clothes was standing with them in the hallway. He was wearing a name tag that identified him as Tom, the lodge manager.

"Are you Shelly Dickerson?" the male officer asked.

"No, I'm Faith Chandler."

Shelly stepped forward. "I'm Shelly. I made the call."

The policeman addressed her. "I'm Officer Holt, and this is my partner, Officer Newton." He focused on Faith. "Do you mind if we inspect the room?"

"Please, go ahead." She tried to calm her nerves while they began their examination.

Shelly and Tom stood nearby, watching with her.

While the policewoman took pictures of the scene with her cell phone, Officer Holt questioned Faith. "How long were you gone?"

Faith released the hair wrapped around her finger. "All day. We left our room at eight for breakfast and haven't been back until now. We're on a guided tour of Yellowstone."

"Have you noticed anything missing, like jewelry or money?"

Faith pointed to the closet. "I locked my earrings and watch in the safe. I haven't checked to see if they're still there because I didn't want to disturb anything."

When Officer Newton had finished talking pictures, she stepped toward Faith. "Go ahead and look."

After opening the closet door, Faith entered her special code on the keypad of the safe in the wall and peered inside. To her relief, her jewelry and watch were undisturbed. "Everything is here." She moved so the police could see.

Officer Newton took a couple more pictures, then turned and pointed to the two unopened bags in the corner of the room. "Whose luggage is that?"

"Mine," Shelly said.

"Why don't you check if anything is missing?"

Shelly walked to her bags and began opening them. She took her small computer case out of the second one and examined it. "It doesn't look like they've been touched." She reached in the pocket of her bag and pulled out a small wad of money. "Even the extra cash I forgot to put in the safe is here."

"Are nametags on all of the luggage?" Officer Holt asked.

Faith and Shelly nodded.

The policewoman's brow wrinkled. "That's odd. Whoever did this went to a lot of trouble for nothing. They didn't take any valuables and only disturbed one set of luggage. It appears they were searching for something. I'll go check the bathroom."

While Faith and the others waited for her to return, Officer Holt switched to a more congenial tone. "I hope you packed for winter weather. It's supposed to turn much colder this week. Who's your guide?"

"Jake Mitchell," Faith replied.

The policeman nodded. "Good. He knows his way around the park, and he's a stickler for safety."

Officer Newton reappeared from the bathroom with a serious expression. "There's no sign of entry or exit in there, but I found a message written on the mirror." When she told the other policeman what it said, they looked at Faith and Shelly. "Do you know what the message is referring to?"

Shelly arched her brow at Faith.

After releasing a heavy sigh, Faith told the police about the note delivered by the boy at the skating rink last night as well as her being pushed into the road earlier that day, and her theory they might be connected.

The two police officers shifted and stared at her. "Did you see who pushed you?" the male officer asked.

"No. It was someone behind me. When I looked around, there was a cross-country skier racing away in the opposite direction, but I only saw him from the back."

The officers glanced at each other, then Officer Holt addressed her again. "Unfortunately, some skiers around here think they own the park and don't like sharing it with pedestrians. I'll make a note of the incident in my report." After texting into his phone, he continued to question Faith.

"Do you have any enemies? An ex-boyfriend carrying a grudge, maybe?"

Jake might still carry a grudge, but he didn't have a malicious bone in his body. "No one who would do something like this."

The officer paused and scratched his face. "It's possible that the person who broke into your room was interrupted and left before he had a chance to go through the other two bags. At least no valuables were taken. I suggest you and your friend move to a different room tonight to be safe."

Tom, the lodge manager, spoke up. "I'll find one for them right away."

"By the way, do you have any security cameras in the hall?"

Tom sighed and shook his head. "They were taken down today so the painters could paint the hallway." He gave Faith an apologetic glance. "I'll see that they're put back up tonight."

Officer Holt shifted back to Faith. "Do you still have that anonymous note?"

"Yes, I'll go get it." She crossed to the nightstand and opened the drawer. Not seeing the note where she'd put it, she yanked the drawer out all the way. A sinking feeling came over her. "It's gone. The intruder must have taken it."

"Don't worry, we'll include that in our report as well."

She described what she remembered about it. "The words were printed on a piece of paper, which was delivered in an unmarked envelope."

"Got it." After the policeman texted into his phone, the officers moved to the door. "Thanks for your time. We'll keep you informed of any new developments. Enjoy the rest of your tour."

Once the officers had left with the lodge manager, Faith and Shelly quickly began cleaning up the place.

"Maybe the manager will find us a room with a shower this time," Shelly said, sounding optimistic.

Faith barely heard her. She kept mulling over the missing

note and the policeman's question about ex-boyfriends. Jake was definitely out of the question. Tad, on the other hand…except *he'd* jilted her. Besides, he was in Dallas.

She couldn't come up with anyone else. It had to be someone who was angry or felt threatened by her. But why?

Using the directions Beth had given over the phone, Faith navigated while Shelly drove them in her SUV through the town of Moose Run. Though Beth had been gracious about them running late, they still wanted to make it to Chip's house on time for dinner and had rushed to pack up and relocate to the third floor of the lodge before they left. At least their new room came with a shower and a tub, and Faith hoped the move would make her feel safer. But so far it hadn't. After being pushed into the road and finding their room had been ransacked, her jitters wouldn't go away.

Arriving at their destination, Shelly parked in front of the modest old house, and they got out. As they strode along the freshly shoveled path to the door, Faith glanced at her watch. Considering the hassle of switching rooms, it was a wonder they were only a few minutes late.

Chip came out and greeted them on the porch. "Glad you didn't get lost."

"No, we had some last-minute things to take care of at the lodge," Faith said.

He tilted his head. "I hope everything is okay."

Not wanting to spoil their evening, she brushed her worries aside and smiled. "It is now."

Two identical little girls, plus a giant St. Bernard, joined them on the porch.

Chip affectionately placed his palms on the children's heads. "These are my daughters, Sandy and Mandy. In case you can't tell them apart, Sandy is in the purple sweater and Mandy is in the pink."

Faith crouched to eye level with the cute, golden-haired twins. "Hello. How old are you?"

They both spoke at once. "Four."

The St. Bernard came between her and the girls, nearly knocking her over.

The girls giggled. "Daddy, Ranger's jealous," Mandy said.

"Ranger, remember your manners," he said to the dog.

Faith smiled and petted the large friendly creature who demanded her attention.

Chip motioned to the twins. "Okay, girls, take Ranger inside and see if Mommy needs help with dinner."

The twins tugged their big pet by the collar and led him into the house.

Faith stood up. "Your daughters are adorable."

"They're little divas, but thanks." Chip opened the door for the women to enter. The tempting aroma of something cooking in the kitchen greeted them as they stepped into the small foyer. It made Faith hungrier than she already was.

He took their coats to hang in the closet.

While he was doing that, Faith admired the family pictures on the wall as the warmth of the house expelled the chill from her body. "It's nice and toasty in here."

Chip closed the closet door and turned toward her and Shelly. "A wood stove is an absolute must in winter." He led them into the next room. An enormous Christmas tree surrounded by presents filled a large portion of it.

Faith moved closer to admire the decorations. Many were handmade, mostly by children. No designer ornaments or perfectly coordinated color scheme. Rather, the tree was a collection of homespun trinkets that only a parent or child could love. Still, it was sweet and heartwarming, and very different from what she would have expected from the uber-ambitious young man Chip used to be.

A plump, pretty woman with curly, golden hair like the twins came into the room, wiping her hands on her apron.

Chip proudly put his arm around her. "Faith and Shelly, this is my wife, Beth."

Faith greeted her with a friendly smile. "Nice to finally meet you."

Beth came and gave her a warm hug. "I feel like I know you already. I hope you're hungry. I've made enough chili for an army."

"That must be what smells so good," Faith said. "I can't wait to try it."

"Me, too. I'm starving," Shelly added.

Chip chuckled. "Nothing like being out in the cold to burn off calories and stir up an appetite."

Faith responded in a light tone. "You mean I could actually lose weight out here?"

Beth gestured to her full figure. "Well, it hasn't worked for me yet."

Chip gave his wife a peck on the cheek. "I think you're perfect just the way you are."

Faith admired the happy couple. Seeing Chip blissfully settled with a wife and family amazed her. She wondered if she'd ever find that kind of love, stability, and contentment.

The dog went to the door and wagged his tail. A moment later there was a knock.

"Are we expecting anyone else?" Beth asked her husband.

"Not that I'm aware of." He left to answer the door.

Faith faintly heard another man's voice, then Jake entered the hall and bent to pet Ranger.

When he saw them in the next room, he froze. "Oh… I didn't know you had company, Chip." He shifted and handed him a paperback. "I only stopped by to return the book I borrowed."

Faith glanced down. The toasty room suddenly felt sweltering, or was it the blood rushing to her face from seeing Jake?

As he started to leave, Chip grabbed his arm. "Not so fast, buddy. Come in and say hello to our friends."

Reluctantly, Jake entered the living room with his cousin.

"How did you like the book?" Chip asked.

Jake glanced at Faith and didn't answer right away. "What was that?"

"The book. Did you like it?"

"Oh…you were right. It's much better than the movie."

"Hey, why don't you stay for dinner? I'm outnumbered here with all these women. I need another guy for moral support." Chip then appealed to Beth. "We have plenty, don't we, hon?"

"Sure." She gave him a warm smile. "I'll set another place at the table." After she left, an uncomfortable silence hung over the four who remained in the living room.

Jake squinted at Chip. "You're sure I'm not intruding?"

"Of course not. Isn't that right, Faith?"

She forced a polite smile. "Right." *There goes my peaceful evening without any more drama.*

Jake sniffed the air. "Is that chili I smell?"

Chip patted him on the shoulder. "You betcha. Now why are we all standing around like a herd of frozen buffalo when we could be eating?" He waved the women toward the kitchen. "Go ahead, ladies. I need to talk shop with Jake for a minute."

Eying Shelly, Faith muttered as they left the men. "I thought you were supposed to protect me on this trip."

"From prowling wolves, not jilted boyfriends," Shelly whispered back. "Besides, whatever transpired between you two happened before you met me, which means I'm absolved of all responsibility."

As they entered the warm, homey kitchen, the savory aroma of Beth's chili filled the air. The twins were occupied at the log-hewn table with crayons and coloring books. When they looked up at Faith, they giggled. "You're pretty," Mandy said to her.

Smiling, she walked over to them. "Why, thank you. So are you and Sandy." She complimented the pictures they were working on and asked if she and Shelly could help them color. The little girls beamed and nodded their heads.

The men soon joined the women in the kitchen, and the twins' faces lit up brighter than the lights on their Christmas tree. Sandy greeted Jake with a big smile. "Are you eating with us, Mr. Jake?"

His eyes twinkled at them. "You know I can't resist your

mother's chili."

"Daddy, I want to sit by Mr. Jake."

Mandy piped up. "No, Daddy, I want to sit by him."

Chip finally ended their dispute. "Mandy, you sit on one side of him, and Sandy, you sit on the other. But first, hand me your crayons and coloring books."

The girls obeyed, then scooted apart as Jake climbed over the bench and sat between them.

He grinned at his two admirers. "If I sit next to you, does that mean I get your dessert?"

"No!" They started giggling.

Chip gestured to Faith and Shelly. "Make yourselves at home and have a seat."

Faith rested on the empty bench next to Shelly and across from Jake and the girls. She was amused and fascinated to watch him tease and play with the twins like a member of the family. Having missed out on a happy home life growing up, a part of her still yearned for that sense of belonging. She couldn't help wondering what might have been had things worked out differently between her and Jake.

Meanwhile, Beth placed the big pot of chili on the table. She then filled the glasses with soda for the adults and milk for the children before she took a seat at the end closest to the kitchen, opposite her husband.

After Chip said grace, Beth began scooping the steaming hot chili into individual bowls and carefully passed them around.

When everyone was served, Faith glanced down and discovered the dog sitting on the floor beside her.

"Ignore Ranger," Beth said. "He likes to meet new people."

Faith scratched the furry beast behind the ear. "He's too cute to ignore." Taking a break from petting the dog to appease her growling stomach, she filled her spoon with the steaming stew and blew on it to cool it off, then she tasted it. "This is pretty spicy, but delicious," she said to Beth. "It's different from the kind I'm used to in Texas. What's in it?"

"Bison meat," Beth said matter-of-factly. "I use it instead of hamburger. It's leaner."

Shelly turned to Jake. "Speaking of bison, that herd we saw today at the Madison River was awesome."

He stopped teasing the twins. "They're hard to miss around here."

"That reminds me," Chip said, "Ned Watson told me there was another bison poaching incident last week."

Jake's expression became more serious. "Do they have any idea who's doing it?"

Chip shook his head. "He thinks it's happening at night. It'd be hard to get out of the park with an animal that size and not be seen or reported in the daytime."

"Yeah, especially this time of year when most of the park access is restricted to permitted vehicles that can travel over snow."

"By the way, a bison charged a tourist yesterday," Chip said. "Tossed him up in a tree, goring his side. Fortunately, the man survived, but they didn't catch the bison."

Faith put down her spoon. "Wow, I didn't realize Yellowstone was so hazardous."

Jake sent her a reassuring look. "Don't worry, bison usually don't attack, unless provoked. If you keep a safe distance away, you'll be all right." His lingering gaze held hers for a moment.

Chip cleared his throat. "Oscar came by to see me today, Jake."

That caused Jake to frown and shift his focus to his cousin at the end of the table. "Yeah? What did he want?"

"I won't use his exact words, but basically, he offered me money if I would fire you."

Faith thought Chip was joking at first until Jake groaned. He didn't appear surprised.

Beth filled her in. "Oscar's daughter is Jillian Prescott, the concierge clerk at the Moose Run Lodge."

Shelly piped up. "We met her at the orientation."

Jake calmly responded to Chip's shocking news. "Sounds like Oscar is still angry at me."

Chip nodded. "I'm afraid you made a real enemy out of him when you reported his company to the park authorities."

"If his sons had obeyed the park regulations like they're supposed to, I wouldn't have. What did you say to his offer?"

"I told him I wouldn't take his money if he paid me a billion dollars."

Jake chuckled. "Maybe you should, if he's offering you that much." He peered at Chip from the corner of his eye. "So, I still have a job?"

"For as long as you want, cuz."

Distracted by the men's conversation, Faith plunged a spoonful of the hot, spicy stew in her mouth without waiting for it to cool off. Instantly, her tongue and throat caught fire. She reached for her soda and chugged the whole glass, which caused her stomach to erupt in a low belch.

The twins giggled.

Chip jumped up. "I'll get more soda."

"Water, please," Faith croaked, her eyes watering and tongue throbbing.

"Bring a whole pitcher, dear," Beth told him.

Faith caught Jake smirking. Indignant, she squinted at him. "I'm glad you're amused."

"It *was* pretty funny." He looked at the twins. "Wasn't it?"

They nodded back.

The girls' infectious giggling made it impossible for Faith to keep a straight face, despite her irritation with Jake.

Chip carried the pitcher of water over and refilled Faith's glass. His eyes shifted from her to Jake. "What did I miss?"

"The twins and I were sharing a joke." Glancing at Faith, Jake's eyes flickered with a teasing glint.

She crossed her arms and glared at him, though she couldn't suppress a grin for very long.

He chuckled lightly then resumed eating his chili. After he'd finished it, he gently patted one of the girls on the shoulder. "Let me out, Sandy. It's getting late and I need to leave."

Surprised and disappointed, Faith's heart cried out. *Don't go—not yet!* What was wrong with her? Only yesterday, she couldn't wait to get away from him and now she wanted him to stay?

Beth rose from her chair. "But, Jake, you haven't had dessert."

"Thanks, but I'll have to pass. I have an early morning." His gaze wandered to Faith. "By the way, a cold front's moving in. Dress warm tomorrow."

Chip stood to walk with him to the door.

After the men left, Faith ate the rest of her chili in silence, while Shelly talked to Beth.

"I'm glad Jake stayed for dinner," Chip said when he returned. "He hasn't been himself since his mother passed away a couple of months ago."

A lump caught in Faith's throat. "Helen Mitchell…is dead?"

Before Chip responded, he paused and exchanged uneasy glances with his wife. "She had a stroke in October. It hit Jake pretty hard. She had moved here a year and a half ago after his father passed away. Aunt Helen even helped out in the office… We all miss her."

"She treated the twins like they were her granddaughters," Beth added.

Warm tears blurred Faith's vision, and her voice was hoarse with emotion. "I didn't realize both of Jake's parents were gone now."

Chip dropped his gaze. "Sorry to be the bearer of bad news, Faith. I know you were pretty close to them, growing up."

She dabbed her eyes with her napkin. Suddenly, her appetite was gone.

Shelly gave her a gentle nudge. "Maybe we should go too."

Faith nodded, then gave Chip and Beth an apologetic smile. "Like Jake said, we need to get up early in the morning."

Beth rose from the table. "I hope you'll come see us again while you're here."

"I'd like that." As Faith moved to get up, she smiled at the two girls who stared in silence with puzzled expressions. "It was nice to meet you, Mandy and Sandy."

They waved goodbye to her with their spoons.

The dog followed her and Shelly to the door, and Faith gave him a pat on the head. "Bye, Ranger."

He raised his paw, and she lightly shook it.

Chip brought them their coats. He paused when he handed Faith hers. "May I speak to you for a minute?"

Shelly caught the hint. "I'll wait for you in the car."

After she'd left Faith alone with Chip in the hall, he stared at the floor, hesitating.

"What is it?"

He paused and scratched his face. "I know it's none of my business, but I care about you and Jake too much to keep silent. Whatever happened between you two nearly devastated him."

She raised her hand to stop him. "Chip—"

He shot her a determined look. "Please, let me finish. I figured that by now both of you had put the past behind you and could make the best of things this week. If you're mad about being assigned to his group, I'm the one to blame, not him. He had nothing to do with it."

"I'm not mad, but it's obvious that he still can't forgive me."

"That's not true. You haven't even given him a chance. Anyway, he's not the one I'm concerned about."

She glanced away, not liking where this was going. "I don't know what you mean."

"I'm just saying, now that I've seen you two together again, I can't help wondering…"

Despite wanting him to drop it, she was compelled to hear the rest. "What?"

"If you can forgive yourself."

# CHAPTER EIGHT

SHELLY'S URGENT VOICE ROUSED FAITH FROM a restless slumber. "Wake up, Faith! It's already six. We'll be late."

"Late for what?" Faith mumbled, rubbing her eyes.

"We're leaving at seven, remember? And we need to eat breakfast before we go."

Opening one eye, Faith slowly focused on her roommate. She was already dressed with her short hair neatly combed, and her face freshly scrubbed.

Faith yawned and raised up on her elbows. "Why is it so hot in here?"

"That old radiator is really putting out the heat." Shelly packed her binoculars in her backpack. "At least we won't freeze."

Faith tossed her a dry look. "No, but we might melt." In her flannel pajamas, Faith dragged herself out of bed and went to inspect the radiator. "We need to report it to the front desk."

"That can wait. First, you need to get ready, and then we need to eat breakfast."

Faith's hunger pangs trumped the radiator. "You're right. It can wait."

Shelly patted her on the shoulder. "That-a-girl. My mission this week is to keep you focused on having fun instead of problems."

"I thought it was to protect me from prowling wolves."

"So far, I don't seem to be having much success at either." Shelly moved to the closet and fetched her coat. "By the way, remember it's supposed to be colder today. I checked the temperature this morning and it's only fifteen degrees, so put on your thermal underwear."

"Fifteen degrees! Oh, that reminds me. My scarf is still in your car. Can I borrow your keys?"

Shelly unzipped a pocket in her backpack and retrieved

them. "I'm going down to get us a table at the Wonderland Diner for breakfast, so hurry up." She tossed the keys to Faith on her way to the door with her backpack.

"Okay. I won't be long."

After Shelly left, Faith quickly went to work washing her face, applying a little makeup, and brushing her hair. Once she had pulled a fleece top and pants over her thermals and laced up her snow boots, she grabbed her parka and backpack to take with her.

It wasn't until she was downstairs exiting the lobby that she realized it was still dark outside. A fresh layer of white powder had added to the accumulation that was now at least a foot deep. Light flakes continued to drift down under the lamplight as she crossed the parking lot to Shelly's SUV.

Using the key fob, Faith opened the rear hatch and found her wool scarf in the back. Next to it was a small canvas bag filled with her mail that she'd brought from home. She'd packed in such a hurry she didn't have time to go through it before they left for the trip, so she took it with her. It suddenly occurred to her that it might contain letters in response to the jobs she'd applied for.

Quickly sifting through the collection of envelopes addressed to her, most of which looked like junk mail, she found a small thickly padded envelope with a Syngexas business return label. *Probably more paperwork to fill out for my unemployment benefits.* She had already received her severance pay via direct deposit in her bank account.

She imagined what Shelly would say. *You actually brought your mail on vacation? There's nothing so important that it can't wait until you get home.*

Heeding the voice inside her head, Faith decided to hold off opening her mail until she returned to Dallas. She stuffed the envelope and her other letters back in the bag to leave in the car. After wrapping her scarf around her neck, she locked the vehicle and started walking toward the diner.

From the parking lot, she turned onto Main Street. Traipsing along the snow-covered sidewalk, she passed the darkened storefronts of businesses that wouldn't open for at least another hour or two.

In the pre-dawn twilight, a shower of snowflakes quietly floated to the empty street like feathers off a molting goose. The wintry scene was hauntingly beautiful. As she admired her quiet surroundings on the way to the diner, she detected a soft crunching from behind some distance away.

It seemed to mimic her footsteps.

She paused and glanced over her shoulder.

A cold gust of air caught her scarf and blew it away.

When she spun around and snatched it, she glimpsed a shadow dart behind a building.

In the dim light, she couldn't make out who or what it was.

Possibly an animal, though it cast a long shadow. A deer or an elk? She wrapped her scarf snug around her neck and zipped her parka as a chill seized her body. The note warning her that she was being watched as well as the break-in with the message on the mirror were still fresh in her mind.

The wind howled again, dropping the temperature a few more degrees. A sudden sense of danger electrified the air.

Heeding her instincts to flee the area, Faith pivoted and hurried away. Whatever was lurking in the shadows wasn't good, and she longed to be in the warmth and safety of the diner where Shelly would be waiting for her.

Faith didn't say much at breakfast. She was running late and wanted to finish her pancakes so she let Shelly do most of the talking. While her friend read from her travel guide about Yellowstone, Faith did her best to shift her thoughts from whatever had spooked her outside to anticipating a fun day in the park. She was probably making something out of nothing—it was most likely an elk. The park was full of them. One must have wandered into town.

By the time she and Shelly returned to the lodge from the diner, it was almost seven. The wide, covered drive-through in front of the lodge hummed with activity as tour buses and vans parked there to load people and outdoor gear in preparation for the day's big adventures.

Faith and Shelly found the other members of the Elk group clustered in front of the Wild Adventures van. Wearing a blue knit cap and a thick winter jacket, Jake was busy on the roof, loading their recreational equipment.

"I need my warmer gloves," Shelly said. "I'm going to run to the room real fast and get them."

"Hurry!" Faith told her.

After Shelly left, Faith waited with the rest of the group to board the van. Staring at the large thermometer mounted on the portico post, she sighed. *Still only fifteen degrees.*

A man spoke from behind her. "It's sixty in Atlanta right now."

She glanced over her shoulder at Alec. The noise from all the activity had kept her from hearing his approach. "It's probably even warmer in Dallas today."

"Homesick?"

"No. I'd rather be here than at home." Shifting in Alec's direction, she noticed Jake loading the last of the skis on top of their van. His gaze met hers, then darted to Alec. After a brief pause, he resumed his work.

It was ridiculous, but she felt a twinge of guilt chatting with Alec.

A grating female voice pierced the cold air. "Phil, what on earth are you doing?"

Faith turned and saw Leslie yelling at her cameraman.

"Get yourself over here now!"

Phil stopped filming the landscape and the lodge. Reluctantly, he followed Leslie with his camera to the poor tourists she had cornered for an interview.

Meanwhile, Jake had climbed down from the van to address the group. "Good morning, everyone. I hope you all dressed warm because we're going to be outside in this weather most of the day." He opened the rear of the van and lifted out a large cardboard box. "I picked up your lunch orders from the Wonderland Diner. When I call out your name, come and get yours."

Faith waited for Shelly near the lodge entrance while the rest of the group gathered around him.

Shelly emerged from the lobby doors and found her. "What's going on?"

"Jake is handing out lunches for today."

He called out Shelly's name, and she went to claim her food.

Eventually everyone had their lunch, except Faith. She never heard her name called.

After setting the box on a bench, Jake moved to open the sliding door of the van. "Okay, everyone, we have a full day, so climb in and we'll head out."

The Elk group quickly lined up to board the van.

Faith spoke to Shelly at the back of the line. "Watch my backpack. I've got to find out what happened to my lunch."

When she passed Leslie, the reporter called her out. "Where are you going? The line is back here."

Ignoring her, Faith marched to Jake, who was busy ushering people into the van. "Why didn't I get my lunch?"

He glanced at her. "Did you put in an order Sunday night?"

"Yes, I checked a peanut butter, banana, honey and raisin sandwich on the form we submitted at the orientation."

"Look in the box over there. There's a sack without a name. I thought they gave us an extra lunch by mistake."

With a sigh of frustration, Faith strode to the nearby bench. A lone sack remained in the box. She opened it and found a sandwich, chips, soda, and a snack inside, exactly as she'd ordered. At least now she wouldn't go hungry, but everyone had already boarded except her and Jake.

Shelly waved from inside the van. "Come on, Faith. I've got your backpack. You're holding us up."

"Okay, okay." Jogging to the side door where Jake was waiting, Faith saw that the first row behind the driver's seat, where Shelly was sitting with Mary and Donna, was already full. With everyone's backpacks and bulky coats, there was no room on the last two rows either.

"We left the front passenger seat open for you," Shelly said.

Studying the empty spot next to the driver's seat where Jake would be, Faith hesitated to get in.

Chip appeared and strode to Jake.

"What's up?" he asked.

"I brought a special treat for your group. Beth made minestrone soup. Can you give me a hand loading it in the back of the van?"

"Aren't you coming with us, Chip?" Faith asked.

He turned in her direction. "Not today. I'll drive my snowmobile to Lamar Valley later and meet your group there for lunch."

As Jake moved to close the sliding door, he paused in front of Faith, waiting.

Realizing she was standing in the way, she quickly stepped aside.

After closing the van, he exhaled impatiently. His puff of vapor drifted to her face. "Is there a problem?"

She shrugged. "No. No problem. I thought someone else might want to sit up front."

He glanced around. "Everyone else is in the van. Feel free to take the seat."

"Okay…" She reluctantly swung open the door. While she situated herself in the front, Jake headed to the rear of the van to help Chip load the soup. By the time he reappeared, she was more relaxed in her comfortable bucket seat.

Getting in on the driver's side, he tossed her a quick glance before he started the engine. "Better fasten your seatbelt."

She glanced at the strap dangling beside her, embarrassed to have forgotten the basics. Jake pointing out her mistake only added to her humiliation. Peering over her shoulder as she buckled herself in, she caught Shelly grinning over her little predicament.

Faith turned around and crossed her arms. How long would it be before their first stop?

Soon her mind switched gears as Jake drove them into the

park, and she saw the breathtaking landscape through the front window. The way the early-morning sunlight glittered across the snow-laden meadows and flocked forests captivated her in childlike wonder.

Jake grabbed the microphone and shared interesting facts about the land they were exploring. Listening to him, she was impressed by his knowledge and the engaging way he shared it with the group.

From the corner of his eye, he caught her staring. He turned the mic off and set it down. "Do you have a question?"

"No. I'm just amazed that you know so much about the park."

The dimple in his cheek deepened. "It's my job."

"It's more than that. The park is your passion." She realized that she'd never felt that way about working at Syngexas. Something had been missing. Could she find it working somewhere else?

Jake interrupted her thoughts. "It must have been tough being let go."

Surprised and touched by the empathy in his voice, she felt more of the ice between them chipping away. "The thing is, I didn't see it coming. If I had, I would have been more prepared."

"Have you heard anything more about the missing woman?"

Faith glanced behind her. Shelly and the other members of the group were absorbed in their own conversations and not listening to the two of them up front. Faith leaned closer to Jake. "Actually, I got a call from an FBI agent yesterday. He's looking into her disappearance as part of an investigation. I think it's connected to the scandal at my former company. Monica worked there too."

Jake's eyes widened and darted in her direction. "So what did he want?"

She shrugged. "Apparently I'm one of the last people Monica tried to contact before she went missing. He thought I might have spoken to her."

"But I thought you weren't friends."

"We're not—at least not anymore." Faith realized she'd probably said too much already. "It's a long story…" There was a time she could tell him anything, yet confiding in him now about an ex-boyfriend's betrayal felt weird, so she changed the subject. "You said at the orientation that you worked in Alaska. What was it like?"

"Not too different from Yellowstone, actually."

"And cold, I would imagine. I should have kept my thermal underwear from Colorado. The stores in Dallas don't exactly have a big selection. I had to buy them online and shipped overnight."

He chuckled, the dimples in his smile reminding her of the boy she used to know.

"What did you do in Alaska?"

"I worked as a geologist for a mining company, but after Dad passed away, I decided to come back to the lower forty-eight to be closer to Mom. During my junior and senior years in college I worked as a tour guide to support myself, so when Chip offered me a job as a guide with his company, I took it—at least until I could find something more permanent. The mining industry wasn't right for me."

His mention of his father's death grieved her. She should have been there for Jake then and also when his mother passed away. "I'm sorry about your father—and your mom. After you left Chip's last night, he told me she recently passed away… I wish I'd known."

He took a long breath and gazed out the side window. "It's strange. Right before she died, she mentioned you."

Faith leaned closer in her seat. "Really? What did she say?"

Hesitating, he focused on the road again. "It doesn't matter now."

Tenderly touching his arm, Faith spoke from her heart. "It matters to me. Your mom was always good to me. I wish I could have told her what a difference she made in my life."

After a brief silence, he finally responded. "She told me I should forgive you."

Faith slowly removed her hand and began fidgeting with a lock of hair. "And have you?"

"I thought I had…until you showed up this week. Now I'm not sure. Maybe if I understood why you did what you did, it would be easier."

He was wrong. If he knew her reasons, it would only drive a deeper wedge between them.

She'd wrapped her hair so tightly her finger went numb. Glancing behind her, she saw the other passengers happily chatting away or gazing out at the scenery, oblivious to the painful discussion going on in the front between her and Jake.

Focusing on him again, it pierced her heart to see the sadness in his face. "Do you mind if I ask you a personal question?"

He shrugged. "It depends. What do you want to know?"

"Did you ever marry?"

His brow shot up. "Now that's a funny thing for *you* to be curious about."

The irony in his tone stung, but she persisted anyway. "Is that a no?"

He glanced in his rearview mirror again. "What difference does it make now?"

She decided she didn't really want to know the answer and shifted toward the side window. "You're right. Forget it."

After a few long moments, he spoke again. "No."

Turning her gaze toward him, she wondered if she'd missed part of what he'd said. "No, what?"

"I never married."

Relief splashed over her like a warm, exhilarating shower.

His gaze briefly fixed on her. "Now, your turn."

She shrugged back. "I guess we're both a pair of lone wolves."

He blinked a couple of times, then stared at the road again. "That's funny. I figured you'd married a rich guy and were living in The Hamptons by now."

"Sorry to disappoint you. I had a boyfriend… He dropped me for Monica. It was the best thing that ever happened to me."

Jake blew out a puff of air, his eyes darting in her direction. "So that's what ended your friendship."

Faith nodded. It surprised her that spilling her guts to him actually felt good. "I think I'm destined to be single. Maybe I should apply to become a nun."

A wry grin hit his face. "I hate to tell you, but you're not cut out to be a nun."

She cast him a sly glance. "Probably not. What about you?"

"I'm definitely not cut out to be a nun."

That got her laughing.

"It's good to see you smile. I was beginning to think you'd forgotten how."

She pouted at his remark. "What's that supposed to mean?"

"Only that you don't seem very happy."

"What? Of course, I'm happy. Why shouldn't I be? I've got a great condo, a nice car, and now that I'm unemployed I've got all the time in the world."

He squinted at her. "What does all *that stuff* have to do with being happy?"

She crossed her arms. "You're one to lecture me about happiness. At least I'm not bitter."

"*Bitter?*" He said it as if the word had soured in his mouth. "You gotta be kidding me."

"Pul-lease, Jake. I got frostbite from your *warm* reception."

His knuckles turned white from his tight grip on the steering wheel. "I was surprised to learn you'd be in my group this week, that's all."

"You and me both." Annoyed, she turned away. As she stared out her side window, Chip's words echoed in her mind. *Whatever happened between you two nearly devastated him.* Convicted, her anger quickly abated, and she felt bad for calling Jake bitter. How could he ever forgive her for the way she'd hurt him? How could she forgive herself?

A herd of elk crossed the road in the distance.

Jake slowed the van and turned on the mic to inform the

rest of the group. "Elk herd, straight ahead. I'm going to pull over for a closer look." Once he parked and killed the engine, he jumped out to assist the people as they exited.

Faith remained in her seat and stared at the majestic creatures clustered together, foraging through the deep snow in search of food. The herd appeared to be mostly female cows with a few older calves.

Shelly tapped on her window and motioned for her to come outside and join them.

Faith signaled to give her a minute. The clear view from her warm, comfy seat tempted her to stay inside. Mostly, she needed a few minutes alone. For years, she'd kept her feelings and regrets safely tucked away. Being with Jake again had released them with a vengeance. *Lord, I'm sorry for the pain I caused him. You know I never wanted to hurt him. Help me to make things right.*

Shelly opened Faith's door. "What are you doing? Get yourself out here before you miss everything."

"Okay, okay, I'm coming." Faith put on her gloves and climbed out of the van.

Shelly was taking pictures of the herd when Faith joined her. "Amazing, aren't they?"

Faith nodded in agreement. Growing up in the Colorado Rockies, she'd seen elk before, though it had been years. Observing the creatures in the wild roused a deep yearning for the connection with nature that had been lost when she moved to the city.

Jake was pointing out the different features of the herd to the others, while Leslie stood a few feet away, speaking into her microphone in front of Phil and his camera. Annoyed by the distraction of the news crew, some of the tour group began grumbling. It was hard for anyone to hear Jake over Leslie.

That's when Jake took control of the situation. Though he kept his voice low and steady for the sake of the herd, his message came across loud and clear. "Leslie, if you don't stop, you'll scare away the elk—and you'll have to find another tour guide."

She glared at him as if she might argue until his adamant expression dissuaded her. Grudgingly, she pivoted to her cameraman. "That's enough for now, Phil."

Shelly poked Faith with her elbow. "I think we should buy Jake dinner tonight."

"And dessert," Faith said. It was the least they could do for the way he'd put Leslie in her place.

Ignoring the reporter's sullen behavior, Jake resumed his talk. "In winter, elk move slower and rest more frequently to conserve as much energy as possible. They need all of their reserves to escape wolves and other predators."

Phil raised his camera to film Jake as he spoke, which prompted Leslie to cross her arms and roll her eyes.

Once the elk herd had moved on, the tour group piled back in the van, and Jake drove them farther toward Lamar Valley, along the only park road passable by car in winter. Shelly had read to Faith at breakfast that morning that they would need to travel the other roads on snowmobiles or snowcoaches like the one Chip drove them in yesterday afternoon.

Eventually, Jake pulled the van into an unplowed parking lot.

After he switched off the ignition, Faith bundled up and stepped outside. Her breath, visible in the cold air, inspired her to blow vapor clouds like a kid blowing bubbles.

Jake led them to a nearby lookout where they could see far across the valley. "At times you can spot the gray wolves from here. They were reintroduced in the park in 1995, after being eradicated from this area by the 1920s."

Faith strained her eyes for a view.

Shelly offered her binoculars. "Here, try these."

Faith took them and placed the attached strap around her neck. Gazing through the lenses, she searched for the wolves in the distance. Focused on the valley, she sensed Jake's presence move behind her before he said a word.

"Off to the right is a herd of bison."

Following his tip, she scanned the landscape until the

animals came into view. "I see them now!"

"There's an eagle flying over the valley. See it?"

She slowly raised her lenses toward the sky. When the bird appeared in her magnifying lenses, it looked so big and close Faith jumped and nearly lost her balance.

Jake caught her. "Are you okay?"

Embarrassed, she stepped away. "I'm fine. It looked like the eagle was right on top of me with these binoculars."

Examining her face, Jake's brows pressed together.

"What?"

"You're flushed."

If she was, it was due to his intent stare. "Must be all of these layers I'm wearing." When the concern on his face didn't go away, she did her best to put him at ease. "I'm fine. Honest."

A hint of doubt lingered in his eyes before he left her to talk to Ruth and Norman.

Faith searched the valley with Shelly's binoculars again, wanting to forget about her clumsy stumble. It wasn't easy with the warmth of Jake's gaze still fresh in her mind. And as much as she tried to concentrate on the wildlife, the sound of his voice while he talked to the others carried directly to her ears, making it hard to focus on anything else. She finally lowered her lenses and watched him point out the bison herd to Donna.

Shelly nudged her and gestured toward the valley. "In case you didn't know, the wildlife is that-a-way."

Ignoring her friend's teasing, Faith turned and raised the binoculars again, searching the snowy wilderness for the elusive wolves. She didn't know if it was the fresh air or the change in scenery, but her senses seemed sharper and more attuned to her surroundings. It had been way too long since she'd felt this vibrant—this alive.

Alec moved beside her. "Any wolf sightings yet?"

She glanced his way. "No. What about you?"

He shook his head. "You'd think with all the hype about them, they'd be more obvious. Maybe they're a myth."

As Faith pointed out the bison herd, a woman's scream

crashed their discussion.

Jake glanced around, then bolted toward the noise.

"Where's Mary?" Donna cried.

Faith let the binocs dangle from the strap around her neck and followed Jake with the others. They caught up to him in a wooded area not far away. He was with Mary, who appeared upset but otherwise all right.

Stepping closer, Faith noticed the woman gawking at the grisly carcass of a female elk in the snow. The head was still intact, and the snow was stained with blood.

"What killed her?" Mary asked as the group circled around.

Jake studied the remains. "Wolves… It's a fresh kill. Probably this morning."

Mary's eyes darted as she scanned their surroundings. "Do you think they're still around?" she asked in a trembling voice.

"Don't worry. They won't bother us," Jake assured her.

She pressed her gloved hands against her cheeks. "I'm sorry I made such a fuss. I spotted a cute little bunny and followed it to take a picture. It's not every day I stumble across a dead carcass."

"That's why it's important to stay with the group and not wander off." His voice was kind, yet firm. "The second rule of survival in Yellowstone is to prepare for the unexpected."

Faith peered at him. "What's the first?"

"Know your limits."

His serious tone sobered her. Stooping down, she studied the animal tracks in the snow. "Look at all these prints. The whole pack must have been here."

"There!" Jake was pointing to something in the distance. "See those two large trees in the middle of the meadow? Wolves are right beyond them."

Faith rose and lifted Shelly's binoculars.

"Do you see them?" Shelly asked from beside her.

Searching in that direction, she detected movement behind the trees. The two creatures were barely discernable, but they were definitely four-legged and on the move. "Yes." She returned the binoculars to Shelly for a look. "They're straight ahead."

Jake had stepped to the other side of Faith. "Here, use these."

She took his binocs and gazed through them.

Carefully reaching over her shoulder, he guided the stronger lenses to the right spot.

Her heart began pounding even before the wolves came into view. When the intriguing creatures appeared, it was like staring at rare diamonds. They were magnificent and fascinating to watch, like playful dogs, yet wild and unpredictable. She wondered what God's purpose was in making predators so incredibly beautiful, complex, and compelling.

Jake spoke to her. "The first time I saw the wolves I thought that if people and wolves can find a way to coexist, there's hope for all of us to get along on this planet."

Faith lowered the lenses and looked at him. "In some ways, the wolves are like us, aren't they?"

"Maybe that's their allure. It's like looking in the mirror."

She handed the binoculars back.

He peered through them with the boyish delight of discovering a hidden treasure. He always saw the miraculous in the simple, everyday things. Now she was beginning to see it as well.

Even Leslie forgot herself and was silent for a moment. It didn't last long. Soon she was ordering Phil to film the animals with his camera.

Faith cringed a little. Capturing the elusive canines on film seemed to cheapen the experience somehow.

Shelly whispered to her. "We *would* get the tour with the news reporter."

"They're leaving," Donna lamented.

Faith stared at the meadow. Without Jake's binoculars, all she could see were two tiny dark specks moving away toward the woods.

Leslie's harsh voice assaulted her ears. "Hurry up, Phil!"

He lowered his camera. "It's too late. They're already gone."

"You're so slow," Leslie berated him. "If you'd set up when I told you to, we would have captured great footage."

"And if you hadn't been ordering me around, you wouldn't have scared them off."

Faith spotted another wolf with her own eyes and pointed. "There's still one left. I wonder why he didn't go with the others."

Jake raised his lenses to see. "That's a lone wolf. He was probably a threat to the alpha male and got booted out. There can only be one alpha male and one alpha female in the pack."

Lowering his binocs, he gazed at the sun's high position. "It's time we headed back to the van." He began escorting Mary to the parking lot.

As the group turned to follow, the lone wolf howled in the distance.

The mournful cry saddened Faith as she trudged through snow behind Jake and Mary. "He sounds lonely. Will he find another mate?"

Jake glanced over his shoulder. "Only if he can woo a female away to start a new pack."

"And if he can't?" Faith asked.

Jake paused to wait for the rest of the group to catch up. "Without a mate, he'll eventually die from starvation, or a pack of wolves will kill him if he encroaches on their territory."

She stepped back, horrified. "That's terrible."

He cast her a grim look. "Which brings me to my third rule of survival—never go it alone."

CHAPTER NINE

As Jake drove the van farther down the groomed road, Faith considered the elk kill that had disrupted their wildlife watching. The carnage left by the wolves was a harsh reminder of the dangers in the wild. At the same time, she knew the wolves served an important role in keeping the elk herds in check. It was a sad fact of life—as long as there were predators, there would be prey.

It reminded her of the threatening note and the hit-and-run skier she believed pushed her in the road. Was the person stalking her like one of those wolves? What if he or she was part of her tour group? Her heart pounded at the terrifying prospect. She anxiously glanced back at the other passengers in the van. They were all too busy sightseeing or talking to notice her scrutinizing them—except for Alec.

He peered in her direction with a subtle grin.

She smiled back, trying to appear calm before quickly turning around. Had he or someone in her tour group rented the ski equipment at Mammoth Hot Springs and pushed her in the road? It was possible… Faith stopped herself. With the exception of Jake and Shelly, she hardly knew these people. Why would any one of them, including Alec, take such a risk? She felt bad for even suspecting them.

Jillian entered her mind again. She also had access to the tour itinerary. It wouldn't be that hard for her to drive to Mammoth Hot Springs, put on cross country skis, and push Faith in the road when no one was looking. But that still didn't explain what it meant *to keep things under wraps*.

Faith sighed in frustration. She hoped the police would soon get to the bottom of it and solve the mystery. Otherwise, she'd spend the rest of the tour looking over her shoulder and worrying about what might happen next.

A short while later, Jake took the mic and informed the

group that they were about to stop for lunch at a former buffalo ranch in Lamar Valley.

Faith was glad for the opportunity to stretch her legs and get some fresh air, even if it was below freezing.

When Jake parked the van at their destination, he tossed her a quick glance. "We'll be gathering at the ranch house. You can go ahead if you want. I need to stay and assist the others in the back."

Still feeling anxious after thinking about the note and the skier, she wanted to stick with Jake and the rest of the group. "I don't mind waiting."

She got out and recognized Chip's Wild Adventures bison logo on a snowmobile parked a short distance away. He must have beaten them there.

Shelly exited the van and handed Faith her backpack.

"Thanks for stowing this behind my seat," Faith said.

"No problem. So how are things in first class?"

"About what you'd expect. It's more comfortable and has a better view."

Shelly nudged her. "You know what I mean."

"If you really want to know, we can trade seats after lunch."

"I wouldn't dream of it. I'm having too much fun watching you two from the cheap seats."

Following Jake and the others, Faith and Shelly took the cleared path toward the largest of the three former ranch buildings. After climbing the steps to the door, they tapped their boots against the outer wall to knock off the snow before entering.

Inside was a spartan room arranged with a couple of long folding tables and chairs. As people filed in, they found a seat at one of the tables to eat their lunch.

Faith sat beside Shelly, across from Donna. The heat from the wood stove on the far wall made the place warm and toasty, and Faith peeled off her gloves and parka.

Soon, the crunching of paper sacks filled the air as people took out their food and began eating. Faith was about to bite into her sandwich when she noticed Chip and Jake carrying in a very large thermos.

They set it on the other table, then Chip addressed the group. "Hello, everyone. I brought my wife's famous minestrone soup to share."

While he and Jake began serving it in the bowls Chip had brought, Faith savored her peanut butter and banana sandwich, listening to Donna tell Shelly about her new job. The passion in her voice drew Faith's curiosity. "What company do you work for, Donna?"

She smiled at Faith. "I work for a nonprofit that helps orphans in third world countries."

Faith set her sandwich down. She hadn't thought of working for a nonprofit. Given the fact that she was unemployed, she couldn't discount any opportunity, though she still hoped to match her recent salary and benefits package. "They wouldn't have any openings for an accountant there, would they?"

"It's a pretty small organization, but I can check when I return to Seattle. I know how hard it can be to find the right job. I was a stock broker on Wall Street before I changed careers."

Faith's mouth fell open. "Really? What happened?"

"I had to quit. Working on Wall Street isn't all it's cracked up to be. In fact, it nearly drove me to a nervous breakdown."

"Oh…I'm sorry."

"Don't be. It made me realize there were more important things in life than the size of my paycheck."

Faith rested her chin on the palm of her hand. "A paycheck is pretty important when you have to pay the bills."

Donna quickly clarified. "Don't get me wrong, I still get paid. Not as much as I did as a stock broker, but there are other aspects of my job that more than compensate for that, like having a sense of purpose and meaning. You can't put a price tag on that. There were signs all along that I needed to make a change, but I ignored them until it became a crisis." She gave Faith a friendly look of concern. "Take it from me, before you accept a job, listen to what your heart is telling you."

Faith considered Donna's advice. Up until now, she'd been consumed with trying to climb the corporate ladder. She'd never given much thought to whether she was really happy or not—a fact that Jake had pointed out earlier. Happiness had seemed irrelevant as long as she had a good job with a decent salary and perks. Maybe while she was in between jobs it wouldn't hurt to give more thought to her future and where God might be leading her. "Thanks. I'll keep that in mind."

"What are you ladies discussing so seriously?" Chip asked as he came to their table.

"Work," Shelly replied.

"*Work?* I thought you came here to get away from that." His good-natured ribbing prompted the women to laugh. "You're supposed to be having fun, remember? This is a vacation."

Faith gestured to him while speaking to Donna. "He's another one who loves his job."

"What's not to like?" he said. "I'm my own boss, and I live in paradise."

Shelly kidded Faith. "Maybe you should work for *him*."

Chip overheard her. "Hey, if you're looking for a job, Faith, I could really use help running my office and finances."

"Perfect. She's an accountant," Shelly said.

His face lit up as he pressed Faith. "When can you start?"

She raised her hand, holding him at bay. "Now wait a minute. Don't I have a say in this?"

Jake brought the big thermos over with a bag of bowls and spoons. "There's plenty of minestrone left. Who wants some?"

Chip raised his finger as Jake began serving the soup. "Hold on a minute, Jake. Faith is considering my job offer."

Jake stopped what he was doing. "You offered her a job?"

Alec appeared from the other table and stood across from Faith. "I came for a second helping of soup. What's so interesting over here?"

Shelly waved her hand. "Shh. Chip offered Faith a job and we're waiting for her answer."

"I'm afraid you're too late," Alec said. "I already offered her one yesterday." He peered at Chip from the corner of his eye. "No offense, but you won't be able to beat it."

Faith jerked her head in Alec's direction, wondering if she'd heard him correctly. He'd only mentioned that he'd take a look at her résumé, and there might be a job opening. It wasn't a firm offer.

Her gaze wandered to Jake.

His brows were pressed down, shading his eyes.

Chip countered Alec. "But Faith would be the V.P. of Finance for my company."

She smiled at her friend's competitive game. "You didn't tell me it was a V.P. position."

Jake scoffed. "That and a nickel won't even buy a cup of coffee. I should know, I'm the V.P. of Recreation."

Chip shot him a stern look. "Please. Can't you see we're in the middle of a serious negotiation?" He earnestly appealed to Faith. "So what do you say?"

"What happened to the previous V.P. of Finance?" she asked.

The gleam in Chip's eye suddenly dimmed as he glanced at Jake and cleared his throat.

Faith peered at Jake. His downcast expression stretched her heartstrings to the breaking point. "What is it?"

Chip changed the subject. "We should get going."

"Wait," Jake said to him. "She should know the truth." Slowly, he addressed her. "Mom took care of all the financial business for Wild Adventures…until she passed away last fall."

The sadness in his eyes made Faith want to cry. "I'm so sorry, Jake. I didn't know."

"It's okay." Pivoting to Chip, he switched gears. "Let's get this place cleaned up."

Faith watched as they quickly gathered the garbage to take outside.

Alec moved to block her view. "Mind if I give you a little professional advice?"

Though she wasn't in the mood, she did her best to be

polite. "What's that?"

"Nothing against Chip or anything but working here for a two-bit tour company isn't a good career move for you. If you joined my firm in Atlanta, you'd have all kinds of perks and opportunities for advancement."

Her head and her heart were both aching, and she felt sick to her stomach. "If you don't mind, I don't want to discuss work right now."

"Understood… However, before you make any decisions, come to Atlanta and visit Underwood-Stanley."

She knew she should show more interest in his invitation, but right now all she could think of was Jake, who was still grieving his mother's death. Finding a new job was the last thing on her mind.

After Alec left her alone, Faith put her head in her hands. Recollections of Helen Mitchell flooded her memory, and she recalled the times the caring woman had sent Jake over with a casserole or pie 'just to be neighborly' or invited her and her Aunt Gertrude over for family holidays and celebrations. It was Helen who took her to church with her family. She even taught Faith's Sunday school class. She'd been like a mother to her, welcoming Faith into her home like one of the family—and Faith hadn't even stayed in touch with her, much less gone to her funeral.

Shelly gently spoke to her. "What do you say we go outside and stretch our legs before we get back in the van?"

Faith raised her head and nodded. After bundling up, she left the ranch house with Shelly and trudged through the snow.

Shelly grabbed her arm. "Come on. Let's check out the other ranch buildings."

When they reached the one closest to the van, Faith waited while Shelly stood on her toes to peek through the windows. Growing restless, Faith wandered along the side of the building toward the van and overheard Jake and Chip talking.

"Sorry about bringing up your mom in front of the others," Chip said.

"Don't worry about it… I was thinking how strange

Christmas will be this year without her."

"You're welcome to spend the holiday with Beth and me and the girls, unless you have other plans."

"Want a shock? Jillian actually invited me to spend Christmas with her and her parents."

"Wow. What did you tell her?"

Before Jake answered, a tap on Faith's shoulder startled her and she jumped.

It was Shelly, appearing equally surprised. "Sorry, I shouldn't have snuck up on you. There are some old saddles and horse gear in the building. Want to take a peek?"

Faith saw Jake and Chip preparing to leave. "No, I'm going back to the van."

Shelly softly touched her arm. "You're not having a very good time, are you?"

*I was doing okay, until the subject of Jake's mom came up, and I heard about Jillian's Christmas invitation to Jake. Had he accepted it?* "I'll be fine. I just need to get out of the cold."

Shelly walked with her back to the van. When they were about to get in, Faith paused and appealed to her. "Why don't you sit up front this time?"

Her friend smiled and took Faith's backpack to stow behind the passenger seat. "Maybe another day. I'm content with my economy seat. You go ahead and enjoy first class." She seemed bent on throwing her with Jake.

After Shelly climbed in, Jake paused in front of Faith. "Looks like you're stuck sitting with me again." He politely opened the front passenger door for her.

Having eavesdropped on his conversation with Chip, Faith felt awkward around him now. "I don't want to monopolize the best seat. Someone else should get a turn."

"No one's complaining except you."

She glanced at the other passengers already seated and waiting, then reluctantly got in.

After closing her door and the sliding one behind her, Jake hurried around to the driver's seat. Once he started the ignition, he turned the van around and started driving in the direction they'd come.

Faith rode in silence, thinking of how close she and Jake once were. The memories of the good times she'd had with him and his family filled her with longing for his friendship and the special bond they'd shared that had blossomed into love.

Could he ever feel that way about her again? Maybe that was too much to ask, even for Jake. After all, his love was based on trust, and she had withheld the truth from him all these years.

# CHAPTER TEN

KEEPING HIS EYES FIXED AHEAD, JAKE wished he could drive faster on the plowed road. It was only about thirteen miles from the Lamar Buffalo Ranch to Tower Fall, but the heavy silence hanging over him and Faith made the drive seem twice as long. He didn't know which bothered him more, that she couldn't stand to sit next to him, or that she was considering working for Alec in Atlanta. Neither were Jake's concern, yet his heart didn't get the message.

No doubt Alec had made her a winning offer. Chip was dreaming if he thought she'd pass up the chance at a lucrative career with Alec's firm to come out here in the wilderness to work for peanuts. Or maybe Chip didn't know the real Faith like he did.

When Jake finally reached the Tower Fall turnoff, he pulled into the snow-covered lot and parked the van. "Okay, everybody out. It's time to do some snowshoeing." On his way around the vehicle to assist the passengers as they exited, he paused by Faith's window. Brushing aside his frustration, he opened the door for her. "Do you remember how to snowshoe?"

She tossed him a light glance as she pulled on her thick gloves. "We'll see. It's been a few years."

"It's like riding a bike, it'll come back to you." Then he addressed the whole group. "You all wait here. I'm going topside to get our gear."

Phil and Norman volunteered to assist him.

While they stood below at the rear of the van, Jake climbed the ladder to the roof and began handing down the equipment. A few minutes later, when everything was unloaded, Jake descended and rejoined them. "Okay, everyone, grab a pair of snowshoes and poles."

After the group picked out their gear, Jake looked for

anyone who might need assistance. He noticed Mary sitting on a tree stump, struggling with the straps of her snowshoes, and headed that way.

"Need help?" he asked her.

"Oh, thank you," she said when she saw him. "I was afraid I might strap my feet together."

He bent on one knee and pulled off his gloves before he began securing the large platforms to her boots. From the corner of his eye, he saw Alec talking to Faith. The brisk air seemed to stiffen Jake's fingers, and he clenched his fists a few times.

Mary tilted her head with motherly concern. "Is anything wrong?"

He shifted his gaze to her. "My hands are cold. I need to warm them up." He vigorously rubbed his palms together, then tried blowing on them. It was strange because he usually had more tolerance to the cold.

"This is my first time snowshoeing," Mary said in an anxious voice.

Jake's hands were more pliable now, and he resumed working with her snowshoes. "There's nothing to it. You'll master it in no time."

A wistful smile touched her lips. "My husband passed away last year. We'd always planned to come here together in winter but never got the chance. I decided to come on my own to fulfill our dream. Today would have been our fortieth wedding anniversary."

The significance of Mary's words caused him to give her his full attention as he secured the last strap. "Forty years! You must have had a wonderful marriage."

She nodded. "We were very happy and blessed, though at the beginning, it was doubtful that we would make it that long. The Lord got us through that rocky season, and I'm so glad, otherwise we would have missed the best years of our lives together. I always tell young couples to hang in there and not give up. It'll be worth it in the long run."

Jake admired the joy she exuded despite the loss of her

husband. He thought of his mom and how much he missed her.

Mary's voice interrupted his thoughts. "My son wanted to come with me but couldn't get away. He's off at medical school."

Jake stood and tugged his gloves back on. "You must be proud."

She smiled. "Very much. I'm sure your mother is proud of you too."

Wistful, Jake gave a humble nod. "Well, you're ready to try your wings now. Just take it slow at first."

He helped her to her feet, then watched as she trod carefully across the snow, like a newborn fawn taking her first steps.

When she got the hang of it, she beamed with delight. "This is fun!"

"You're a natural, Mary."

"Jake, help me next." The voice sounded like Leslie's.

He pivoted in that direction and found her sitting on a log bench. After he came over and saw how she had bungled her straps, he scratched his head. "What's going on here?"

"I can't figure out which strap goes where."

Jake bent down to fix the mess.

"I'm curious, what's a guy like you doing in a place like this?"

He continued working on her snowshoes without looking up. "Same as you. I'm working."

"Yes, but how did you become a guide in Yellowstone?"

By now, he suspected her request for help was really a ruse to interview him. It was one thing for the nosy reporter to do a feature on Yellowstone, but delving into his private life was off limits. He did a quick search for Phil and spotted him trying out his snowshoes. He wasn't filming for once.

Since Jake wasn't being recorded, he decided there was no harm in answering her question. "Chip and I are cousins. He offered me a job, so I moved here."

Interest flickered in her green eyes. "What do you do for

fun when you're not working?"

He cast her a deadpan look. "What? This isn't fun?"

"You know what I mean. I want to know about your social life. Do you have a girlfriend?"

He gave the strap on her snowshoe a firm tug.

She flinched. "Ow! That's too tight."

"Oops. I'll let it out a bit. There, that should do it." He stood and helped her to her feet. "How does that feel?"

She took a couple of steps. "Fine, I guess. But you never answered my question."

"I don't see how it's relevant to your feature on Yellowstone."

Flashing her teeth, she appeared to take that as a direct challenge. "I'm very resourceful, you know. If you won't tell me what I want to know, I have other ways of finding out."

He remained cool, despite her manipulation tactics. "I'm sure you do. Now if you'll excuse me, I have a tour to lead."

Faith hadn't worn snowshoes since she moved to Texas seven years ago. The long, wide platforms felt awkward and foreign at first. Soon, however, she remembered to walk slightly bow-legged to prevent them from tangling. Not the most graceful thing, but snowshoes definitely made it easier to walk in deep snow.

She wrapped her scarf around her neck to block the chill and followed with the group as Jake led them on a trail freshly groomed by cross-country skiers that morning. It caused her to think of the hit-and-run skier at Mammoth Hot Springs again. As much as she wanted to believe the policeman's theory that it was only an overzealous person in a hurry, it definitely felt more like a shove than a nudge or a bump.

More and more, she suspected it was the same person who ransacked her room. The intruder could have come anytime between when she had left for breakfast yesterday morning and when she returned from Mammoth Hot Springs late that afternoon. At least nothing of value was stolen, unlike the break-in of her car right before this trip when her laptop was taken.

The policeman's theory that the intruder who had ransacked her room had been interrupted and left suddenly was certainly possible. However, there was time enough to write that threatening message on the mirror and take the note from her drawer. Too bad there weren't any security videos. Until the person was caught, it would be hard for her to completely relax and enjoy the tour.

While Shelly forged ahead, Faith moved at a more leisurely pace. Her new snow boots had started to bother her feet, so she stayed in the middle of the pack. It gave her an opportunity to get to know Donna better and find out more about her radical career change. As they chatted, they stopped now and then to adjust the straps on their snowshoes and appreciate the scenic beauty around them. Occasionally, they spotted animal tracks in the snow and tried to identify them as those of deer, elk, or bison.

Faith noticed the group was spreading out as the hike progressed. Alec and Rick were somewhere up ahead with Jake and Shelly, probably halfway to Canada by now. Mary, Leslie, and Phil had fallen behind, and Faith had completely lost track of Ruth and Norman, which concerned her because they were considerably older than the rest.

Coming out of a wooded area with Donna, Faith saw the trail descend through a series of switchbacks along a steep ravine. Staring down the side of the hill, Faith spotted Jake standing on the crest of the second set of switchbacks, waiting for the rest of the group to catch up. She and Donna carefully began their descent along the trail. When it narrowed, Faith let Donna go ahead of her.

After Faith finally cleared the first set of switchbacks, Jake greeted her. "Any problems coming down?"

She stopped and loosened her scarf. "No, but have you seen Ruth and Norman? I lost track of them a while ago."

He chuckled lightly. "They're way ahead of us. I told them to wait for the rest of you at the bottom of the trail."

The irony caused her to laugh too. "Wow, I hope I'm that fit at their age."

"You seem to be holding your own. It'll be tougher going uphill on the way back. Maybe you can give them a run for their money."

"I doubt it. Skiing is more my speed."

"I remember." A ray of sunlight twinkled in his eyes.

"You're holding up the line," Leslie's voice barked from behind Faith.

Glancing over her shoulder, Faith saw the news crew waiting on the trail with Mary.

"Sorry," Faith told them, "I didn't mean to create a traffic jam." She sent Jake an apologetic shrug, then quickly made her way down the rest of the trail.

By the time she reached the bottom, the others who were ahead of her, including Ruth and Norman, were all there, looking spry with satisfied expressions.

Shelly grinned. "What took you so long?"

Faith bent to whisk the snow off her snowshoes. "My feet are bothering me in these new boots. Besides, what's the rush? Haven't you been telling me I need to relax and take it easy?"

That made Shelly laugh. "Well, while you're here, you should check out the view from the suspension bridge."

Following her friend's suggestion, Faith continued on the trail until she found the tethered bridge that stretched across a canyon. After removing her snowshoes and leaving her poles with them, she tentatively ventured out on the teetering planks suspended by ropes. It felt strong yet reacted to the weight of her body like a taut spring. With childish delight, she bounced with each step until she reached the center of the bridge. From there, she stared into the flocked canyon below.

Inhaling the fresh, crisp air, she wished she could bottle it up and bring it home with her to Dallas. Too bad she couldn't take this spectacular view home as well. It would make the perfect picture for a Christmas card. She wished she'd brought her cell phone to snap the image but had left it in her backpack in the van. She'd have to ask Shelly to share the pictures she'd taken with her wide-angle camera after they returned home.

Turning to leave, Faith saw Jake at the edge of the bridge, gingerly escorting Mary toward her.

"How about that view?" he said to Faith when their paths met. "You ought to stay and enjoy it for as long as you can."

Faith paused and lingered, while he coaxed Mary to the center for a look at the canyon.

The pristine beauty of this remote winter wonderland was the perfect antidote to Faith's stress-filled life. She'd forgotten how liberating it felt to be in nature like this. How had she gone without it all these years?

Donna, Leslie, and Phil joined them on the bridge.

Jake pointed out a few landmarks and shared interesting trivia about the area with them. He really was a wealth of knowledge, as well as kind and patient with Mary, who seemed to be enjoying herself despite her fear of heights.

After he ended his talk, he addressed Mary. "Ready to head back?"

Her voice was wistful. "Do we have to? It's so beautiful here. I'd like to stay."

He glanced at the sky. "I'll give you a few more minutes, but it's getting late, and it'll be harder climbing up."

By the time everyone had taken all the pictures and video they wanted, the temperature had plummeted with the setting sun, and they were ready to return to the van.

Having put her snowshoes back on and collected her poles, Faith followed Jake and Mary toward the ridge. As they trekked uphill, his slight limp caught Faith's notice. He was an experienced guide. It was unlikely his snow boots were the problem.

At the first set of switchbacks, he let Mary and the others go ahead of him while he waited for Faith.

Faith wondered if he was all right. "I noticed you limping, Jake. Did you hurt your leg?"

He stepped aside to let her pass. "I'm fine."

The subtle tension in his jaw belied his terse response. It was clear he didn't want to discuss it—at least not with her.

Moving on, she soon discovered that Jake hadn't exaggerated one bit about the return climb being challenging. Mary and Donna struggled to catch their breath on the difficult hike, so Faith tried to stay close despite her sore feet to make sure they were all right.

Further complicating matters, the earlier sunshine had melted the snow, causing it to cake on the crampons attached to the bottom of Faith's snowshoes. It made it difficult to gain any traction. The way her new snow boots rubbed against her feet gave an additional challenge, especially with the steep incline and slippery conditions. Limping in pain, she fell behind Mary and Donna, as well as Leslie and Phil.

When she reached the last series of switchbacks, she stopped to rest her sore feet and gazed at the scenic landscape below as Jake caught up to her.

"What's wrong with your feet?" he asked.

"Blisters, I think." She looked at her boots. Dirt and snow suddenly sprinkled down on them from overhead. At the same time a crashing sound came from somewhere near the top of the ridge.

"Rock slide!" Norman's gruff voice shouted from a few switchbacks above.

"Everyone, take cover!" Jake immediately swept Faith under a protruding ledge by the trail, shielding her body with his own. "Cover your head!"

Bracing against the rock wall, she dropped her poles, ducked, and raised her arms to protect herself.

Seconds later, the sprinkling pebbles and debris became a shower that poured over the sheltering ledge. Then came low thumps and rumbles of what sounded like falling rocks tumbling above them.

Faith prayed the stone outcropping would hold as she braced for impact.

A rock the size of a beach ball shot over the ledge, inches away from them. More rocks hurtled down like an out-of-control bowling alley.

For a moment, she thought the canyon wall would collapse

and flatten her and Jake into pancakes.

Then the noise stopped.

Jake's protective arms held her close while they waited a few seconds longer until the coast was clear. "I think it's over," he said in a soft voice.

Trembling from the shock, she slowly peered up at him.

His low brows, tightly-pressed, revealed deep concern. "Are you okay?"

She slowly nodded, unable to speak.

They stared at each other in stunned silence. She wasn't sure if it was the exhilaration of still being alive—or his close proximity—but anticipation tingled through her like an electric current. As she gazed into his eyes, she became a teen again, discovering love for the very first time.

The sound of approaching voices jolted them to the present.

Jake released her and slowly backed away.

Feeling lightheaded, she pressed against the canyon wall for support and took a deep breath. Falling rocks and hit-and-run skiers weren't the only hazards on this tour. It was clear she'd also have to guard her heart where Jake was concerned.

When they stepped out from under the ledge and peered up, Mary and Donna were staring down at them from a higher switchback. They looked as shaken as Faith felt, but they appeared unharmed.

Jake shouted in a loud voice. "Is everyone all right?"

"Ruth and I are okay," Norman replied from a higher section of the trail, where he stood next to his wife.

"I'm okay too." Shelly scurried past Mary and Donna and descended the last slope. She rushed to Faith and gave her a big hug. "Thank heavens, you're all right. You had me worried. It's a miracle you weren't hurt."

Now that she was safe, questions plagued Faith's mind. It didn't seem possible that the rock slide was manmade, but after being pushed in the road and finding her room ransacked, she was starting to become suspicious of everything. "Did you see what started the slide?"

Shelly shook her head. "I was a little way up when I heard Norman call out from above. Then I saw that big rock break free from the top of the ridge and head straight for you. Good thing you and Jake took cover, or we'd be peeling you off the trail right now."

Faith heard Leslie's distinctive voice and lifted her eyes. The reporter and Phil were standing to the side of the trail farther up, filming them below.

"Look at those two," Faith said to Shelly. "Think this will go viral?"

"It is a first." Jake said, handing Faith her poles. "Nothing like this has happened on my tours before."

Warmth flooded her cheeks from his intense gaze. Was he talking about the rock slide or their close encounter under the ledge? At least in this cold it wouldn't be as obvious that she was blushing. She looked around. "Where are Alec and Rick?"

Shelly shrugged. "I haven't seen them since we left the suspension bridge. They must be at the top."

Jake left Faith and Shelly and climbed the next switchback where Mary and Donna were lingering with anxious stares. He coaxed them up the rest of the trail.

"Are you ready to go?" Shelly asked Faith.

"I need to take care of these snowshoes first." Faith unstrapped them from her boots. After tucking them under her arm, she prepared to carry her poles in her opposite hand. "What I wouldn't give to leave my boots behind."

When she continued to struggle up the hillside, she saw Jake stop and let Donna and Mary go ahead of him. He studied the craggy remains at the top rim of the canyon where the big rock had broken free until Faith and Shelly caught up. As they approached, he turned and reached for Faith's snowshoes. "Here, let me carry those."

Since she needed both hands to hold the poles and keep her balance on the slick trail, she gladly relinquished the snowshoes. "Thanks."

He collapsed his poles and fastened them to his backpack so he could carry the snowshoes unhindered.

Moving past them, Shelly tossed her a sly grin.

Ignoring her friend, Faith gingerly resumed her ascent on a wider section of the trail. As Jake hiked beside her, she was still concerned about his slight limp, though it was hardly noticeable and didn't seem to slow him down. She was probably the only one aware of it.

"Sorry about the incident back there with the rock slide," he said.

"It's not your fault. That's why we signed a waiver when we registered for this tour, right?"

The lines on his face softened, though some of the tension remained. "It's almost like…"

She paused and glanced at him. "Like what?"

His long exhale formed a vapor cloud in the cold air. "Nothing. The important thing is that you're okay."

With raw blisters on her feet and old passions stirred up, she was anything but okay. "So what's the rule of survival for what just happened?"

A gleam flickered in his eyes. "Always keep an eye out for danger."

She smiled and nodded. "Good advice. I'll have to remember that one." Feeling more at ease with him, she decided to probe an earlier subject. "Why are you limping, Jake—and don't tell me you're fine."

He hesitated for a moment, his brows pinching together. "It's an old injury acting up."

She couldn't tell if his pained expression was due to his hurting leg or the memory of what had cause it. "What kind of injury?"

"It was when I was a seasonal firefighter in the Rockies. I got in the way of a falling tree."

Faith's heart lurched. "Oh, Jake."

He glanced at her from the corner of his eye. "It's all right. Actually, I came through pretty well. I wasn't sure I'd be able to walk again, much less hike or ski. It could have been much worse."

She knew he didn't like to dwell on his problems. Still, it

was hard for her to see him limping now. He had always been strong and athletic. "I remember the first summer you worked as a firefighter. I was scared to death that something bad might happen to you."

He chuckled. "If I'd had my way, I would have stayed on permanently. After the accident, that wasn't an option. That's when I switched to giving tours to pay my way through college."

Wanting to lighten the mood, she spoke in a more cheerful tone. "You always loved being outdoors and exploring. I can see why you like being a tour guide."

"I have to admit, coming to work at Yellowstone every day isn't a bad way to earn a living. Of course, it doesn't pay as well as a firm like Underwood-Stanley."

At his mention of Alec's firm, Faith felt conflicted. Having grown up with very little money, she'd devoted her life to her career with the goal of becoming financially secure. Assuming Alec was serious about making her an offer, she would be crazy to turn down a golden opportunity like that. On the other hand, the idea of working for him in Atlanta triggered a recurrence of the burning sensation in her stomach that had started during her time at Syngexas.

When they reached the top of the hill, Alec and Rick were waiting with the others in their party near the overlook.

Alec strode up to meet them. "What happened? We were beginning to think you were hurt in the landslide."

Weary from the climb, she let Jake respond.

"Faith's got blisters on her feet."

Ruth and Norman were standing nearby. "Don't worry," Ruth said. "Back at the lodge, I have a special ointment that does wonders for blisters."

"Here's a Band-Aid." Shelly pulled it from the pocket of her backpack and handed it to her.

Soon the small crowd gathered around Faith, offering their best blister remedies.

Touched by their concern and attention, she raised her hand. "Thanks, everyone. It's really no big deal."

Grandmotherly concern shone in Ruth's eyes. "It will be if you don't take care of them right away."

"I will as soon as we return to the lodge."

The group traipsed across the snow in the unplowed parking lot. When they reached the van, the men helped Jake re-load the snowshoes and poles on the roof before boarding to leave.

Glad to be settled in her warm front seat again, Faith could finally relax and give her feet a break. She'd begun untying the laces of her snow boots when Jake hopped in behind the wheel.

"I've got a first aid kit in the back, if you need it."

She smiled, appreciating his offer. "No, thanks. People have already given me more bandages than I know what to do with."

He chuckled as he started the engine and stepped on the accelerator—but the van hardly budged. "Uh-oh." His smile faded, and he shifted to a lower gear before lightly pressing the gas pedal again. There was still no movement, and an ominous swishing sound came from the back.

"What's wrong?" she asked.

"The tires are spinning out." He shifted into reverse and tried to back up, then attempted to go forward again. After he repeated the action a couple more times, the van was still stuck.

He twisted in his seat to address the people in the back. "All right, I need everybody out. I want the men to help push."

Faith groaned as she quickly re-tied her laces. After slipping on her gloves again, she exited the van and joined the others huddled outside.

Jake tried a couple more times to ease the van forward with the men pushing from the rear, but it didn't work, and the right-side tires had dug deeper into the snow causing the van to tilt.

Leaving the motor running, he jumped out to inspect the situation. "Well, folks, it looks like we're going to be here for a bit. I'll try one more thing. If it doesn't work, I'll use the radio to call for a tow truck."

"It's freezing cold," Leslie complained. "Do we have to

stand outside?"

"I'm afraid so. The van is leaning too much. Keep moving around to stay warm."

While he headed to the driver's seat, Alec began to grumble. "If I were driving, we'd be out of here and halfway to the lodge by now. We almost had it moving. He gave up too soon."

Faith didn't like his complaining. "If he waits much longer to call for help, it will be dark before the tow truck gets here. I think he's smart to not take that chance."

Alec crossed his arms. "I think you're giving him too much credit."

She wanted to argue with him, but that would only make things worse. Throttling back her temper the best she could, she marched away.

That's when a flying white ball zipped past her and knocked off Norman's cap, exposing his thinning, gray hair.

Norman brushed the snow off his head and spun around. "Who did that?"

Peering around the van, Jake grinned.

The older man scooped snow in his mittens and lobbed it at him.

Jake ducked just in time. Another snowball smacked him on the shoulder. "Hey!"

Ruth wore a triumphant smile as she flexed her bicep muscle. "Never pick on your elders, sonny."

Faith laughed and gave Ruth a high-five. A snow missile pelted Faith on the arm.

Smirking, Jake taunted her. "That's for laughing at my expense."

"Oh, yeah? Game on!" Faith headed to a small mound away from the van and waved to Shelly. "Get over here. This is war."

Shelly hurried to help her build the white bombs behind the protection of the snowdrift.

Suddenly, they were assaulted from the rear. They twisted around and saw Phil and Rick giving each other congratulatory fist bumps.

Mayhem ensued. The sky rained snowballs the size of baseballs. With all the snow flying, Faith couldn't see well enough to aim. Having lost track of time in the pandemonium, she noticed Jake had disappeared. A short while later, someone snuck behind her and shoved snow under her collar.

Screaming from the shock, she spun around and pounced on the rascal. Jake skillfully shifted out of her way, causing her to lose her balance and do a face plant in the snow. She couldn't let him get away with that. Lying still with her eyes closed, she heard the soft crunch of his foot beside her.

"Come on, Faith, get up." He gently rolled her over.

Before he could react, she plastered snow on his face. "That's what you get for messing with me." While he wiped it off, she quickly jumped to her feet and stepped away.

"Now you're really in for it." He lunged and playfully grabbed her wrists, wrestling with her.

Taunting and pushing back at him, she couldn't stop laughing.

Then he paused suddenly as if he'd forgotten himself. His exuberance cooled, and he released her. "My revenge will have to wait. While you were waging war in the snowball fight, I shoveled out the van. We should leave before it gets dark."

As he walked away, she sighed and fell back in the snow. That's when she realized she was no longer cold. The snowball fight had invigorated her. Pushing up on her elbows, she saw the others gathered around the van, their faces flushed and cheerful. They were no longer complaining about the cold but were joking with each other.

She smiled to herself. Jake was a genius. He must have known the snowball fight would not only take their minds off of the situation but would keep them warm while creating fond memories they could take home with them. She'd had such a good time she almost forgot about her blisters, the rock slide, and her other worries.

Leslie walked past and arched a brow at her, her green eyes flashing like a fox eying a rabbit.

The cold returned to Faith's body and traveled up her spine, threatening her heart. If the nosy reporter found out about her history with Jake, it could hurt him all over again.

Shelly came over and gave Faith a hand up.

Wincing from her blisters, she rose to her feet. "Thanks. It's not easy to get up in these boots."

"I noticed that little scuffle between you and Jake."

Faith smiled. "He was paying me back for shoving snow in his face."

"Well, it's a good thing he didn't kiss you. That would really be torture."

She gave Shelly a light punch in the arm. "Let's go. I'm starting to get cold again."

"I guess that's my cue to mind my own business."

"You're catching on." *If only Leslie would do the same.*

## CHAPTER ELEVEN

By the time Jake had delivered his tour group back to the lodge in Moose Run and parked the van, the sun had set. Though his work was done for the day, he knew Chip was short-handed, so he walked to the Wild Adventures office to lend a hand.

His cousin rose from behind his desk as Jake came through the door. "Long day?"

Jake blew out a deep breath. "Yeah, you could say that. We had a rock slide and then the van got stuck."

"Rock slide?"

He quickly told Chip about it and assured him that everyone was all right.

"That's a relief," his cousin said, dropping into his chair.

"You're telling me! I checked things out afterward but couldn't determine what caused it. I radioed the ranger station from the van to let them know. Until they determine that the trail is safe to use again, we should skip that part of the tour."

Chip nodded. "I'll notify the other guides and tour companies and give them a heads-up."

"If Faith and I hadn't ducked under a ledge, it could have been catastrophic. It still bothers me that I didn't see it coming."

Chip leaned forward and peered over the computer monitor on his cluttered desk. "Don't be hard on yourself. I'm sure you did everything you could. Our customers know there's an element of risk that comes with being in the wilderness. That's why we have them sign a waiver."

"I know, but it's the first time something this bad has happened on one of my tours."

"It was a freak accident, Jake. Don't dwell on it." Switching back to his office work, Chip opened a desk drawer and searched inside. "I've been looking for this month's receipts.

Have you seen them?"

"Nope." Jake moved to Chip's desk to help him find them.

Chip groaned as he and Jake rifled through the papers on his desk. "They're probably buried under all this mess." He glanced at Jake. "I want you to know I'm planning to make Faith a serious job offer. I can't keep this company going much longer without more help."

Jake decided his cousin needed a reality check. "I wouldn't hold my breath about her accepting it."

Chip paused and rose from his chair. "Why?"

Shifting to the small desk where his mother used to work, Jake leaned against it. "For one thing, there's no way she would move out here to Moose Run to work for a struggling tour company for a fraction of what she's probably used to being paid."

Chip frowned. "Thanks a lot."

Not wanting to insult his cousin, Jake softened his tone. "Sorry, I know you want to hire her, but you need to face facts."

"Don't underestimate my powers of persuasion. I've offered her a V.P. position, you know."

"You're wasting your time."

Chip squinted an eye at him. "I think you're hoping she won't take the job."

Jake shook his head and pushed off the desk. "Even if you could afford her—which you can't—as long as I'm here, she'll never say yes."

"So it's either you or her, huh?"

"Pretty much."

Chip fell back into his chair and sighed. "You're probably right."

Now that his cousin had finally come to his senses, Jake turned and sat in front of the other computer screen. He began responding to the inquiries and bookings from the company website, hoping the task would take his mind off of Faith and the potential job offer from Alec. It didn't. Memories of her alluring gaze after the rock slide and her girlish laughter during the snowball fight invaded his thoughts anyway.

The sound of the door opening was followed by a gruff male voice. "Working late, I see."

Lifting his eyes, Jake saw Oscar Prescott, Jillian's father, and silently groaned.

After rising, Chip went to meet him by the door. "What can I help you with, Oscar?"

The tall, beefy man gave him a brief wave. "I'm here to see Jake."

Chip tried to stall him. "Anything I can do for you?"

"No, this is between me and him." Oscar lifted his palm in a peaceful gesture. "Don't worry, I'm not here to cause trouble."

Jake stood, wondering why on earth Oscar would want to see him. They hadn't exactly been on friendly terms since Jake complained to the park officials about Oscar's tour company's repeated park violations. From what Chip had said last night at dinner, the man was still angry about it. Jake turned to Chip. "It's getting late. Why don't you go on home to Beth and the girls? I'll lock up."

Chip scratched his head. "Well…all right." He disappeared into the back room. A moment later he returned, carrying his coat. Pausing before he left, he peered at Jake and Oscar. "Be good, you two."

After Chip left them in the office alone, Jake decided the best way to deal with Oscar was to be direct. He crossed his arms. "Okay, what did you want to talk about?"

"I hear you're dating my daughter, Jillian."

Surprised, Jake realized she must have told him that. "We're not dating, Oscar. We work together—that's it."

"Whatever. I'm here to make you a peace offering. You see, Jillian is my only daughter, and for some reason, she thinks you can make her happy."

"Oscar—"

"Let me finish." The man examined the small, cramped office. "I can see why you want a new job. This place is a dive."

His condescending attitude ruffled Jake. "Who said

anything about wanting a new job?"

"Jillian told me. I'm here to help."

Jake was confused and indignant. "Why would you do that?"

"I told you. I want my daughter to be happy."

Scrutinizing the shrewd man, Jake was wary. "Yesterday, you offered to pay Chip to fire me."

Oscar shrugged. "Jillian persuaded me to give you a second chance." He pointed a finger at Jake. "But I want my daughter to be with a man who has a future."

It was time to put an end to this nonsense. Jake rubbed the back of his neck, searching for the best way to let him down easy. "Look, Oscar—"

Raising his hand, the overbearing businessman cut him off. "Hear me out. Why don't you come work for me as a tour guide? Whatever you're making here, I'll pay you more, and you could eventually run the business with my sons."

Oscar couldn't seriously be offering him a job. Jake sighed, hoping he could avoid a major argument with the man. "That's very generous, but as I said, I'm not dating Jillian, so this conversation is pointless."

"All right, forget about dating my daughter. The job opportunity still stands. All I ask is that you overlook a few minor park transgressions."

Jake had a feeling he wouldn't bury the hatchet that easily. "They aren't minor. Your sons have been speeding through the park on their snowmobile tours and allowing your customers to harass and scare off the wildlife."

Oscar scowled. "Now you listen here, young man. I run a legitimate, law-abiding business. I won't let you undermine it because we're successful and Wild Adventures is floundering. If you ask me, the park regulations are too strict to begin with. I'm not going to lose my permits because of you or anyone else." He stormed to the door. "And let me give you a word of advice. If you want to find another job in this area, you'd better mind your own business and stop meddling in mine."

Faith emerged from the bathroom in a red sweater and black jeans. She gingerly hobbled on her bandaged bare feet to the dresser to find a pair of thick socks.

Lying on her bed with her travel guide open, Shelly peered at her. "Finally. I thought you might stay in the bathroom through dinner."

"I could have soaked in that tub all night. It felt so relaxing."

"So now that we have a shower, you're becoming a bath person?"

"Only when I need to thaw out from the cold." Faith gazed in the mirror over the dresser and hummed a happy tune while she combed the tangles out of her wet hair. "You know, I'm glad you invited me to come on this trip."

From the mirror, Faith could see Shelly roll to her side and raise up on her elbow. "Really?" she said, resting her cheek on her palm. "Have you suddenly discovered that you like being outdoors in the cold?"

"For your information, I've always liked the outdoors. I've just been too busy to enjoy it much."

"Or you've taken a renewed interest in an old flame."

"That's ridiculous. Besides, I think something is up with him and Jillian."

"Judging from how attentive he was to you today, I doubt that."

"He's our tour guide. He's paid to make sure we have a good time, and knowing Chip, he probably offered Jake a big bonus if we write a nice review after the tour. They're not giving away tours free for nothing, you know."

Shelly rolled her eyes. "You're such a cynic—and stop deflecting. Why is it that in all the years we've known each other, you've never told me what happened between you and Jake?"

Faith sighed. "I did tell you. We broke up. I moved to Texas. End of story."

"This is your best friend you're talking to. I know there's more to it than that."

Ignoring Shelly's remark, Faith resumed detangling her hair. "You'd better hurry and get ready or we'll be late for dinner."

"Yeah, yeah." Shelly got up and passed Faith on her way to the closet. After grabbing her robe, she stopped and gently touched Faith on the shoulder, gazing into the mirror at their reflections. "It's good to see you enjoying yourself. It's been a long time since I've seen you this happy."

Jake had made a similar comment when she laughed at one of his jokes in the van. Maybe she really did need this vacation. And so far, having him for a tour guide wasn't near as bad as she'd thought it would be.

At the Bison Grill for dinner, Faith studied her menu while she and Shelly waited for someone to come and take their order. From the corner of her eye, she saw Alec approach with Rick.

"Mind if we join you?" Alec asked.

Faith glanced at Shelly, who responded with a tepid shrug.

After the men seated themselves across from each other in the two empty chairs at the table, a brawny man with a full beard appeared, carrying four glasses of water. He seemed to belong in the wild, not waiting tables. "Is this all together?"

Alec replied before Faith and Shelly had a chance. "Yes. It's on me."

Faith spoke up. "No, we can't let you do that, Alec."

"Why not?"

"You already paid for our dinner Sunday night and lunch yesterday." She addressed the waiter in an adamant tone. "Separate checks, please."

When they'd finished ordering, Rick spoke to Shelly, seated next to him. "What do you think about that freak rock slide today?"

She shuddered. "Too close for my comfort. I'm glad no one was hurt."

Alec chimed in. "I wish we had a better guide. I don't think the snowshoe trail was challenging enough."

Rick sipped from his glass. "Yeah, and there was too much waiting around."

The men's griping about Jake irritated Faith. She cleared her throat. "The waiting around was my fault, not Jake's. The blisters on my feet caused me to fall behind."

"If he wants to stay behind with the stragglers, that's okay," Alec said, "as long as he lets the rest of us go at our own pace."

"But he's responsible for all of us. He can't let the group get separated."

Alec shrugged that off. "Why not? We signed a waiver removing any liability from the tour company."

Shelly interjected. "Look, I don't like having to wait any more than you guys do, but if I wanted to do my own thing, I wouldn't have come on this tour. Besides, I'm here to have fun, not break speed records."

Faith was proud of her friend for sticking up for Jake.

Shelly jerked her head discreetly, trying to gain her attention.

Following the hint, Faith glanced around until she spotted Jake, sitting only two tables away. He was with a young, attractive brunette, who couldn't be much more than twenty.

Alec's voice broke in. "Faith, I meant what I said earlier about you coming to Atlanta to visit my firm."

She shifted her focus. "Why don't you tell me more about the type of work I would be doing there?"

Instead of describing a specific job, he began boasting about some of the firm's biggest clients as well as his recent business trips to exotic places.

She tried to listen, but whatever was going on between Jake and the woman at the other table kept distracting her.

Jake was still fuming over Oscar's warning for him to mind his own business. The manipulative man was the last person he would want to work for, though Oscar did have considerable clout and connections. Hopefully, his threat to keep Jake from finding another job was only bluster, and he wouldn't sabotage Jake's chances for the park service position.

April Brooks, Jake's coworker and friend, peered over her menu at him from across the table. "Is anything wrong? You seem distracted."

Jake blew out a long breath. "Before you stopped by the office looking for Chip, I had a run-in with Oscar Prescott." After his dustup with the underhanded businessman, Jake was glad to see a friendly face and had invited her to join him for dinner.

April put down her menu. "That must have been fun. What happened?"

"Let's just say, I don't think he'll be sending me any Christmas cards this year."

She laughed. "Speaking of running into people, I saw our friend Rory Fisher yesterday. He said he might be leaving his job as a game warden."

"He did? Why?"

"He's applied to become Ned Watson's apprentice."

Jake was surprised, and a bit worried. Rory had always seemed happy in his work. His experience and connections as a game warden could give him a big advantage over Jake in landing the job. He couldn't think about that now. "So how does it feel to be back in Yellowstone?"

His question elicited a cheerful grin. "Great so far. I really missed it while I was away at college last fall. I'm glad Chip was able to hire me during the Christmas break. I can sure use the extra money."

"You're helping us out. The other snowcoach driver quit last month, and I don't have a license to drive one of those rigs."

Something captured April's interest, and she gestured to another table. "Do you know the people sitting over there?"

Jake turned his head and spotted Faith and Shelly having dinner with Alec and Rick. They looked very chummy—too chummy. "They're in my tour group this week."

A perceptive smile crossed April's face. "The pretty woman with the long hair has her eye on you."

Jake cast his dinner companion a dry look. "I seriously doubt that."

April leaned forward. "Listen, I know what I'm talking about. I read an article about body language, and hers is begging you to come rescue her from the guy sitting next to her."

In his heart, Jake wished that were true. However, his mind reminded him that he'd already been burned once by Faith. Getting his hopes up would not only be naive, but utterly ludicrous.

After finishing her meal, Faith indulged in a piece of carrot cake. She'd been wanting to try it ever since Jake recommended it Sunday night. He and the woman he'd had dinner with had already left the restaurant. The man certainly didn't lack for female companions.

Alec's voice interrupted Faith's thoughts. "I hear there's a pub down the street with live music. What would you ladies say to joining Rick and me there after we finish dessert?"

Faith was ready to ditch Alec and head straight to her room. Despite boasting about his firm and himself through the entire dinner, he still hadn't shared any specifics about the job he supposedly had in mind for her. It caused her to wonder if he was really interested in hiring her or merely leading her on. "Actually, I think I'll head back to the lodge and turn in early. Tomorrow is another full day."

"Me too," Shelly said, a tad too eagerly.

When the women rose from the table, the men escorted them outside the restaurant. "Sure I can't change your mind about coming with us tonight?" Alec asked.

Faith politely shook her head. "My feet still need to recover from the hike today."

After the men said goodnight and started to head down the

shoveled sidewalk, Faith and Shelly walked in the opposite direction toward the lodge.

"I'm glad you said no," Shelly told her. "I couldn't have listened to Alec brag about himself or his company one second longer. I know you need a job, but you're not that desperate. What about Chip's offer?"

"It sounds like he needs more of an office manager than an accountant, plus I would have to work with Jake on a daily basis."

"And that's a problem? You didn't seem to mind playing in the snow with him today."

Faith cast her a sideways glare, and Shelly wisely changed the subject. "Let's go ice skating tonight. What do you say?"

"With these blisters?"

"Oh, I forgot. Well, at least come to the rink with me while I skate."

Not wanting to deprive Shelly, Faith agreed to go with her. "As long as we don't stay out too late."

Shelly snapped her fingers. "That reminds me. We need to pick up our cross-country skis for tomorrow."

They stopped at the lodge to rent the outdoor equipment at the front desk.

Faith was browsing the park brochures on a stand nearby when she heard a woman at the counter speak to her friend. "Hi, Shelly, what can I help you with?"

While Shelly told the attendant the equipment she needed and what size shoes she wore, Faith picked up a map of the Old Faithful area and studied it. She heard the voice of the woman at the counter again.

"Here you go."

Glancing at the front desk, Faith saw Jillian hand Shelly a pair of skates and ski gear, then Shelly stepped away to a nearby chair to try on the skates.

Jillian had spotted Faith as well. The blonde's cool gaze didn't feel very inviting for someone who worked in hospitality. "Hello, Faith. See any wolves today?"

Putting on a pleasant front, Faith approached the desk.

"Yes, in Lamar Valley."

Jillian nodded. "Jake always knows where to find them." She leaned over the desk as if sharing a secret. "Good thing you're on the tour this week since it's probably his last with Wild Adventures. My father has offered him a job with his company. Promise you won't tell Chip. He doesn't know yet."

Shelly rejoined them and cleared her throat a little louder than necessary. "Sorry to interrupt, but Faith needs to pick up her ski equipment also."

The blonde resumed her professional tone. "Of course. What is your shoe size, Faith?"

After she told her, Jillian disappeared in the back and returned shortly with her equipment. "Here, these should work for you." She handed the skis, poles, and boots to Faith.

Hands full, Faith and Shelly took the elevator to their room to drop off their outdoor gear before going down to the ice rink.

"What was Jillian saying to you about Jake?" Shelly asked as soon as the elevator door closed.

Faith glanced at her friend. "Promise you won't tell Chip?"

Shelly nodded.

"She said her father offered Jake a job, but I got the impression she was sending me a message."

"She's jealous of you, you know."

"Why should she be jealous of me?"

"Maybe Jake told her about your past relationship, or she's sensed the obvious chemistry between you two."

Faith released a rueful sigh. "While we were at the buffalo ranch today, I overheard Jake tell Chip that Jillian had invited him to spend Christmas with her and her family."

"Oh..." Shelly quickly switched to a more upbeat tone. "That doesn't mean he's interested in her romantically."

"Maybe not yet, but if he goes to work for her father, who knows?"

A short while later, when they'd arrived at the frozen pond, Shelly quickly put on her skates and hit the ice, while Faith hovered near the large bonfire, hoping to chase the chill away—more from what Jillian had said than the cold. Was she goading her about Jake working for her father? At least if it were true, Faith wouldn't have to worry about facing him every day if she worked for Chip, though that didn't make her feel any better.

Standing near the ice rink again prompted the memory of the boy who handed her the suspicious note two nights ago. She looked around but didn't see him there now. And the piece of paper had been taken from her room. She hoped the police were closer to tracking down the person responsible.

An eerie sensation prompted the hair on her neck to stand on end. Was someone watching her now?

The crunch of footsteps from behind made her jump, and she spun around.

The sight of Jake approaching instantly calmed her nerves and chased away her fears.

He joined her next to the bonfire and warmed his hands. "How come you're not on the ice with Shelly?"

"The blisters on my feet wouldn't let me."

His brows pressed together. "They're still bothering you?"

"Not too much. What are you doing here this late?"

"I stopped by the office for a while, and now I'm on my way home." Staring at her feet, he rubbed his chin. "It's going to be a rough week if you already have blisters. Do you have an extra pair of boots you can wear?"

"Only sneakers."

"Tomorrow, we'll be cross-country skiing. The boots for that will be more broken in and easier on your feet."

That put her more at ease about the next day. "Good to hear, though I still kind of wish we were going downhill skiing instead."

The dimples in his cheeks deepened. "I never could keep up with you on the slopes. Do you still ski?"

"Not since I left Colorado. I told myself I didn't like the cold but being here has made me realize how much I miss the winters in the mountains."

He inclined his head, his expression thoughtful. "How's

your Aunt Gertrude? I heard she sold her house in Rockville and moved after you left town."

The mention of her aunt brought up bittersweet memories. "She died three years ago."

Jake lowered his gaze. "Sorry, I didn't know."

"She had health problems, so I urged her to move closer to me. Of course, she missed the mountains." Faith paused and glanced down for a moment. "Do you still keep in touch with old friends in Colorado?"

"As much as I can. I try to get back once a year and visit the ones who still live there."

"Like who?"

"Dylan Veracruz."

Faith recalled the name. "Wasn't he your engine captain when you were a firefighter?"

"Yeah, he married a former professor of mine from Alpendale U. Now he's a pastor at a local church. Both he and his wife were a big help to me while I recovered from the accident with the falling tree. I went to their church my last two years in college."

Faith regretted she wasn't there to help him recover too, but she was thankful he'd had good people in his life who were. "Who else do you stay in touch with?"

"Well, there's Trey Tanner—"

"Wait. You don't mean the football star?"

Jake chuckled. "We're actually good friends. In fact, he came on my tour last summer. Now that he's on the Seahawks football team he lives in Seattle."

"Really." She appealed to Jake in a persuasive voice. "Maybe you can get him to autograph a ball cap for me. Shelly has family in Seattle and is a huge Seahawks fan. I'd love to give her the cap for her birthday."

"I'll see what I can do." He was silent for a moment and shifted his stance. "What do you think about Chip's job offer?"

She smiled. "To tell you the truth, I don't know what to think. He never gave me anything in writing."

"I'm pretty sure he plans to."

That put things in a new light. "Let's say he does; how would you feel about working with me?"

The flare of firelight in Jake's eyes seemed to challenge her. "I can handle it, if you can."

She sidestepped his dare and turned the tables. "By the way, I heard a rumor today that you might not be working for Chip much longer."

He frowned. "Who told you that?"

"Is it true?"

Crossing his arms, he stared at the sky, the vapor of his breath floated toward the heavens. "I applied for a job with the park service."

Her mouth fell open as her heart rallied that it wasn't with Jillian's father's company. "That's great. What type of job is it?"

"It's an apprentice for the acting land resources manager. Whoever gets the job will eventually backfill his position when he retires in a few years."

She arched a brow. "Sounds important."

He nodded. "Though it's a bit of a longshot for me."

"No, it sounds perfect—but how will you break it to Chip?"

"I told him when I came here that being a tour guide was only temporary until I found something where I could use my degrees in Geology and Wildfire Science."

"Two degrees. I always knew you were an overachiever."

Her remark drew a smile. "You know, if I get this job, we wouldn't have to work together, if that's a factor that would keep you from accepting Chip's offer."

Did he want her to move here and work for Chip? "I'll keep that in mind, but frankly, I don't think it's the right fit for me."

Jake's grin faded, and he slanted his head. "Why? Is the pay not high enough?"

His remark struck a tender nerve, and she bristled. "I know you probably think money is all I care about, but there's more to it than that."

"I didn't mean to offend you."

"I'm not offended. I told you, I have a great life."

"I know, I know. You have a plush condo, expensive car, a 401K, et cetera."

"Now you're mocking me. Why is it so hard for you to believe that I'm happy?"

"Sounds to me like you're the one who needs convincing." With that, he turned to leave. "See you in the morning, bright and early. Remember to glide on your cross-country skis like you're skating." He mimicked the motion as he walked away.

Watching him disappear in the moonlight, she felt his words convict her heart. The truth was, the only time she could ever remember really being happy was with him. After that, she'd resigned herself to a second-rate life.

The ominous feeling of icy fingers crept up her spine, and it wasn't from the cold.

*Someone is watching me.*

She glanced at Shelly, who was still skating with a few others. A small cluster of spectators were standing near the rink. As Faith scanned them in the dim light, a person bolted and bumped into a man in the group.

"Hey!" the man cried. "Watch where you're going."

Faith followed the fleeing figure with her eyes until it disappeared in the dark.

"Who was that?" a woman asked the man who had been hit.

"I don't know. He was wearing a ski mask."

Faith recalled the cross-country skier who pushed her into the road at Mammoth Hot Springs. Was it the same person? The frightening prospect triggered a shiver. She rubbed her arms, realizing her earlier instinct was right—someone had been spying on her at the rink, and it was the masked man.

## CHAPTER TWELVE

FAITH STARED OUT THE WINDOW AT the falling snow under the streetlights. She'd been awake since five a.m., unable to get her conversation with Jake—or the masked menace at the ice rink—out of her mind. For nearly half an hour now, she'd been sitting up in bed, gazing at the pretty scene outside.

The serene pre-dawn landscape brought back happy memories of the winter morning on her twelfth birthday. It was right after a blizzard, and the snow was deep. Jake had thrown a snowball at her window to wake her and urged her to come out and play with him and Joey.

Not wanting to disturb her aunt, Faith sneaked outside for a snowball fight, and afterward, they built an igloo and a snowman. It was one of her happiest birthdays, though she received very few gifts.

She heard Shelly's voice from the other side of the room. "This is a first—you're awake before me."

Faith pointed to the window. "Look, it's snowing."

Shelly jumped out of bed and came over for a closer view. "Super! We'll have fresh powder this morning. I can't wait." She stared at the snow a couple more seconds, then she glanced at Faith. "What did you and Jake talk about at the skating rink last night?"

"Nothing much."

Shelly pouted. "Fine, don't tell your best friend. See if I care."

Faith broke into a grin. "If you really want to know, we were arguing. He thinks I'm a shallow, unhappy person."

"He didn't say that, did he?"

"Not in so many words, but he implied that the only thing I'm looking for in a job is a high salary."

Shelly sat on her bed. "Well, what else do you want?"

"That's the problem. I'm not sure."

"You know, if you continue to let Alec go on and on about his firm and himself, he's going to think you want to work for him, or you're interested in him. Either way, it's a lose-lose for you. Besides, there are more important things in life than working in a fancy downtown office with fringe benefits."

"Such as?"

"Self-respect and happiness. You had all those perks at Syngexas, but it still didn't make you happy."

Her friend's remark hit the same tender nerve Jake had probed earlier. "You sound like Jake."

"Maybe you should listen to us." A knowing glint flickered in Shelly's eyes. "He's the reason you can't sleep, isn't he?"

"You never give up, do you?"

"Of course not. That's what friends are for."

After breakfast, Faith and Shelly gathered their ski equipment and backpacks from their room and brought everything down to the lobby. Stepping outside the main entrance, Faith recognized the Wild Adventures van already parked in front of the lodge. Chip was handing the ski gear to Jake, who secured them to the top of the van.

As soon as Faith and Shelly handed over their equipment to Chip, Alec showed up.

"You should have joined us last night. The band wasn't too bad considering this is a small town in the middle of nowhere."

Jake climbed down from the van and grabbed his backpack from a nearby bench. "Excuse me, Alec, I need to speak to Faith for a moment."

Alec frowned and gestured to the van. "I thought we were about to leave."

Jake checked his watch. "We still have a few minutes while Chip is checking the air pressure in the tires."

Intrigued and happy for the interruption, Faith grabbed her backpack and left Alec to go with Jake toward the lodge entrance. "What is this about?"

"I'll tell you inside." He held the door open for her. When

they were both in the lobby, he kept his tone professional. "How are your blisters this morning?"

Her excitement deflated like a popped balloon. All he wanted to talk about were her feet. "They're fine."

"I'd like to see them for myself. If you're not careful, they could become infected."

"Look, Jake, I appreciate your concern, but it's really not necessary."

The determined glint in his eye told her he wouldn't take no for an answer.

"All right, Dr. Mitchell." She found a nearby chair, put her backpack down, and took a seat. While she untied the laces of her ski boots, Jake pulled up an ottoman and sat in front of her.

"This is silly. They're only blisters, and I hardly notice them in these boots."

His eyes flared impatiently.

Grudgingly, she removed her boots and socks, then shoved her bare foot at him.

He caught it and pulled it toward him as she straightened her leg.

She rolled her eyes. "This is such a waste of time."

"If you don't stop squirming like a two-year-old, I'm gonna glue your toes together."

Pausing, she squinted at him. "You wouldn't dare."

He returned a sly grin. "It wouldn't be the first time."

The memory of his prank at church camp when they were teens caused her to erupt in laughter. "It took a whole week for that stuff to wear off."

After he finished examining her first foot, she lifted the other one for him to inspect. The tingle of his touch made her leg jerk.

"Be still," he ordered.

"You're tickling me."

"This scar on the ball of your foot. I remember the day you got it. You stepped on a tent spike at a church retreat, and I had to carry you all the way to town because the battery in the church van was dead."

She smiled at the memory. "I'm surprised you still remember."

"Whenever I get a backache, I think of you."

"Thanks a lot."

A twinkle shone in his eyes. "That was some trip. We couldn't have been more than…"

"Sixteen," she said.

He smiled, still cradling her foot in his hand. "Remember Mitzi and Hank?"

"You mean our so-called friends who started the popcorn fight in the movie theater in Rockville that got us all in trouble? Aunt Gertrude wouldn't let me see a movie for the rest of the summer." She inclined her head. "Whatever happened to them?"

Jake resumed his inspection of her other foot. "They got married and moved to Denver."

"Oh." Faith recalled the four of them hanging out together on Friday nights after high school football games. They'd shared their plans and dreams with her, and she didn't even know they had married or where they lived. She'd been too busy working in Texas to stay in touch. That wasn't true. She hadn't wanted to stay in touch because they would have reminded her of Jake.

He released her foot and pulled a tube of ointment from his pack along with medicated bandages. "Put these on your blisters." After giving them to her, he unzipped a pocket and retrieved a sheet of soft, padded material with self-adhesive on the back. "This moleskin will help protect your feet from your shoes rubbing against them."

When he pulled out a pocketknife, Faith teased him. "I hope you're not planning to do surgery with that thing."

"If you don't take care of your feet, I might have to. This is for you to cut off smaller pieces of the moleskin."

She stared at the knife he handed her. "Wait, isn't this the Swiss Army knife I gave you for your eighteenth birthday?"

The corner of his mouth lifted slightly. "Yep."

"And you still use it?"

"Why not? It's a good knife. I never go anywhere without it."

She was touched that he still had it. As he stowed the other medical supplies in his backpack, she was reminded of his firefighting injury. "How is your leg today?"

He zipped the pocket of his backpack, not looking up. "Okay. It only flares up now and then."

Slowly, he rose from his chair. "By the way, we'll be leaving in five minutes."

"I'll return the knife to you as soon as I'm finished wrapping my feet."

"No, hang on to it and the moleskin this week, so you won't get more blisters."

After he left, she opened the attachments of the knife, recalling when she'd bought it for him. And he'd kept it all these years.

She quickly bandaged her feet. As she stood to leave, she glanced toward the front desk and caught Jillian watching her. She must have seen Jake with her—and judging from the blonde's thin lips and narrowed eyes, she wasn't the least bit happy about it.

## CHAPTER THIRTEEN

Eager to leave the lobby and Jillian's prying eyes, Faith ducked out with her backpack and hurried to the van where Chip was handing out lunches and assisting the last members of her group to board.

He greeted her with a friendly wave. "Good morning, Faith. Here's your lunch." He handed her a small paper sack. "Looks like you'll have perfect ski conditions with all this fresh snow."

"Why don't you come with us?" she urged him.

"Not today. I've got too much work to do in the office. Speaking of which, have you given any more thought to my job offer? I could sure use your help."

She inclined her head. "You haven't told me how much it pays."

He bit his lip. "Oh, that… I'll be honest with you. I can't compete with the salary and benefits package you're probably used to. We're a small outfit, but growing. I will promise you that I'll be fair and lenient with time off, and there are other fringe benefits as well."

"Like what?"

He waved his hands as he circled around. "Like working here, for starters."

She laughed. "Too bad you aren't in the used car business."

An earnest glint shone in his eyes. "It's a serious offer, Faith. I'm used to confirming an agreement with a handshake, but for you I'll put it in writing. How does that sound?"

She appreciated him wanting to hire her, though doubted he could convince her to take the job. Still, she wanted to keep her options open. "Thanks. I promise I won't accept any other offers until I've seen yours first."

"Fair enough."

After quickly stowing the lunch in her backpack, she

peered inside the van to find a place to sit. Leslie had taken the passenger seat up front, and it appeared the only space available was on the very last row.

Toting her backpack with her, Faith squeezed through the narrow aisle to the rear, trying to avoid stepping on anyone's feet or belongings in the process.

Shelly, sandwiched on the first row between Mary and Phil with his camera equipment, spoke as Faith passed her. "Where have you been?"

"Jake was doctoring my blisters."

Alec was in the second row with Rick and Donna. "He certainly took long enough."

Faith ignored his remark and finally made it to the back, where she wedged herself beside Ruth, who was sitting next to her husband Norman.

Ruth handed her a tissue to wipe the fog off the window so she could see out. "How are your feet, dear?"

"Better today, thanks."

"I've certainly had my share of blisters, haven't I, Norman?"

Her husband nodded.

Once Faith was settled, Jake got in behind the wheel and pulled the van out of the drive.

Between Ruth telling Faith about her grandchildren and great-grandchildren and Jake up front pointing out interesting features of the park, the time passed quickly as they traveled through the winter wonderland.

Eventually, they arrived at a snow-covered parking area for Tower Fall. While the group exited the van, Jake strode to the rear of the vehicle and climbed the ladder to hand down the skis and poles from the roof. Phil and Norman assisted him in distributing the gear to the members of the group. As each person got their equipment, they hung out near the van, testing out their skis until Jake came down and joined them.

Faith was pressing her boot to lock it in place when her ski slipped out from under her, causing her to lose her balance.

Jake's strong hand steadied her. "Skiing used to be second

nature for you."

"That was a long time ago." She pushed her foot hard against the ski until she heard the click of the bindings engage. After she did the same with her other ski, she felt more stable. "Thanks. I've got it now."

"Jake," Leslie called. "I need help."

He groaned at the annoying reporter's voice, causing Faith to giggle. She didn't buy the woman's helpless act, and from his humorous reaction, Jake wasn't falling for it either.

After he left to assist Leslie, Faith noticed Ruth and Norman already gliding on their skis with ease. The senior couple could give her a lesson or two.

She then spotted Shelly and Phil trying out their skis and headed in their direction. Alec and Rick were inspecting their skis as she passed by, and she heard Alec complaining. He showed his skis to her. "Look at this. These skis are too short and heavy. They're for beginners. It's like having training wheels on your bicycle."

Poor Jake, having to contend with Alec, who was always complaining about something.

Jake glided in front of the group. "When everyone's ready, we'll go up that road a little ways. There's a recreational area with picnic tables at the top of the hill. That's where we'll stop for lunch."

Once all the members of the group were comfortable enough on their skis, they gathered around him, and he started to lead them toward the road.

Skiing with the others, Faith found it easier to glide in the grooves of the two parallel tracks forged by previous skiers. Soon the group split along the two groomed lanes.

Faith quickly caught up to Leslie, who was in the lane across from her.

The reporter saw her and called out. "What were you and Jake doing this morning in the lobby? It looked like he was giving you a foot massage."

Apparently, Jillian wasn't the only spy in the lobby that morning. Faith laughed it off. "He was examining the blisters on my feet." Breaking away from her, she hurried to catch Shelly, Ruth, and Norman.

A loud thud sounded from behind. When Faith glanced over her shoulder, she halted.

Leslie was flat on her back, her skis tangled up.

Fighting the urge to keep going, Faith skied back to help her.

Like an eagle, Jake soared in their direction and dug his skis in the snow, coming to an abrupt stop in front of them. "Are you okay, Leslie?"

"Yes, yes. I just slipped and lost my footing."

He shifted to Faith, who had successfully detached Leslie's skis from her boots. "Let's help her up. You take her right side, I'll take her left." Together they lifted her to her feet.

Indignant, Leslie yanked her arms free of them and brushed the snow from her backside. She caught Phil filming it all and yelled at him. "What are you doing? Cut that thing off."

Ignoring her, he kept the camera rolling. "This is classic. Our ratings will jump sky high with this footage."

"No, they won't, because no one is ever going to see it."

While Leslie argued with Phil, Jake sent Faith a daring glance. "Race you to that tree?"

She followed his gaze to the tall evergreen at the bottom of the hill that the others in the group were now ascending. "You're on."

They took off on the parallel tracks like two race horses sprinting for the finish line. Though Faith knew she wouldn't win, she loved the feel of going full bore on her skis. The brisk air stung as it filled her lungs and chapped her face, invigorating her as she broke into a light sweat.

Once Jake made it to the tree, he waited for her. When she reached him, he glided effortlessly beside her as they approached the long slope leading to the recreation area. "What happened back there between you and Leslie?"

"We were talking and the next thing I knew she fell."

Amusement flickered in his eyes. "What were you discussing that literally knocked her off her feet?"

"You, actually." Faith lifted her brows.

He scoffed at that. "Me?"

"She saw us in the lobby this morning and was probing me about it. You should know that she's determined to get the scoop on you. She thinks you're hiding a deep, dark secret." The two of them stopped skiing, and Faith raised her poles for dramatic effect. "*Man Escapes from World in Winter Wonderland.* Don't you see the headline?"

He shrugged, unimpressed. "Doesn't sound very interesting to me. Besides, what does she think I'm escaping from?"

"Me, I suppose. Leslie found out we knew each other in high school. I think she suspects something is still going on between us."

"Well, she won't find much of a story there."

*As long as she doesn't dig too deep.* "Even so, I don't want to be blindsided with my picture on the evening news."

"That's ironic coming from you."

"What?"

He cast her a sideways glance. "As I recall, once upon a time, you did a pretty good job of blindsiding *me.*"

Faith sighed and gazed at the cloudless sky. "Can't we simply enjoy the day without bringing up the past?"

He stabbed his poles in the snow. "You mean wipe the slate clean for a day?"

"Yeah. Let's pretend we just met each other for the very first time."

He thought it over. "You mean, like this?" He extended his hand. "Allow me to introduce myself. I'm Jake Mitchell."

She smiled and shook hands. "And I'm Faith Chandler."

"It's a pleasure to meet you, Faith."

"Likewise, Jake."

Continuing their silly banter, they ascended the long hill. When they eventually reached the picnic area, Faith could hardly believe it. Time had passed so quickly.

Shelly was already seated across from Ruth and Norman at a picnic table under the pavilion. She grinned as Faith arrived with Jake.

Knowing she'd be interrogated later, Faith was having too much fun to care. After gliding to the pavilion, she stopped to remove her skis. Jake caught her arm and held her steady while she released her boots from their bindings.

Still playing the game, she gazed at him with a coy expression. "Thanks, uh…"

"Jake," he said. "Let's do this again sometime."

"By all means." Watching him ski away to greet the others, warmth radiated through her like sipping hot chocolate next to a wood-burning stove. She brushed the snow off her skis and leaned them against one of the wooden posts supporting the shelter.

When she sat beside Shelly at the picnic table, her friend leaned close. "What was that all about?"

"It's a game we're playing."

Shelly laughed and astutely dropped it. "You know, I'm impressed with how quickly you got the hang of those skis."

Ruth, who had been listening, smiled. "Yes, you looked like a pro out there, Faith."

"Thanks," she said to the older woman. "I could say the same about you. You're putting the rest of us to shame. How do you stay in such good shape?"

"Oh, Norman and I have been cross-country skiing for years." The couple exchanged fond glances, and Ruth patted her husband on the arm before she addressed Faith again. "We didn't take up cross-country skiing until we retired. It's a great way to stay in shape."

"It's kind of hard to do in Texas. We don't get a lot of snow."

"Better move to the mountains then," Norman said. He retrieved his lunch out of his backpack. "I'm starving. I think we should go ahead and eat."

"Me too," Shelly seconded. "I feel like I've burned a million calories this morning."

Faith felt the same way. After she and Shelly removed their lunches and thermoses from their backpacks, they unwrapped their sandwiches.

Shelly looked at Faith's. "What kind is that?"

"Same as I had yesterday, peanut butter and banana with honey and raisins." Faith held it up so Shelly could see. "What about you?"

"A club. Want to trade?"

Faith clutched hers to her chest. "Not on your life. I've been looking forward to eating this all morning. It was my favorite when I was a kid." After sending a silent thanks to God for the beautiful day and good company, she took a big bite.

Alec and Rick appeared from the woods instead of the road and settled at the empty picnic table next to Faith's.

Between Leslie's fall and playing make-believe with Jake, Faith had lost track of them. They must have been ahead of the group and gone exploring.

While everyone else was at the picnic tables eating their lunches, Leslie finally arrived with Jake.

Faith realized he must have gone to assist her.

Once he helped Leslie disengage her skis, she stomped toward the pavilion as if she might bite off the head of the first person who spoke to her.

Faith was glad the temperamental reporter chose to sit at Alec and Rick's table instead of hers.

When Jake finally joined the rest of the group under the pavilion, he surprised Faith by sitting in the vacant spot beside her, spurring her heartrate. Glancing at her sandwich, he cast her a wry grin. "Peanut butter and banana, huh? You've been eating that since grade school."

"You're not supposed to know that, remember?"

Ruth smiled at them. "You went to school together?"

He gave the older woman a deadpan look. "A long time ago. I tried to get rid of her, but she keeps following me."

Faith rolled her eyes. "That's not the way I remember it."

"So you were childhood sweethearts," Ruth said in a wistful voice. "How darling."

Jake opened a bag of chips. "More than that. We were engaged to be married."

Faith nearly choked on a piece of banana.

Shelly's mouth fell open as Ruth beamed at them. "How wonderful that you've found each other again."

Faith chugged water from her thermos to clear her throat. "It's not like that. We just happen to be in the same tour group."

"But you make such a cute couple," Ruth said. "Why didn't you tie the knot, if you don't mind me asking?"

Shelly leaned in. "Yes, please don't keep us in suspense." Her eyes flickered at Faith, wide with curiosity.

Jake also stared at her. "I'd like to hear this myself."

All eyes at the table were on Faith now, and a strange buzzing filled her head. "We were too young," she said, shrugging.

Norman piped up. "Nonsense! Ruth and I married at eighteen. Been married fifty-eight years this month. Got four kids, eight grandchildren, and two great grandkids."

Surprised by the great-grandfather's defense of youthful marriages, Faith's face burned under their inquisitive stares. "Sounds like you were the exception."

"But now you have a second chance," Ruth told her. "After all, neither of you are married, are you?"

Faith exchanged glances with Jake, and they slowly shook their heads.

"Well," Ruth continued, "Now that you're here together, you can make up for lost time."

Faith detected a slight glimmer in Jake's eyes. She was surprised he found it amusing.

As she resumed eating her sandwich, Shelly whispered in her ear. "Looks like the cat's out of the bag."

That's when Faith noticed Alec and Leslie observing them from the next table—Alec was scowling, and Leslie wore a sly grin.

# CHAPTER FOURTEEN

WHEN JAKE HAD FINISHED HIS LUNCH, he got up from his seat next to Faith and stood in front of the pavilion to get the group's attention. The winter picnickers soon stopped talking amongst themselves and turned their focus to him.

"The trailhead to see the waterfall is only a short distance away," he said. "You won't need your skis. They'll be safe here until we return. After you've cleaned up your tables and stowed your trash in your backpacks, we'll gather right here where I'm standing."

Soon everyone mustered there except for Leslie.

"Aren't you coming?" Jake asked her.

Still seated at the picnic table, she rested her chin on her fist, looking bored. "I've had enough fresh air for one day. I need to make a few calls at the lodge. Can you call someone to pick me up?"

Jake suspected her bruised ego from her earlier fall and her difficulty climbing up the long hill in skis had more to do with her not wanting to go than work. "By the time I call someone to pick you up and they arrive, we'll be finished with the hike. Besides, the road we skied up is closed to vehicles."

"Well, I don't want to hike to the waterfall," she said.

"I'll wait with her," Alec volunteered. "I didn't want to do the hike anyway."

Rick grudgingly shrugged. "I'll stay here too. It'll give me a chance to hone my skiing technique."

Though Leslie wouldn't be alone, Jake still wasn't thrilled with the idea of the group splitting up.

When he hesitated, Alec sneered. "Lighten up, Mitchell. Nothing bad is going to happen."

Leslie called to her cameraman. "Phil, you're staying with us. I want footage of me on skis for my feature."

"*Now?*" he said.

"Yes," she replied in a demanding voice.

Phil sent Shelly a rueful glance before he trudged away toward his boss.

Since there was nothing Jake could do to change their minds, he decided to make the best of the situation for the sake of the others. "All right, for those of you who aren't going on the hike, stick together and don't leave this area. We won't be gone long." Then he motioned to the rest of the group. "Come on, hikers, let's hit the trail."

Standing with Shelly at the first overlook, Faith stared in wonder at the view in the distance. The enormous cascade of water, known as Tower Fall, had frozen into an icicle chandelier, the thunder of its rushing waters silenced by the cold. Below the snow-draped canyon walls, geothermal steam rose from the edge of the Yellowstone River, giving the place a mysterious, ethereal appearance like a hidden fantasy world.

Descending deeper into the canyon via steep switchbacks along a narrow trail, Faith got a closer view of the 132-foot frozen column. It stood proudly, like a giant ice sculpture, sparkling in the sun. Marveling at the beauty of the crystalized waters nestled in the cleft of the canyon, she felt as if she'd discovered a rare treasure that had been miraculously preserved through time.

By now, the rest of the group had caught up to her. As they crowded close together to take pictures, Jake explained the origins of the canyon from lava flows.

As he spoke, Faith could easily picture him as a park administrator. With his knowledge and enthusiasm, he'd be a perfect fit for the position he'd described to her. She hoped he got the job.

When he'd finished sharing about the canyon and waterfall, he led them farther down the trail to a view of Tower Creek where it flowed into the Yellowstone River.

Breathing in the clean, brisk air, Faith surveyed the vast winter wilderness. It moved her like words to a favorite poem she once knew by heart. Hearing a high-pitched whistle in the air, she lifted her gaze to a magnificent bald eagle soaring overhead.

As if sensing her reverie, Jake spoke softly over her shoulder. "Most of the eagles leave for winter, but a few like that one choose to stay."

Despite the bitter cold, his presence drove the chill away like standing next to a hot spring. Their earlier game of pretend had given her an inkling of what might have been, and how she missed their special bond that went beyond friendship. His kind, steady disposition could have brought the elusive balance she needed in life.

A tap on her other shoulder interrupted her thoughts. "Excuse me, Faith. I want to take a picture before we leave here." Shelly moved in front of her with her camera.

Jake stepped away and called out to the group taking pictures and enjoying the scenery. "When you're finished here, head back up the trail. I'll meet you at the top."

While Shelly and the rest were focused on the view of the rivers, Faith quietly followed him to the last overlook, waiting until they were alone to speak. "I can see why you love it here, Jake."

He stopped and turned around. "It's very different from Dallas, I imagine."

"Yes, but similar to the Rockies."

Raising a brow, he slanted his head. "Is that good or bad?"

She desperately wanted him to know the truth, at least as much as she dared share with him. "Jake, despite what you think, I never wanted to leave Colorado—"

He interrupted her. "I know… It wasn't Colorado you were running away from. It was me."

She winced at the sharpness of his words. Though they were true, it still hurt to hear them from his lips.

"Sorry, I forgot we were starting from a clean slate. It doesn't leave much for us to talk about."

His lighter tone put her more at ease. "Sure, it does." As she tried to think of a safe topic, one came to mind. "Like your new job."

"I haven't even been contacted for an interview."

"It doesn't matter. I know you're going to get it, Jake."

A glimmer of amusement shone in his eyes. "You do, huh? What makes you so sure?"

"Because of your knowledge and passion for the park. They'd be crazy not to hire you."

A shadow of doubt touched his brow. "Thanks. I wish I had your confidence. Good jobs like that don't come around very often, and when they do they're in high demand. I have stiff competition." He shifted toward her. "Speaking of job prospects, Chip really hopes you'll come work for him."

She gazed down at the snow on the trail. "I'm considering it, but I'm not ready to make any decisions yet." Since Jake had shared about his job opportunity, she felt she could confide in him. Lifting her eyes, she spoke openly. "I've never had the kind of passion for my work like you do for yours. The truth is, you were right. I haven't been happy for a long time, especially at work. That's why I want to make sure my next career move is the right one."

He nodded as if he understood. "Listen to that inner voice. It'll tell you what to do."

"It's funny you should say that. It wasn't until I came here that I started to hear it again."

Inclining his head, he regarded her intently. "And what's it saying to you now?"

*Tell him the truth, Faith.* Gazing into Jake's eyes, she resisted the voice. This wasn't the time or the place. "I'm getting cold. I think I'll head back to the van."

As she moved to pass him, he touched her arm. "Please wait."

She stopped and slowly turned around. The earnest expression on his face made her wonder what more he had to say.

"Despite what you think, I don't hate you, Faith." His eyes searched hers. "I only wish that you would tell me the truth."

The words prompted her to shake her head. "No, you

don't."

Her resistance didn't dissuade him. "I want to know. You owe me that much."

She gazed down at their footprints in the snow, unable to face him.

Tenderly, he lifted her chin toward him. "What did I ever do to make you distrust me so much?"

A rogue tear escaped her eye and froze against her cheek.

Voices below signaled the approach of the rest of their party. After a moment's hesitation, he withdrew his hand.

She abruptly turned and began marching up the trail, dabbing her eyes and face with her scarf. *How can I tell him the truth without hurting him all over again?*

When Faith arrived at the picnic pavilion ahead of the rest, Jake's plea to tell him the truth continued to convict her. Maybe one day she'd tell him what he wanted to know. She couldn't bring herself to do it now. Still lost in her thoughts, she heard his urgent voice.

"Where are Leslie and the others?"

Faith scanned the area. She didn't see them anywhere. Their ski equipment was gone as well.

Jake began calling their names. Faith did the same.

By now, the rest of the group had joined them in combing the area.

After ten minutes of fruitless searching, worry and frustration lined Jake's face. "Hopefully, they're waiting for us at the van."

Faith quickly engaged her boots in her skis and began gliding down the trail ahead of Jake and the five remaining members of her group.

Shelly caught up to her. "Where did you and Jake disappear to at the falls?"

Faith kept her eyes forward. "We didn't disappear. I followed him up the trail."

"And?" Shelly probed, interest resonating in her voice.

Not wanting to talk about it, Faith used her poles to push off, leaving Shelly behind.

The afternoon sun had melted the snow a bit, making it smooth and slick. Faith's skis glided along the tracks almost effortlessly. The exhilaration of gliding downhill temporarily freed her mind from thoughts of Jake and her self-imposed bondage of regret.

She was far ahead of the others by the time she reached the van. They weren't even visible from the parking lot. Taking advantage of the momentary solitude, she skied closer to the woods where she spotted a small fox wandering at the edge.

While she admired the little creature from a distance, the sound of a motor disrupted the quiet.

Shifting her focus, she saw a red and black snowmobile crossing the parking lot at breakneck speed. Surprised, she stared at the oncoming vehicle, expecting it to stop.

When it didn't, she dove out of the way right as it veered where she'd been standing.

The snowmobile stopped, and the driver's head turned in her direction. His face was hidden behind a helmet and goggles.

The force of her fall had disengaged Faith's skis. Dazed and confused, she stared at the red and black body of the motorized sled as it spun around, engine revving.

A moment later, it raced toward her again.

She leapt up from the snow. The van was closer than the woods so she made a run for it. Sprinting as fast as her legs would carry her through the deep powder, she scanned the ski trail. Still no sign of Jake or the others. She wanted to scream for help, but it would only deplete the dwindling supply of oxygen in her overtaxed lungs. She couldn't evade her pursuer for long. She needed a plan.

Spotting the ladder on the back of the van, she wondered if she could make it there in time.

The sound of the engine grew louder as it closed in.

Pushing herself as hard as she could, she felt her chest and throat constrict from the cold air and extreme exertion. Like an elk chased by a wolf, she was in a race for her life. Her legs and lungs burned, begging her to stop, but she refused to listen—her survival depended on making it to the van.

Lunging toward the ladder, she grabbed hold of it and scrambled up.

As she glanced over her shoulder, she caught sight of her assailant swerving to avoid crashing into the van.

After she hoisted herself to the roof, Faith scooped a fistful of snow and hurled it at him. "You crazy—"

She was interrupted by Jake's voice shouting in the distance. "Hey, you! Leave her alone!"

Turning her head, she felt the tightness in her chest ease as he flew toward her on his skis. Shelly and Norman were close behind.

The maniac quickly U-turned and sped away.

Inhaling a deep breath to fill her depleted lungs, Faith watched her nemesis zip down the road until the snowmobile disappeared.

Shelly skied to the van and peered up at her. "Are you okay?"

Relieved to see her friend, Faith slowly descended the ladder. "I'm still in one piece."

Jake had followed the snowmobile a short distance before he doubled back. He came to an abrupt halt on his skis at the rear of the van. "What happened?"

Faith pivoted and gestured toward the road. "That snowmobile came out of nowhere and started chasing me. I'm pretty sure the driver wanted to kill me."

Jake stared at her, his eyes wide and his face ashen. "Are you all right?"

She nodded, though she was still trembling inside. "The driver was wearing a helmet and goggles, preventing me from seeing his face. The only thing I got a good look at was the red and black snowmobile."

Wanting to ease Jake's worries, she tried a dose of humor. "Maybe I should have purchased travel insurance for this tour."

He didn't laugh. Instead, he scanned the parking lot. "Have you seen Leslie and the other three?"

Faith shook her head. "I was the only one here before the snowmobile showed up."

After removing his skis, Jake did his best to appear calm. She knew how frustrated and upset he must be. Hopefully, the four missing people would show up soon.

About fifteen minutes later, Rick emerged from the woods nearby and skied to where the group was waiting.

Jake crossed his arms. "Where have you been?"

He gestured behind him. "Exploring a trail in the woods."

"What happened to the other three?"

"Leslie and Phil skied down the hill with us and caught a ride with someone who pulled in the parking lot to turn around. I didn't see who it was. Leslie told us they'd see us at the lodge." Rick peered in the distance. "Alec said he was going to ski down the road a bit. I thought he'd be back by now."

Jake raised his voice at Rick. "You were supposed to stay with the group."

Unfazed, the other man shrugged it off. "We didn't go far." He pointed to a figure skiing toward them. "See, there's Alec now."

Before the group departed from the parking lot, Jake radioed the ranger station from the driver's seat of the van to report the snowmobile incident to his ranger friend, Noah Fulton.

After Jake gave a brief summary of what happened, Noah followed up with questions. "What was the name of the woman again?"

"Faith Chandler." Jake glanced outside the van at Faith talking to Shelly. "The snowmobile was painted red and black. Neither one of us saw the driver's face."

"What else can you tell me?"

"Not much since I didn't see exactly what happened. By the time I got here, Faith was on the roof of my van, and the snowmobile was speeding away."

"Too bad there were no witnesses. Without a description of the driver or anyone to corroborate her story, it'll be hard to find and arrest the person responsible. And if we do, it'll be her word against his. Do you believe she's telling the truth?"

Jake stared at Faith through the window. When she walked out on him seven years ago, she broke his heart and his trust. Instead of having the decency to tell him in person, she sent him a text, of all things. He still remembered it word for word.

*I'm sorry, but I can't marry you, Jake. I've decided my career has to come first. That's why I'm transferring to another university with a better business program.*

*The last thing I ever wanted was to hurt you. In time, you'll see that this was the best thing for both of us. I hope you'll understand that my mind is made up. Please don't try to find or contact me.  —Faith*

He never did buy her lame explanation. And while the breakup might have been the best thing for her, to receive her text on the heels of his brother's tragic death was definitely not the best thing for him.

Regarding Noah's question about the snowmobile incident, however, Jake couldn't think of any reason for her not to be truthful. "Yes, I believe her."

"Is there anything else you'd like to add to the report?"

The skier Faith had said pushed her at Mammoth Hot Springs entered Jake's mind, as did the rock slide on the snowshoe outing yesterday. "Actually, there is." He quickly told Noah about the other bizarre close calls.

"You think the same person is responsible?" the ranger asked.

"I can't say for sure, but after what happened today, I'm beginning to think it's possible."

The near-miss with the snowmobile had shaken Faith more than she'd let on to either Jake or Shelly. It had given her a splitting headache too.

Shelly was talking to her as they carried their ski equipment through the lobby of the lodge to turn in at the front desk. "I'm glad Jake notified the ranger about that snowmobile driver. I feel better knowing they're keeping an eye out for him." She raised a brow. "Hey, if you couldn't see the person's face, maybe it was a woman. It could have been Leslie, trying to scare you off so she could have Jake all to herself."

*More likely Jillian.* Faith brushed off the pestering thought. "I'm pretty sure it was a man." Probably the same one who was spying on her at the rink last night and shoved her into the road at Mammoth Hot Springs. "Hopefully, the police can trace the snowmobile to him."

While they waited for someone to help them at the front desk, Shelly gave her a pep talk. "The important thing is that you're all right. Don't let it spoil your vacation. Try to relax and things will look better in the morning."

*Relax! Easy for her to say. How could she relax when someone wanted to kill her?*

# CHAPTER FIFTEEN

IT WAS ELEVEN AT NIGHT, AND Faith lay awake in bed. She wondered if she might be safer somewhere other than Yellowstone, but where? She didn't feel good about being home alone in her condo. At least with her tour group she was with other people, and that made her feel a little more secure.

Tomorrow the Elk group would be moving to a different lodge, deep inside the park. Maybe by then, the person harassing her would have been caught.

Rather than stare at the ceiling all night, Faith decided she might as well do something productive. She'd noticed a laundromat downstairs in the lodge. It was probably her best opportunity to do laundry before they relocated to their next destination. She wanted to make sure she had enough clean wool socks and thermal underwear for the rest of the week.

After quietly slipping on her sweats over her pajamas and stepping into her shoes, she gathered her things to leave. She also grabbed her cell phone and turned it on in case Shelly awoke and called to find out where she was—or if Faith encountered anything suspicious and needed to call 911.

Carrying her laundry bag and a small packet of detergent she'd brought from home, Faith cautiously opened the door and peered into the hallway. Satisfied that no one was lurking, she tiptoed out of the room.

Downstairs, the lobby was empty, except for the female attendant at the front desk. Faith smiled and said hello when she passed by. It was good to know someone was on duty, and Faith felt more secure as she made her way down the hall.

Entering the laundromat, she found an available washer and dumped the contents of her laundry bag in it along with the detergent. When the wash cycle began, she moved to the window and gazed outside. The brilliant moon reflected off the sparkling snow, illuminating the vacant street in wintry twilight.

Alone with her thoughts, Jake's words at the waterfall echoed in her mind. *What did I ever do to make you distrust me so much?* They plunged her heart deeper in the sea of regret, as if that were possible. "Oh, Jake, if only we could go back in time and start over."

A solitary car slowly traveled down the road.

Watching the taillights fade in the distance, she noticed a light on in the Wild Adventures office, next door. Staring at the building, she glimpsed Chip walk past the window. Rather than hang out by herself killing time until her laundry was done, she wanted to pay her old friend a visit and find out why he was still at the office.

On her way through the lobby again, she waved to the woman at the desk before heading outside. Braving the cold in only sweats worn over her pajamas, she made a dash next door.

As she entered Chip's office, he peered up and immediately rose from his desk, his eyes wide with surprise. "Faith? What are you doing here at this hour?"

She quickly closed the door behind her and moved to the space heater to warm up. "I couldn't sleep, so I'm washing my clothes at the lodge. What's your excuse?"

He released a weary sigh. "End of the year bookkeeping. I'm terrible at it. Aunt Helen somehow managed to keep things in order and accounted for, but nothing ever balances when I do it. You know I was always better at marketing than math. I'm trying to get as much of it done before Christmas because I want to take next week off and spend it with my family."

She admired his valiant efforts to be with his wife and kids. "That's sweet. You're blessed to have such a great family."

"Thanks, though Beth deserves most of the credit." He grabbed the empty chair in the corner and brought it closer to his desk for her to sit.

"You know Jake was always good at math," Faith said as she relaxed in the chair. "I'm sure he could help you."

Chip moved behind his desk and sat down. "Yeah, but I don't want to take advantage of him, plus I want him to stick around as long as possible. Between you and me, I think it's only a matter of time before he finds another job."

Not wanting to confirm Chip's suspicions, she carefully guarded her words. "What makes you say that?"

"Ever since he had to quit his job as a firefighter in Rocky Mountain National Park, he's always wanted to work for the park service again. To tell you the truth, I think the only reason he's still working here is because he doesn't want to leave me in the lurch."

Chip slanted his head, his brow creasing. "By the way, I hear you've experienced some pretty bizarre incidents on this trip. Jake told me about the rock slide yesterday and the crazy snowmobile driver today. That's pretty upsetting, but I'm sure the rangers will find the guy and revoke his license. I hope it hasn't ruined your vacation."

Since Chip had been generous in giving away the free trip and seemed to have enough problems of his own to deal with, she shrugged it off and didn't bring up the skier who had pushed her in the road, or the note and break-in at the lodge. "Nah, I refuse to let it get to me."

She glanced at the clock on the wall. "While I'm waiting for the washer to finish, would you like me to look over your books?"

Chip's face lit up. "Really? That would be great."

"I'm not promising miracles, though I am pretty good at balancing ledgers. If you show me your data, I'll get started."

He rose and motioned for her to take his chair in front of the screen. "It's all up on the computer. While you're doing that, I'll fetch us coffee."

"Decaf for me, please," she said. "I'm still hoping to catch a few winks."

While he stepped away, she analyzed the spreadsheets. By the time he returned with the coffee, she'd zeroed in on a discrepancy. "I found one problem," she told him as he set her cup on the desk.

"That was fast."

He peered over her shoulder, and she pointed out the error. "This was entered as a credit instead of a debit."

"You're right. Who knows how long it would have taken me to find that? Thanks."

"Since I'm here I can look over the rest of your books to see if anything else might be a problem."

"Super! That reminds me…" He walked to his printer in the corner of the office and retrieved a piece of paper. When he returned, he handed it to her. "Here is the official offer for the V.P. of Finance position in writing. It may not be exactly what you're looking for, but it could be a port in the storm, at least until the right job comes along. Then maybe you could help me find your replacement."

She scanned the offer. From what she'd seen in the ledger, the salary was more than he could afford. "This is very generous, Chip. I don't know what to say."

"How about 'yes'?"

"I wish it were that simple. There's a lot to consider."

He raised a brow. "If working with Jake is a problem, I can arrange it so the two of you rarely see each other."

She shook her head. "No, the problem is me. The truth is, I don't know what I want to do or where I want to work. Before I came here, I thought I had it all figured out. Now I feel like I'm starting from scratch."

Chip dropped the sales pitch and displayed more brotherly concern. "You know, this is a pretty good place to find answers, away from all the hubbub of a big city. When I need direction, I like to go into the wilderness to be alone with God. Spending time with Him helps put everything into perspective and makes it easier to see what's really important. What I usually discover is that what I think I want isn't what I actually need."

While Chip moved to the other desk to work, Faith sipped her coffee, thinking about what he'd said. It reminded her of what Jake had told her about listening to her inner voice. She had never really sought God's will for her life and now everything was a mess. At this point, what did she have to lose?

She paused for a moment to pray. *Okay, Lord, I'm turning my future over to you.* As soon as she'd finished, she felt better, more at peace. It seemed too easy to pray and expect everything to work out. She was used to making things happen. Believing in God was one thing, trusting Him with practical day-to-day matters like finding a job stretched her faith more than she was used to.

A little while later, when Faith was studying Chip's financial records, she noticed more errors in the bookkeeping. The timing coincided right after Jake's mother passed away. The business had barely made enough to cover expenses. Still, Faith found a few opportunities to improve the company's bottom line and jotted them on a pad of paper.

She wondered what it would be like to live and work here. The town was nice enough, but what if Jake dated Jillian—or that pretty young woman he had dinner with? The thought made Chip's coffee turn to acid in her stomach. No, that would be a deal-breaker.

Her cell phone rang from her pants pocket, startling her. Thinking it must be Shelly, she answered it immediately.

A frantic woman's voice surprised her. "Faith, it's Monica."

*Monica is alive!* It took a moment for it to sink in. "Where on earth have you been?"

"I only have a minute. I didn't want to involve you, but I had no choice. You're the only person I can trust—"

"What are you talking about?"

The sound of pounding and a distant siren came over the phone—followed by a loud clatter.

"Monica? Monica!" Faith called. Trepidation spiked her heartrate when no one responded.

A moment later, the line went dead.

Faith immediately tried to call her back with no success. She then dialed 911 and reported her fears that Monica might be in danger. Hopefully, they could trace her phone number to find her location.

As soon as she'd finished with the 911 operator, Faith texted the FBI agent who had contacted her at Mammoth Hot Springs and informed him about Monica's disconnected call. Other than praying she was all right, Faith didn't know what else she could do.

Chip spoke from the other desk. "I couldn't help overhearing. What was that all about?"

She'd almost forgotten he was there. She told him about Monica's disappearance and the federal agent's investigation into her former company.

He stared at her in disbelief. "Good thing you don't work there anymore. It sounds like a shady operation."

She shrugged. "I always thought it was on the up-and-up."

It was two a.m. when Faith snuck back into her room with her clean clothes.

By the time her laundry was dry, she had managed to square away most of Chip's finances. She'd also handed him a list of suggestions for cutting costs and increasing profits. He was so delighted he offered her another free vacation tour in the summer. She thanked him and told him that wasn't necessary. She was simply doing a favor for an old friend.

Not wanting to wake Shelly, Faith quietly set her folded clothes on the dresser and pulled off her sweatshirt in the dark.

"Stop!" The lamp clicked on, and something lightweight hit Faith's backside.

Startled, she spun around and squinted into the glaring rays.

Her roommate was armed with another slipper, ready to launch.

"Shelly, it's me. Faith."

After blinking hard, Shelly fell back on her bed. "I thought you were the burglar."

"If I were, that slipper wouldn't stop me."

Sitting up again, Shelly eyed Faith's sweat pants and pajama top. "Where have you been?"

"Doing my laundry."

"At this hour? If I'd known you needed to do your laundry that bad, I would have come with you."

"It's okay. I managed to keep myself occupied giving Chip

a hand with his finances."

Shelly frowned and shook her head. "You really can't leave work behind, can you?"

"It's not like that. I was doing him a favor to pass the time until my laundry was done."

Her friend cast her a sly look. "Was Jake there too?"

Annoyed and tired, she answered in a clipped tone. "No. Now go to sleep." Crawling into bed, Faith buried herself under the covers.

Shelly continued talking. "Why didn't you ever tell me that you and Jake were engaged? I'm your best friend. I couldn't believe it when he told Ruth today at lunch."

Faith sighed and rolled toward her friend. "It's hard for me to talk about, even now."

"You still care about him, don't you?"

"I never stopped caring. He thinks I went away to college and forgot all about him. The truth is hardly a day went by that I didn't think about him."

Shelly responded in a sisterly tone. "Then you need to tell him what you just told me."

Faith was doubtful. "It's too late. Why would he bother with me when he could have his pick of women here?"

"Because you were his first love, the one he wanted to marry."

When Faith finally drifted off to sleep, she dreamed she was going to a wedding. She arrived at the church late and saw Jillian at the altar with Jake.

"Jake!" she cried, her heart breaking. "You were supposed to marry me."

*"I warned you not to marry him, Faith."*

She pivoted toward the male voice and recognized a face she hadn't seen in years. "Joey?"

The young man gave her a rueful grin, then disappeared.

Jake stared at her. "What have you done with my brother?"

All at once, she was outside in the snow. A red wolf

emerged from the woods and began to stalk her.

She turned and ran, but the wolf was closing in. Glancing back, Faith tripped and fell in the snow.

With a jolt, Faith woke herself from the nightmare. For a moment, she wasn't sure where she was. She flipped on the light to reorient herself and was relieved to see Shelly sound asleep in the other bed.

As the pounding of Faith's heart subsided, it became clear that she couldn't put it off any longer. Until she told Jake everything, the past would continue to chase her like that red wolf, and she'd never have any peace.

## CHAPTER SIXTEEN

EARLY THURSDAY MORNING, FAITH YAWNED AS she waited with her and Shelly's luggage outside the entrance of the Moose Run Lodge. A crowd of people were standing around from different tour groups, including her own. A bus would soon pick them up and drop them off at the snowcoach station. From there, her group would be shuttled deep inside the park to the Old Faithful Snow Lodge, where they would stay for the next two days. Their luggage would be transported separately.

Faith had woken early to pack her things and was running on very little sleep. Her earlier jitters from Monica's call and the vivid nightmare quickly subsided in the bright yet bitterly cold morning, and she felt safe surrounded by people. The masked skier wouldn't dare try anything as long as she stuck to her group.

Since Shelly wasn't around, Faith reached for her phone and scanned her messages. Nothing new from Monica or the FBI agent. She didn't know if that was good or bad.

When she spotted Shelly walking toward her after checking out of the lodge, she turned off her phone and hid it in the pocket of her overstuffed backpack. "I was afraid you might miss the bus. Was there a line at the front desk?"

"No, I stopped by my car to get my other hat. By the way, you left this in the back. I thought you might want it." She handed Faith the small canvas bag with her mail.

"Thanks, but I stashed it there because I didn't want to keep up with it. I don't have any room left in my backpack."

"Oh, well. It's too late now. That looks like the luggage van pulling up." Shelly reached for the canvas bag. "Here, I'll put it in my backpack."

As soon as she had stowed it away, the van parked in front of them and two young men jumped out.

"Make sure they load my things," Shelly said to Faith. "I

need to stop by the restroom in the lodge."

Once Shelly had left, Faith reached for her heaviest suitcase to hand to the workers loading the van.

"Here, let me." It was Jake, standing next to her. He lifted her luggage and gave it to one of the men, then he made sure they loaded Shelly's as well.

The bags taken care of, Jake paused and stared at Faith's feet. "How are those blisters today?"

"Much better." Remembering the decision she'd made after the nightmare, she sucked in a deep breath, mustering her courage. "Jake, do you have any time today? There's something I need to speak to you about."

He paused to think for a moment. "How about this evening, after we arrive at Old Faithful?"

Relieved that their talk would have to wait until then, the tension in her body relaxed. "That sounds good—oh, by the way, here's your Swiss Army knife." She reached in her pocket to give it to him.

He raised his palm. "Hang on to it until Saturday. The tour isn't over yet, and it might come in handy." He sent her a quick smile before leaving to help Mary load her luggage.

Shelly returned. "Was that Jake?"

Faith watched him from a distance. "Yes, he helped me with our bags." The two strolled together toward the bus. "I'm going to talk to him tonight and tell him everything."

Shelly patted Faith's shoulder. "You're doing the right thing."

Alec approached and pointed at Faith. "There you are. I just got off the phone with the Human Resources manager at my firm. How about having dinner with me tonight, and I'll fill you in on the job opening she told me about? I think you'd be perfect for it."

Shelly clutched Faith's arm and whispered in her ear. "Be strong." Before her friend headed for the bus, she shot her a stern look.

Heeding the warning, Faith started to decline his dinner invitation. "I don't think—"

"By the way, I saved this for you." He handed her a newspaper.

Her eyes flew to the headline: *Syngexas Executives Suspected of Fraud and Cover-up.* Her pulse throbbed in her temple as she read further.

*In addition to the CEO and several executives under investigation, the disappearance of Monica Wallace, who was an employee with the company, is also being looked into. It is believed that she had access to certain documents pertinent to the case.*

Shelly's voice called from a distance. "Faith, hurry up!"

When Faith tried to give the paper back to Alec, he waved his hand. "No, you keep it," he told her.

She thanked him, then hurried to the bus to board.

Shelly was waiting for her by the steps. "What took you so long?"

Faith glanced at Alec, who had caught up and was standing behind her now. "Why don't you go ahead, Alec? I want to talk to Shelly for a minute."

"I'll save you a seat," he said, moving past them.

After he climbed into the bus, Faith thrust the paper at her friend. "I was reading this."

Shelly skimmed the article. "This isn't your problem anymore, remember?" She handed it back.

Faith spoke in a low voice. "But it's so shocking. Did I tell you that Monica called me last night while I was doing my laundry?"

Shelly's brows shot up. "She did? What did she want?"

"I don't know. We got disconnected. I texted the FBI agent who contacted me at Mammoth Hot Springs to make him aware. I hope she's all right. After that email she sent me, I've been worried something bad might happen to her."

"Wait a minute." Shelly squinted at Faith. "What email?"

"Oh." Faith realized she hadn't told her yet. "I didn't find out about it until Sunday night. It was in my junk folder. Monica said she needed my help and to contact her right away.

I tried, but her phone number and email address had been changed so I wasn't able to. She also asked me not to tell anyone. That's why I haven't told you until now. Also, I didn't think I should mention it because of the ongoing FBI investigation."

"You poor thing. That mess with Monica, Tad, and Syngexas keeps haunting you, even out here in the wilderness."

By the time they boarded the bus, the other tour groups had filled it up and only two seats were unoccupied, one next to Alec and the other a few rows ahead of him.

He motioned for Faith to sit in the empty spot beside him, on the same row with Rick.

Shelly grabbed her arm. "Wait. Sit with me."

"Where? There aren't any seats together."

Her friend frowned like a worried big sister. "I'd rather you stood the whole time than sit with him."

Faith heard Jake's voice and glanced toward the front, where he was talking to the bus driver. She turned and spoke to Shelly again. "I have to sit somewhere. Don't worry." Leaving her friend, Faith sat beside Alec on the aisle.

While she stowed her backpack under the seat in front of her, he leaned over. "I get the impression your friend doesn't like me."

Faith simply shrugged, not wanting to tell him that he reminded Shelly of Tad.

Alec pointed to the newspaper she was holding. "What did you think of the article?"

"It's very strange and hard to believe."

"It said a woman who worked for Syngexas is missing. You didn't know her, did you?"

Avoiding the question, Faith glanced forward and saw Shelly cast her a pointed look. Shifting her gaze, Faith smiled politely at Alec. "If you don't mind, I don't want to talk about the investigation. Why don't you tell me more about the job opening you mentioned?" She'd already ruled out working for his firm, but it should keep him off the subject of Monica for the rest of their ride, especially once he started talking about himself, which he inevitably would.

Eventually, their bus pulled into the lot for the transit station, and everyone began the process of de-boarding in order to catch their next ride. For the Elk group, that would be a snowcoach which would take them to Old Faithful.

Faith grabbed her backpack and followed the crowd toward the front of the bus.

Alec followed, continuing his story about how he won the golf tournament his firm sponsored last year.

When she reached the door, Jake was outside and had just finished assisting Mary down from the bus. In a hurry to get away from Alec, Faith quickly descended the steps on her own.

At the bottom step, she slipped on the ice and lost her balance and her backpack.

Jake caught her, breaking her fall.

Her gaze traveled to his arms holding her. Surprised and embarrassed, she quickly stood on her own and steeled herself against the lightheadedness that had nothing to do with the fall. Stepping away, she brushed a hand over her hair, attempting to regain her composure. "You could have warned me about that last step."

He picked up her backpack and handed it to her. "I would have, if you hadn't been in such a rush."

"Jake," a woman called, "the snowcoach is ready for your group to board."

Faith turned in the direction of the voice and recognized the cute young lady walking toward them—Jake's dinner date from the other night. She was wearing a parka exactly like Faith's.

The younger woman approached the group with a friendly smile. "Hi, everyone."

As Faith slowly backed away, Jake took her arm before she could escape. "Faith, I'd like you to meet April Brooks."

Faith said hello, then gestured to their identical parkas. "I like your taste in coats."

April laughed. "Thanks, you too. We'll have to be careful not to mix them up. We're going to be spending a lot of time together the next couple of days."

Puzzled, Faith slanted her head. "Why, are you taking over for Jake?"

"Oh, no," April replied. "He's still your tour guide. I'm only the snowcoach driver."

"You're more than that." Jake pivoted to Faith to explain. "April has worked here during her college breaks for the past three years. She knows Yellowstone better than I do."

"I wouldn't say that. Jake is the resident expert." She smiled at him, then gave a wistful sigh. "I will miss this place when I start veterinary school next fall."

"Vet school." *A naturalist and a vet—the perfect couple.* Faith appealed to Shelly for moral support. "Impressive, huh?"

Shelly caught her distress signal. "Very."

April motioned to them. "If you're ready to board, follow me."

Faith dragged her feet, falling behind the other Elk group members. Why did April have to be so sweet, in addition to being cute and perky? *Where can I board the next bus to Florida right now?*

April led them to her snowcoach, an odd-looking, sturdy conveyance with oversized snow tires that appeared to Faith like something out of a tractor-pull or a demolition derby. Some other vehicles at the transit station had tracks instead of tires, like the one Chip had driven on Monday. April's snowcoach appeared to be a newer version of the oversnow vans.

The college student unfolded the steps to the door.

As the Elk group mustered to go in, Faith stood at the end of the line.

When her turn came to board, Jake offered her a hand to climb the steps. After her previous blunder, she swallowed her pride and took it.

The inside of the passenger vehicle was like a small bus. She headed for the very last row, not wanting to be anywhere near April and Jake in the front.

Alec left his seat on the second row and sat beside her.

"What's up with your ex and the co-ed?"

Faith tried to sound casual. "What do you mean?"

"There's obviously more going on between them than snowcoach tours."

"I wouldn't know." She eyed him directly. "Why are you so interested?"

His lips curled in a cunning grin. "I always size up my competition before going after what I want."

She didn't like his tone and decided it was time to be frank with him. "If you're referring to me working for your firm, Alec, I think you should know that I'm not interested—the same goes for anything else you might have had in mind."

That silenced him and erased his smug expression. *Good.* Now all she needed was an effective strategy for stopping the menace harassing her on this tour, and dealing with whatever Jake's relationship was with April.

CHAPTER SEVENTEEN


STARING AT THE STUNNING SCENERY FROM her window, Faith listened to Jake and April take turns entertaining the group with stories of their personal adventures and folklore about the park. She couldn't help thinking again that they were perfect for each other. It didn't make her happy, but at least April seemed genuinely nice compared to Jillian.

Meanwhile, Alec hadn't spoken a word since her rebuff. He seemed to be giving her the cold shoulder. That didn't bother her, except she wished she had more pleasant company to share the ride with.

When the snowcoach finally stopped at Norris Geyser Basin, the group prepared to take a short sightseeing hike to stretch their legs. Jake told them they wouldn't be there long, so Faith decided to leave her cell phone behind in her backpack.

Outside in the elements, it felt much colder than at Mammoth Hot Springs, and people were covering their faces with scarves for protection against the biting wind.

Faith's parka did a good job shielding her from the brunt of the frigid temperatures. The wind gusts, however, made it difficult to move as she shuffled through the snow. Relieved to be away from Alec, who was somewhere behind her, she stayed in the middle of the pack with Shelly.

The first trail they took was to Porcelain Basin. In their bulky clothing, the group moved like spacemen canvassing a foreign planet. Following the snow-covered, boardwalk maze, they descended into the steaming valley where geysers spewed boiling water from the earth like miniature, angry volcanoes.

Faith pulled her scarf close around her neck and face, careful not to slip in her athletic shoes on the ice-crusted snow. Her blisters were better today, but she hadn't wanted to agitate them with the snow boots.

Though the geyser basin was truly stunning, she was glad

her group was taking a relatively short hike along the two boardwalk trails in the extreme cold, and that there were no reckless snowmobiles or masked cross-country skiers in sight.

After they'd finished admiring the breathtaking views at Porcelain Basin, Jake led them on the Black Basin boardwalk trail. There they stopped to admire the green color of Emerald Spring, which Jake told them came from sulfur deposits combined with reflective blue light.

Their next stop was another colorful thermal pool named Cistern Spring. Shelly took pictures of Mary and Donna in front of it, then Donna used Shelly's camera to take a picture of Faith and Shelly together. Once they'd finished posing for the camera, Shelly took Faith aside. "What happened between you and Alec? I saw him glaring at you earlier."

"I basically told him I wasn't interested in the job at his firm, or in him."

Shelly smiled. "Good, I'm proud of you! It's better than letting things drag out, though from the way he's been scowling at you, he's obviously not happy about it. You should try and avoid him as much as you can."

Faith planned to do exactly that. She looked down at the spring and studied its deep blue waters, so clear she could see to the very bottom. Edging closer, she felt the hot steam drifting off its surface like a sauna in the middle of a freezer. Relishing the warmth on her chilly face, her gaze wandered to Jake, who was standing a short distance away.

As he removed the blue scarf that covered his nose and mouth so he could speak to the group, the bitter cold's effects were evident in his ruddy complexion. "It might be tempting to jump in this water to warm up, but it's not a hot tub. These springs and pools can reach over 400 degrees. Needless to say, if anyone fell in, they wouldn't survive."

The somber tone in his voice silenced the chatty group as they considered the dangers that lurked beyond the beauty of this place.

Faith stared at the deceptive waters. *One false move and I'm literally toast.*

Jake then led them to a large, conical-shaped rock. "This is Steamboat Geyser, the largest geyser in the park and very unpredictable. Last year, I was leading a tour group here when suddenly the ground shook and rumbled like an earthquake before it erupted. It was one of the most amazing things I've ever seen, though it scared the living daylights out of me."

Faith smiled behind her scarf at the image of Jake jumping out of his skin from the mountain of water gushing unexpectedly. It reminded her of the time Joey dropped water balloons on him from their old tree house. In retaliation, Jake grabbed the hose and sprayed his brother until he was soaked. She hadn't thought of that in years.

On the way back to the snowcoach, Faith stopped for one last look at the steaming blue waters of Cistern Spring.

Leslie's voice from behind startled her. "That warm water is inviting in this cold weather, isn't it?"

Faith tossed her a sideways look. "And deadly. I hope you're not thinking of diving in."

"Me?" Leslie laughed. "The only thing I care about diving into right now is a good story—like the one behind Syngexas and Monica Wallace."

At the mention of Monica and her former company, Faith bit her tongue. Dipping a toe in the boiling springs was probably safer than talking to Leslie right now.

That didn't stop Leslie from talking to her. "I've done a little digging and discovered that you and Monica both worked in accounting at Syngexas. You must have crossed paths at some point."

"I don't want to talk about Syngexas. I'm not employed there anymore, remember?"

"That's right," Leslie coolly replied. "You were let go. Maybe it was a blessing in disguise. Otherwise, you might have been caught up in that messy investigation."

Wishing the woman would go away, Faith responded in a snarky tone. "Funny, it never occurred to me to think of losing my job as a blessing."

Leslie smirked. "By the way, I overheard that you and Jake

were engaged. You almost had me fooled, but now that I'm wise to your 'we're old friends' act, I bet I'll find a story there if I do enough digging."

Faith balled her fists, fighting to control herself. Was there no limit to the woman's audacity?

Jake called to them from a distance. "Hey, you two, hurry up! It's time to board the snowcoach before we head to Old Faithful."

As they rode farther south in the park, Jake glanced behind him at Faith sitting next to Shelly in the back of the snowcoach. He wondered what Leslie had said to her by the hot spring. Whatever it was, it obviously upset her. Faith had been staring out the window and fidgeting with her hair ever since.

Alec seemed to be brooding about something too, and he wasn't sitting next to Faith this time. It appeared Shelly had switched seats with him. Had he and Faith had a falling out? Jake hoped so, for Faith's sake.

Through the rear window, a group of snowmobilers came into view. Jake pointed them out to April, who was driving.

She peered in her side mirror as the group caught up to them, then she pulled the snowcoach over to let them by.

Speeding past, the rowdy bunch whooped it up like a pack of hooligans.

Jake noticed their black snowmobiles. The one that had chased Faith at Tower Fall was red and black. He recalled that the snowmobiles Oscar Prescott's company rented for their tours had those same colors, though it didn't seem likely that he or his sons would do something like that. As far as Jake knew, they had no connection to Faith.

On the other hand, what if Faith wasn't the real target? If any member of Jake's tour group was seriously injured, it could put Chip's company out of business. It was no secret that Oscar held a grudge against Jake for reporting his company's violations to the park officials, but would he put innocent people at risk as payback?

The more Jake thought about it, the more it troubled him. He glanced at his tour group engaged in idle chatter, everyone except Faith oblivious to the potential danger. Until the wanted snowmobile driver was found, Jake would need to be extra vigilant for the rest of the tour to make sure that nothing worse happened.

# CHAPTER EIGHTEEN

After Faith arrived at the Old Faithful Snow Lodge with her tour group, she waited by the fireplace while Shelly stopped at the front desk to check in. The journey there from Norris Geyser Basin was much more enjoyable sitting next to Shelly instead of Alec. Faith owed her friend dinner for asking him to change seats with her when they boarded the snowcoach.

Thawing out from the cold in front of the glowing embers, Faith looked around the comfortable, festive lobby. Over the mantle hung a lighted evergreen garland, and in the corner stood a giant Christmas tree. Above her, rustic log beams crisscrossed the high vaulted ceiling, which complemented the charming wood and stone décor on the lower level. Designed to resemble the nearby historic Old Faithful Inn, which Jake had informed the group was closed for winter, the modern snow lodge was only a short walk from the famous geyser for which it was named.

Though Faith had enjoyed staying at the Moose Run Lodge, she was glad for the change of scenery and to be away from where all the disturbing incidents had taken place. As a precaution, she had instructed Shelly to tell the desk clerk not to give out their room number or let anyone know they were staying at the lodge.

Now that Jake was at Old Faithful, he decided he should notify Chip about his new concerns and suspicions regarding the safety of his tour group. He found a quiet spot in the dining room of the snow lodge to make the call. As he pulled out his phone, he noticed a new text from Jillian.

*Sorry about our little tiff the other day. I hope you'll reconsider and change your mind about spending Christmas with me and my family.*

He hadn't changed his mind. If anything, he was even less inclined to spend the holiday with the Prescotts. If the strange incidents this week were any indication, it might be hazardous to his health.

When Faith and Shelly entered their new room, all of their luggage was already there, the biggest pieces set on luggage racks against the wall. The simple wooden desk and bedroom furniture gave the small living space a cozy, rustic feel. Faith dropped her backpack on the floor and made herself at home by increasing the heat setting to warm the place up. "No radiators this time."

Shelly removed her coat and gloves and tossed them on the far bed before disappearing into the bathroom. Moments later, she popped her head out. "You'll be happy to know we have both a shower and a tub."

Relieved, Faith collapsed on the nearest bed. "Good. I can't wait to take a hot shower."

Returning from the bathroom, Shelly opened her suitcase and began unpacking a few of her things.

Hungry from being in the cold all day, Faith sat up on the bed. "What do you say we grab an early dinner in the lodge?"

Shelly stopped what she was doing. "Sounds great, but what about your hot shower?"

"It can wait." Faith rose to fetch her backpack. She set it on the desk, unzipped the pocket, then reached for her cell phone. Plunging her hand deep inside, she felt around. *It wasn't there.* After searching all the pockets, she grimaced at Shelly. "My cell phone—it's gone. Have you seen it?"

"No, not since this morning, before we left Moose Run."

"I was sure I put it in my backpack."

"Maybe it's in the bag with your mail." Shelly grabbed her backpack and set it on the bed. After retrieving the canvas bag, she handed it to Faith.

Faith quickly dumped the contents on her bed and sorted through the mail. "It's not here either."

"Maybe you left it in the snowcoach. Why don't you ask Jake or April to check?"

A disturbing thought crossed her mind. "You don't think anyone would have taken it, do you?"

Shelly shook her head. "Why would they? Don't worry, I'm sure it will turn up."

Faith hoped her friend was right. On the bright side, without her phone, Faith wouldn't be tempted to check her messages about her job applications—or receive any more calls from the FBI agent. Monica wouldn't be able to reach her either, which worried her a little.

Turning to her mail on the bed, Faith sighed at the collection of junk and bills scattered on the comforter. Eventually, she'd have to sell her condo and possibly her car to pay the bills. Now that she'd burned the bridge with Alec, Chip's job offer was her only alternative. Though the salary was more than he could really afford, it was considerably less than she'd made at Syngexas, and there wouldn't be much upward mobility for her career.

Gathering the letters to stuff back in the bag, she paused at the small padded envelope with the Syngexas business return label and was reminded again of the FBI investigation. She remembered Leslie telling her that losing her job at Syngexas might be a blessing in disguise. At the time, Faith resented the woman's remark, but now Faith was beginning to see some truth in it. Since she was no longer tied to her old job, she was free to start fresh with a new one that might be more rewarding. The prospect began to excite and reenergize her.

Twenty minutes later, when she and Shelly were seated near the window in the spacious dining room of the lodge, Faith peered over her menu. "Order whatever you want, Shelly. Dinner is on me."

"Why? What's the occasion?"

"Consider it a thank-you for being a good friend and switching seats with Alec on the snowcoach today, and for inviting me to come on this tour with you."

Shelly smiled fondly at her. "Aw, you'd do the same for

me."

Faith affirmed that with a nod. "We're also celebrating my uncharted future. After turning Alec down, I feel like I've been released from a gilded cage."

Shelly set her menu on the table and clapped her hands in a hearty cheer. "Yay! You've finally ditched the golden handcuffs." Raising her menu again, her lips curled in an impish grin. "And since you're paying, I think I'll order the prime rib."

"Good choice. I'll have the same."

When their food was served, Shelly picked up their earlier conversation. "Now let's see if we can discover what your dream job is. What did you want to be when you grew up?"

Faith considered the question. "I had a favorite teacher in high school, Ms. Washburn. She taught math and always made it fun and interesting. I remember thinking it might be nice to be a teacher like her one day." Faith shrugged. "But that was before college."

"Maybe you could work as an accountant for the school system." Shelly continued to suggest types of jobs for Faith while they enjoyed their delicious food. It seemed they discussed every profession under the sun without coming to any conclusion. When they'd finished the prime rib, they ordered cheesecake for dessert.

Faith broke off a piece of the rich treat with her fork. "I think this may be the best meal I've ever had." As soon as she'd said it, she noticed a man staring at her from across the room and couldn't believe her eyes. *Tad.* Rain clouds suddenly darkened her sunny mood. "What on earth is he up to now?"

Shelly turned her head to see who Faith was talking about. "Oh, brother. How did he know how to find you?"

"Good question." Faith shot up from her chair. "I'll be back in a minute."

"Wait!" Shelly cried. "Don't go over there."

"I have to find out what he's up to. He might know what's happened to Monica." Faith marched to his table by the river rock fireplace and halted in front of him. "What are you doing here, Tad?"

"That's a coincidence. I was going to ask you the same question. This place is colder than an igloo in Siberia. Couldn't you have run off to a resort on a private island instead?"

She planted a hand on her hip. "You didn't answer my question. Why are you here?"

His grin faded as he dropped the act. "Why do you think? I came to see you."

"How did you find me?"

A shrewd grin stretched across his lips. "We have a mutual friend."

She scoffed. "I doubt that."

"Does Alec Underwood ring a bell?"

"*Alec.*" She released a long breath. "I should have known." She pulled out the chair across from him and dropped in it.

"His firm did consulting work for Syngexas a few years ago, and we've stayed in touch. I couldn't believe it when he called this week and asked if I knew you. Said he was thinking about offering you a job with his firm." Tad gave her an approving nod. "Way to go, Faith. Of course, I gave you a great reference."

Shelly had come over and tapped her on the shoulder. "Everything okay?"

Tad waved. "Hi, Shelly. Pull up a chair and join us. We were discussing Faith's job prospects."

Her friend snorted and spoke again to Faith. "You want me to stay?"

Faith glared at Tad's smug face. "No. This won't take long. I'll meet you back in the room."

Slowly, Shelly started to leave, but not before she hurled a harsh look at Tad.

When she walked away, he rolled his eyes. "Never was a big fan, was she?" He picked up his menu. "Care for a cup of coffee? Dessert maybe?"

"Cut to the chase, Tad. What do you want?"

He set his menu down, his cordial expression becoming dead serious. He leaned toward her and lowered his voice. "I'm here about Monica. It's very important that you tell me if she's contacted you."

The deep ripples in his brow and the slight tremble of his fingers told her he was worried about something. *Very worried.* "If she had, why should I tell you? For all I know you're the reason she disappeared."

His face twitched from her remark and he shifted away. "Look, I know you don't trust me, and I guess I can't blame you, but you've got to help me find her." He inclined his head slightly. "Did she give or send you anything?"

"Like what?"

He hesitated as if debating how much he should tell her. "I just need your help finding Monica."

The newspaper article about the investigation into her former employer entered Faith's mind. "Is this about the scandal at Syngexas? An FBI agent called me this week and asked if I'd heard from her."

Tad nervously scanned the room. "I've got to go." As he rose, he appealed to Faith once more. "If she contacts you, promise me you'll let me know before you inform the FBI."

Faith shook her head. "If you're in trouble, Tad, you need to go to the FBI and come clean. One thing I've learned is that running away from your problems only makes things worse."

That reminded her she still needed to come clean with Jake, and tonight was the night.

Tad's face twisted. "What if they won't believe me?"

"You'll have to take that chance."

# CHAPTER NINETEEN

When Faith returned to her room, Shelly wouldn't be satisfied until Faith told her what she and Tad discussed. After she did, the two prayed together for him to have the courage to do the right thing. Praying for Tad somehow seemed to lessen her hurt and anger from his betrayal. She hoped that God would give Jake the same grace to forgive her for the way she'd hurt him.

By the time Faith and Shelly ventured out in the elements to see Old Faithful, it was almost sunset. The wind had died down, making the cold more tolerable, though it wasn't much above zero.

Following the groomed walkway to the famous geyser, they saw a small crowd gathered around it, waiting for the next eruption. While they stood in the cold with the other spectators, Phil joined them. "How long until show time?" he asked.

Shelly checked her watch. "Only a few minutes. Where's Leslie? I'm surprised she's not filming this."

"She's eating dinner. By the way, she's not my keeper. When I'm not working, I do have a life."

"That's good—does Leslie know that?"

When steam and boiling water began splashing from the geyser's crater, Faith interrupted Shelly and Phil. "Look, it's time!"

The climbing fountain sloshed and sprayed, reaching higher and higher until it shot up in a towering column.

Faith gasped at the sheer height and spectacle of it. For the next few minutes, the showy geyser amazed and awed with its power, beauty, and mystery.

"I still get a rush watching Old Faithful blow."

The sound of Jake's voice took her attention away from the geyser. He was standing next to her, staring at the tall plume.

Surprised and delighted to see him, she felt like a kid again and couldn't resist making a joke. "And to think they named it after me."

He gave her a dry grin. "You're not that *old*."

"Very funny."

His eyes twinkled back at her. "Despite the name, it's not as faithful as it used to be. Earthquakes altered the channels underground, and now it only erupts every 60-110 minutes."

As if a huge water main had been shut off, the giant column of water quickly shrunk to a gurgling, spitting spring.

Shelly and Phil had disappeared into the crowd that dispersed, leaving Faith alone with Jake.

When she slowly faced him, he took a small step forward and tied her hood more snugly over her head and zipped the top of her parka to keep out the cold. Gently resting his hands on her shoulders, he spoke in an amiable tone. "You'll freeze in these temps if you're not careful."

The warmth of his gaze quickly melted her heart. At that moment, she could no longer deny her feelings for him. She could only accept them, as one accepts hunger or thirst.

He lifted a brow. "You said you wanted to talk to me?"

The voice inside urged her not to wait, but she couldn't spoil the moment. "I seem to have lost my cell phone. I may have left it in the snowcoach."

"Oh…" Withdrawing his hands from her, he stuffed them in the pockets of his jacket. "I'll check with April and see if she's come across it." He paused and glanced at the clear twilight sky. "You know, there's supposed to be a full moon tonight. I'm going skiing later." He inclined his head and peered at her. "Want to come along?"

"Night skiing?" She smiled at the notion as her heartbeats quickened. "Sounds like fun." Then she remembered that someone was targeting her. "But maybe I shouldn't, at least not until the person who tried to plow me down at the Tower Fall parking lot is found. I don't want to put you at risk either. In fact, I've been thinking maybe I should leave. I just don't know where else to go."

Concern reflected in his eyes. "Whoever is harassing you won't try anything as long as you're not alone. You saw how fast that snowmobile blew out of the parking lot when the rest of us showed up."

She lowered her gaze. "Even so, I couldn't live with myself if anyone got hurt on account of me." Joey's face flashed in her mind as the painful memory of his death stalked her like that wolf in her dream. No, she couldn't put it off any longer. She had to tell Jake tonight.

"I won't let that happen. I'm staying at the lodge instead of the staff dorm to keep a closer eye on things." He gave her a reassuring smile. "Want to hear my fifth rule of survival?"

She grinned and nodded.

"Never let a predator know you're afraid."

"That's a good one, but not very easy to do."

Jake chuckled. "Come on, I'll walk you back to the lodge. I have a few things to take care of this evening. How about I meet you in the lobby at nine?"

"I'll be ready." Feeling giddy as a schoolgirl, she tried to temper her hopes that it was a real date in case he didn't see it that way.

When they reached the entrance to the snow lodge, he opened the door for her. "I'll walk you to your room."

"That's not necessary. I don't want you to feel like you have to be my personal bodyguard. Now that you've safely delivered me here, I'll be perfectly fine inside with people around."

"Are you sure?"

"Yes. Don't worry about me."

Her words seemed to reassure him. "Then I'll see you at nine. You can pick up your skis at the outfitters store in the lodge."

After he left, Faith walked through the lobby on a cushion of air. Pushing the hood of her parka away from her head, she crossed to the fireplace. Basking in its rejuvenating heat, she was soon lost in a daydream about being with Jake.

Leslie's mocking voice burst her bubble and brought her back to the earth. "You must share your secret, Faith. Is it your sweet, girl-next-door looks, or your knack for keeping men at arm's length that attracts them to you?"

Annoyed, Faith narrowed her eyes. "I don't know what you're talking about."

The reporter smirked as if she got her kicks from provoking her. "Here's a friendly word of advice, don't cross Alec if you can help it. He doesn't have a good track record with women who get on his bad side."

Leslie's words surprised Faith and unsettled her since she'd already rebuffed him. "Why are you telling me this?"

"I thought you should be forewarned. You see, I did a little digging and discovered he was married. His wife died in a suspicious boating accident. Supposedly, she fell off their yacht. There was an investigation and Alec was the prime suspect. Of course, his family hired the best lawyers, and since there wasn't enough evidence to charge and convict him, the case was dropped."

Despite the disturbing news, it didn't mean Alec was guilty. "Sounds like it could all be a tragic coincidence."

"That's possible. However, his wife had filed for divorce and was seeking a huge settlement, including a sizable interest in Alec's firm. That makes me think something more sinister took place." Leslie's eyes flashed like green flares.

Faith inhaled a deep breath to calm the pounding in her chest. "In any case, I hardly know Alec, so I doubt he'd come after me."

"Just the same, watch your step."

It was hard for Faith to know what to make of the hard-nosed reporter expressing concern for her safety. The fact that Leslie was a successful journalist with a reputation for telling the truth added some weight to her warning, especially with the menace snowmobiler at large. "Thanks for the tip, but again, it shouldn't be a problem."

Leaving Leslie, Faith headed down the corridor to her room. Turning the corner, she paused as a disturbing thought entered her mind. Alec didn't hike with them to Tower Fall, nor was he waiting at the van like Jake had told him to. Instead, he'd left on his own, supposedly to do a little sightseeing. That would have given him ample opportunity to get on the snowmobile, attack her, then ditch the machine so he could show up on his skis a few minutes later.

She didn't like to presume a man was guilty without proof. On the other hand, she couldn't risk being naive about Alec either. From now on, it was best to heed Leslie's warning and steer clear of him altogether.

# CHAPTER TWENTY

On the way to her room, Faith stopped by the outfitters store in the lodge to rent her ski gear for the evening. When she tried to pay, she was told it had already been taken care of—she assumed by Jake. Touched by his thoughtful gesture, her hopes began to rise that this might be a real date after all.

When she'd dropped off the gear in her room, she returned to the lobby and found Shelly sitting at a table with Ruth and Norman in the long hallway between the lobby and the restaurant. The three invited her to join them in their game of dominoes.

After accepting their invitation, Faith played until a quarter of nine, then excused herself to leave before the game was over.

Ruth peered at her as she drew her dominoes from the pile. "Where are you off to in such a hurry?"

"I'm going skiing."

The older woman reacted with a worried frown. "Alone? In the dark?"

"Don't worry. I won't be alone, and there's supposed to be a full moon tonight."

Shelly stared at Faith with a knowing glint. "You're going with Jake, aren't you?"

Faith grinned automatically, confirming she had guessed correctly.

Ruth's face beamed as she responded in a wistful voice. "How nice. You and Jake make such a cute couple. Don't they, Norman?"

He grunted as if he'd woken prematurely from a nap. "What? Is it my turn?"

Faith waved to them. "Well, have fun without me."

Shelly jumped up and caught her in the hallway. "Are you going to tell him tonight?"

"That's the plan. Say a prayer for me."

"I will," Shelly assured her. "Be strong, and stay safe."

From the lobby, Faith strode to her room to get ready. After she had changed into warmer clothes, she grabbed her parka, scarf, and ski gear, then hurried out the door.

When she turned the corner in the hallway, she froze.

Alec was coming toward her, reading his cell phone.

She gazed at the floor, hoping to pass him unnoticed.

He suddenly moved in front of her, blocking her path. "Aren't you even going to say hello?"

Lifting her eyes, she coolly acknowledged him. "Hello."

He gestured to her skis. "You're going out? Is it a private party, or may I come along?"

Leslie's warning about Alec replayed in Faith's mind, as did Jake's advice to never let a predator know you're afraid. She rested the lower end of her skis on the floor and straightened her shoulders. "I'm meeting someone, and you're in my way."

He didn't move. "Whoever you're meeting tonight can wait—did you know that we have a mutual acquaintance?"

"If you mean Tad, yes, he told me. Now let me pass." When she tried to squeeze around him, Alec stuck out his arm and re-planted himself in front of her. "You're going skiing with Jake tonight, aren't you? I saw you with him earlier."

Anger overtook her fears, and she stared him straight in the eye. "That's none of your business. However, here's what you should be concerned about—if you don't let me pass, I'll tell Leslie Turner all about you harassing me. I'm sure she'll be interested in more drama for her story. And once it's on the news, you probably won't be too popular at the country club anymore. It won't help your consulting business either."

He grudgingly removed his arm and shifted out of her way.

As she hurried down the hall to the lobby, his voice echoed behind her.

"Watch out, Faith. I hear there's going to be a full moon, and you never know when one of those wolves might show up."

While Jake waited for Faith by the door in the lobby, he regretted there was so little time left on the tour. It was Thursday night already. The tour would be over by Sunday. Instead of feeling like celebrating, the prospect depressed him. Now that he and Faith had found each other again he didn't want to lose her.

The irony made him chuckle. Wasn't he the one who complained when Chip assigned her to his group? Now he wanted to convince her to stay. But why should she? She had an exciting future waiting for her in the big city, working for a prestigious consulting firm and making more money than she would know what to do with. All he could offer was a simple life, and a devoted heart.

Suddenly, Faith rushed into the lobby.

Seeing the tension on her flushed face, Jake grew concerned. "What's wrong?"

Turning her eyes to him, her expression brightened. "I had a run-in with Alec in the hall just now. He tried to stop me from meeting you."

Jake frowned and pivoted in that direction. "That's it! It's time somebody taught him a lesson."

Faith grabbed Jake's arm. "No, please don't. I've already handled it. Besides, I'm looking forward to skiing with you, and I refuse to let him ruin it."

Jake paused and stepped toward her, his expression softening. "I half wondered if you'd show up."

"How could I not, especially since you picked up the tab for my skis? Thank you, by the way." She smiled fondly. "Besides, it was either this or an all-night dominoes party."

He laughed as he escorted her to the door. "You don't like dominoes?"

She tossed him a humorous look. "Not when I'm in last place."

Walking outside with Jake, Faith wrapped her scarf around her face and neck to guard against the cold, while the rest of her body stayed surprisingly warm in her winter parka and snow bibs.

At Jake's suggestion, they carried their skis and hiked to Old Faithful to watch another eruption before setting out. Despite the bitter weather, it was a beautiful night. The brilliant, silvery moon reflected off the snowy landscape, illuminating the entire Upper Geyser Basin region.

They reached the viewing area of the mighty geyser right in time for her next performance, and she did not disappoint. By day, the giant fountain awed and dazzled with her power and spectacle. By moonlight, her water exploits became an enthralling, romantic dance, suspended between heaven and earth.

As Faith watched the column of steam and boiling water leaping through the air toward the starlit sky, her gaze wandered to Jake standing next to her.

He looked her way at the same time, the vapor of their breath mingling in the air between them. "Are you staying warm enough?"

She nodded, then peered at the sky. "It's been a long time since I've seen this many stars. They're brighter out here."

"It's the higher altitude and no city lights. Sometimes you can actually see the aurora borealis from here."

The geyser soon ran out of steam. A few minutes later, only a frothy fountain remained.

Jake shifted toward Faith, excitement gleaming in his eyes. "Ready to hit the trails?"

His boyish zeal was contagious and made her eager to begin their adventure. "Whenever you are."

They quickly locked their boots in their skis and took off toward the geyser basin. Reaching the main path, they encountered a number of people walking around the geothermal features, despite the frigid weather.

Traveling along the perimeter of the Upper Basin, Faith and Jake stopped to check out the geysers and pools. As he shared personal stories and trivia about the region, she felt like she was a VIP on a private tour.

Continuing their trek, they encountered other cross-country skiers on the trail, which made Faith nervous. Sensing her hesitation, Jake glided around and positioned himself between her and the skiers. Feeling more at ease with him shielding her from the oncoming traffic, she picked up her speed as they moved on to Morning Glory Pool.

From there, they traveled beyond the Upper Basin and took a long, level trail that followed the Firehole River toward Biscuit Basin. With the full moon illuminating the snowy landscape in silvery splendor, Faith settled into a steady rhythm beside Jake.

The constant motion of her feet alternately pushing and gliding invigorated and kept her warm despite the bitter temps. Away from the splashing and roaring of the geysers, only the gentle whoosh of their skis and the sound of their breathing touched her ears. Gliding across the moonlit landscape filled her with a peculiar mix of quiet and exhilaration, like swimming underwater. It gave her time to mentally rehearse what she would say to Jake when the opportunity presented itself.

He halted at the edge of the woods, and she slowed to a stop to see what he was pointing at.

It took a moment for her eyes to focus in on the huge, dark mounds in the distance—a bison herd. She and Jake observed them a few more minutes before moving on.

After they crossed a bridge over the river and passed through the woods, Jake gestured to a bench near the trail. "Let's take a break over there."

Faith followed him, and they detached their skis from their boots before sitting down.

Resting against the hard bench, she was still a little breathless from her workout, but had never felt more alive. When she removed the scarf from around her face and throat, a distant howling pricked the tranquil atmosphere.

She looked around in wonder and slight trepidation.

Jake loosened his scarf and listened.

Another wolf responded from the opposite direction. A few seconds later, the entire wilderness erupted in howling.

The hair sprung from the nape of Faith's neck. "They're everywhere. It sounds like we're surrounded."

Jake nudged her. "You're not scared, are you?" Boyish delight twinkled in his eyes like the stars above.

She jutted her chin. "Me? Of course not."

His knowing glint indicated he wasn't buying it. "Well, let's hope they aren't hungry."

"If that was a joke, it wasn't funny," she said in a light tone. "If a pack of wolves attacks me, don't expect an endorsement for Wild Adventures."

"Don't worry. You're not in any danger. The wolves are only letting everyone know they're around."

"As a warning?"

"Kind of, though it's intended for other wolves, not humans."

The howling soon died down, and she felt more relaxed. As she gazed up, a bright streak crossed the dark sky. "Look, a shooting star! Make a wish."

Jake stared at the heavens. "I said a prayer instead. It's more effective."

She smiled. "I like that. What did you pray for?"

His gaze drifted to her. "For more times like this."

Excitement tingled through her body, but she was afraid of reading too much into what he'd said. "I know what you mean. It's so beautiful here."

"Yes, it is." Shifting toward her, he touched a long lock of her hair. "But I meant more times with *you*." A significant spark flickered in his eyes.

"I want that also."

Her words seemed to embolden him. Leaning closer, he pressed his lips to hers. In his loving embrace, she finally felt safe and content. Savoring the rejuvenating warmth and sweetness of the moment, she wanted to forget about the past and start over. Yet what kind of future could they have if she kept the truth about his brother a secret?

Slowly, she withdrew from him, praying for courage. "There's something I need to tell you."

He responded in a tender voice. "Is it what you wanted to talk to me about earlier?"

She lowered her gaze and nodded.

After releasing a long breath, he leaned against the bench. "If it's about why you broke up with me, none of that matters anymore. All I care about is that we're back together again."

It would be so easy for her to sweep it all under the rug, but she couldn't do that to him. He deserved to know the truth, and it was now or never. Emotion gripped her throat, making it difficult to speak. "You have no idea how much that means to me, Jake. As much as I would love to pretend it never happened, I can't. I have to be honest with you."

With a light shrug, he conceded. "Then I'm all ears."

She gazed at the starlit sky, searching for the words to begin. "Do you know that I still have scrapbooks of every little card, gift, and keepsake you ever gave me? In middle school, you were my best friend, and in high school, the love of my life. The day you proposed was like a dream come true. I could hardly keep it to myself until we told your family right before Christmas—that's when I learned that not everyone was happy about it."

Deep lines formed on Jake's brow. "You mean your Aunt Gertrude?"

She shook her head. "I'm talking about your brother...Joey."

"Joey?" The light dimmed in Jake's eyes. "Go on."

Faith stared into the woods as the haunting memories replayed in her mind. "Late that night, after you brought me home, Joey came to see me."

A mixture of confusion and doubt cast a shadow over Jake's face. "Why? What did he want?"

Her muscles tightened as she recalled his unexpected visit. "He wasn't himself. He was angry and told me I was making a mistake marrying you. He said we would both regret it." A tear froze at the corner of her eye. "I was shocked. I didn't know what he was talking about. I never suspected he had feelings for me…until he tried to kiss me." It was hard for her to look Jake in the eye as she summoned the strength to continue her story. "I pushed him away and told him to leave."

She'd never wanted to hurt Joey. He was like a brother. If she had known how that one night would devastate them all and alter the course of their lives, she would have handled things differently, but she was only nineteen.

"Did he go?"

"Yes… But I'd never seen him so angry and hurt. He raced away in that souped-up car of his, and that's the last time I saw him alive. The next day I heard about the accident."

A strange faraway stare struck Jake's face. Finally, he responded. "You've carried this with you all these years?"

She lowered her gaze and nodded. "I didn't realize until a few years ago that Joey's accident had resurfaced the trauma of my parents' car crash. It took months before I came to terms with both incidents. By then, I figured you had moved on, and I didn't have a right to intrude on your life again because of what I'd done. I know now that as soon as Joey drove away, I should have called you and your parents and warned you that he was upset, but I didn't want to explain why he came over in the first place."

She pulled at her scarf in her lap. "If only I had stopped him from getting in that car… I couldn't face you or your family after that night. I kept wondering, what if it wasn't an accident? What if he meant to drive off the bridge, because of you and me?"

"Shh." Jake tenderly placed a hand on hers. "The police investigated it. A witness said Joey was speeding. He hit a patch of ice and lost control. That's why his car skidded off the bridge into the river. It wasn't your fault." After a long, heavy silence, Jake removed his hand from hers. Squeezing his eyes shut, he spoke in a rueful voice. "I knew something was bothering him. He was moody and always picking fights. Now I understand."

A cold wind brushed against Faith, chasing away the lingering warmth from their kiss. The sudden awareness of a growing chasm between her and Jake displaced the relief she should have felt from learning the crash was an accident. He would need time to process everything, but how would he feel about her when he did? Would she become a constant reminder of that terrible night? "You have no idea how much I wish I had been there for you and your family, instead of running away."

He rubbed his forehead. "We've both had a lot of growing up to do, haven't we?"

Neither of them said another word as a veil of sadness hung over them, dropping the temperature a few more degrees.

The silence was broken with a woman's blood-curdling scream.

"That's not a wolf," Faith cried.

Jake sprang to his feet and reached for her hand to pull her up. "Come with me. We'd better check it out."

Faith quickly re-engaged her skis before they backtracked toward the woods at a breakneck pace. The screams grew louder and led them to the river on the other side of the trees.

A man dressed in black, wearing a ski mask, struggled with a woman wearing a hooded coat on the water's edge.

Jake yelled at him. "Let go of her!"

The man looked up and released his victim. Then he ran into the woods and disappeared.

Faith followed Jake to the woman's side.

He froze when he got closer. "April?"

In the moonlight, Faith made out the college student's pale face. She was wearing her matching parka.

April pointed toward the woods, stammering. "T-That man was trying to throw me in the river."

Faith shivered at the thought of the younger woman falling into the chilly waters. Though the Firehole River never froze due to the geothermal springs that fed it, it was still cold enough that no one could survive in it for very long.

April's voice quivered as she peered at Jake. "I don't understand."

He bent to help her to her feet. "What's that?"

"That man kept demanding I tell him where the Lone Star file is. That's why he was threatening me. I don't even know what he was talking about."

# CHAPTER TWENTY-ONE

CARRYING THEIR SKIS, FAITH AND JAKE trudged back to the lodge in silence. April's attack on the heels of Faith's confession about Joey had left them both drained without much to say. By now, April had been safely delivered to the staff dormitory by the ranger on snowmobile who had responded to Jake's radio call.

Like the suspicious person at the skating rink, the man who attacked April also wore a ski mask, and Faith recalled that April's parka matched hers exactly. Could it have been a case of mistaken identity? The possibility caused Faith to break out in a cold sweat despite the freezing temperatures. She hoped the rangers would track down the assailant while he was still in the area and put an end to this nightmare.

When she and Jake reached the lodge entrance, he pulled his scarf from his face and opened the door for her. "If you leave your skis and poles by the door, I'll return them with mine."

After she had done that, she pushed back her hood and removed her scarf to speak to him in the lobby. "I can't stop thinking about what happened to April."

He pulled off his gloves. "The guy's sick, probably out of his mind."

"That would almost make me feel better. What if it was the same person who tried to run me over with the snowmobile and pushed me into the road at Mammoth Hot Springs?"

Jake squinted at her. "Why would you think that?"

Then she told him about the anonymous note, her room being ransacked, and the masked man at the ice rink.

His jaw tensed as he stared at her. "You should have told me sooner."

She gave him an apologetic shrug. "I told the police already. I didn't want to burden you with more bad news. The point is the parka April was wearing is the same as mine. What if I was the target instead of her?"

Rubbing his chin, Jake considered her theory. "I hadn't thought of that. I need to call the ranger back and tell him there might be a connection with the other incidents…" An ominous look darkened his face. "There could be another explanation—the perp may be targeting our tour group and not you specifically."

She frowned, trying to make sense of it. "Why would anyone want to do that—and what about the file?"

"I don't know about the file, but I can think of one or two people who wouldn't mind seeing Wild Adventures go out of business."

"That's terrible! You really think this could be a plot against Chip's company?"

Jake blew out a long breath. "I don't know what to think."

When they moved near the fireplace to warm up, Jillian walked into the lobby. "There you are, Jake! I've been waiting for you all night." She ran up and planted a big kiss on him.

Appearing flustered, he freed himself from her clutches and stepped away. "What are you doing here, Jillian?"

She draped her arms over his shoulders and spoke in a syrupy-sweet tone. "I missed you, Jakey. I took off work to see you. I'm staying with my friend Susan in the dorm here tonight."

He extricated himself from her again.

"Uh-oh, you're still upset with me. I'm sorry about that little misunderstanding we had earlier this week. Let's forget it ever happened. After all, it's almost Christmas."

A wave of revulsion rocked Faith's stomach.

Jake moved beside her. "Jillian, you remember Faith, don't you?"

The tall blonde assessed her with a haughty stare. "Yes, of course. Hello, Faith. I'm sure by now you're sick of the winter weather and can't wait to be home for Christmas." The woman's tone was more biting than the air outside.

Faith felt sick all right, but it wasn't because of the weather.

"It's getting late. I think it's time for me to go."

"Good night," Jillian musically replied with a whisk of her hand.

"Faith, wait!"

She ignored Jake's voice and began walking.

He caught up and strode beside her. "What happened back there with Jillian is not what you think."

Faith paused, keeping her gaze fixed on the floor. "It's been a long day, and I'm exhausted. Good night, Jake."

As she started to cross the lobby, a deep bass voice stopped her. "Faith Chandler?"

Turning around, she saw a bald, black man dressed in a sport coat and jeans, standing near the front desk. "Yes?"

He walked toward her, pulled out his badge, and flashed it before her eyes. "I'm Special Agent Gordon Baxter with the FBI. I spoke with you on the phone a few days ago."

He was built more like an offensive lineman than how she pictured an FBI special agent. "I don't suppose you came all this way to celebrate Christmas at Yellowstone?"

"No, I moved from Chicago to Dallas because I can't stand the cold and snow." His subtle sense of humor softened his intimidating appearance.

Faith sighed. "Then I assume you're here about Monica Wallace."

He nodded. "After I got your text that she contacted you, I decided I should take a little trip up north and see you in person. I tried to reach you earlier today, but you didn't answer or return my call."

"I lost my phone. Can't this wait until I'm back home?"

He shook his head. "Believe me, I'd much rather be decorating my tree with my family. Now if you don't mind, I'd like to have a word with you. *Alone.*"

Jake broke in. "Is everything okay, Faith?"

The fortyish agent pivoted and politely introduced himself.

Faith felt she needed to explain. "He's the FBI agent investigating Monica's disappearance."

"Oh," Jake said. "In that case, I'll leave you alone." Before he left, he glanced at her once more. "Call me if you need anything. I'll see you in the morning." He turned and strode toward the lobby entrance. Once he'd gathered their skis and poles, he disappeared down the hall.

Faith felt the sickness in her stomach spread to her heart. She looked around and saw to her relief that Jillian was gone as well. Faith turned to the agent. "The lobby appears empty now. Let's sit by the fireplace, if that's okay."

The man nodded, and she led him to some lounge chairs close to the hearth. The agent sat in the one across from her.

She gently started the conversation. "Have you found Monica yet?"

"No, but I'm following up on a few leads."

Connecting the dots, she leaned forward and lowered her voice. "You think Monica is here in Yellowstone."

"I didn't say that. However, we tracked her to Jackson Hole, Wyoming yesterday. Either she gave our agents the slip or somebody got to her first. It happened last night around the time she contacted you and her call was interrupted."

That explained the sirens in the background and possibly the banging on the door. Jackson Hole was less than a couple of hours south of Yellowstone. "I still don't know how I can help you."

"It appears she was privy to Syngexas financial information that was used to blackmail company executives. I believe your boyfriend, Tad Winters, was one of them."

"*Ex-boyfriend.* Let me get this straight. Monica was blackmailing the executives?"

"That's what it looks like."

Faith remembered how strange Tad had acted when she saw him earlier that afternoon, like he was afraid of something. Was it Monica he was afraid of? "That's all very interesting, but what does it have to do with me?"

"One of the Syngexas executives told us he was threatened that the compromising information about him would be made public if he retaliated against his blackmailer."

Faith swallowed hard. The agent obviously suspected that

Monica had sent her the incriminating material.

The investigator's eyes narrowed. "Did you know that Tad Winters is here?"

Taking a deep breath to steady her escalating pulse, Faith nodded. "I ran into him earlier today, but without my phone, I couldn't contact you."

Gordon's scrutinizing gaze made her uncomfortable. "What did he want?" the agent asked.

Faith shut her eyes, wishing this would all go away. After a long sigh, she responded. "He wanted to know if Monica had tried to contact me."

"What did you say?"

"I didn't tell him one way or the other."

"Did either Monica or Tad mention anything about a missing file?"

*File. April said her attacker wanted a file.* "No… What file?"

"It's called the Lone Star file. It supposedly contains confidential information about key corporate Syngexas accounts based in Texas. It may be the source Monica used for the blackmail. Have you heard of this file?"

Faith's heart pounded like war drums. This was starting to make sense, and not in a good way. "I hadn't until tonight. Our snowcoach driver, April, was attacked by a man she said demanded to know where the Lone Star file was, but she didn't know what he was talking about."

"What's her name again?"

"April Brooks."

He took out his phone and entered the information. "Thanks. Has anything else suspicious happened since you've been here?"

Faith took a deep breath, then told him about the anonymous note and the break-in at the Moose Run lodge, as well as the masked skier and crazy snowmobile driver. She also mentioned the rock slide in case it wasn't a freak accident.

After she finished, he stared at her with an intense frown. Then he reached in his pocket. "Here's my card. Call me if you think of anything else that might be connected to the case."

She took the card and glanced at it. "Thank you. How long do you plan to be here?"

He rose from his chair. "It depends. Hopefully, not long. Oh, one more thing." Concern touched his serious expression. "Be careful. I believe Monica disappeared because her life is in danger. If so, yours may be too."

Instead of going to his room at the lodge, Jake skied alone on the moonlit snow, consumed with his thoughts. He couldn't get the attacks on April and Faith off his mind. If his group was in danger, the safest thing would be to cancel the tour. That meant Chip would need to refund the participants, and his cousin was counting on this last tour of the year to cover his remaining expenses and provide Christmas for his family.

Jake wanted to be certain about his suspicions before taking such drastic action. The park rangers were already on high alert after he reported the incident with April. Thankfully, nothing more serious had happened, and he was determined to keep it that way. However, life in the wilderness came with inherent risks, especially in winter. It was impossible to protect people from everything—even when his rules of survival were followed.

Joey's accident came to mind—and Faith's revelation about what had transpired before his death. Though it still hurt, time had given him the maturity and perspective to understand why she'd kept it to herself. He also realized she too had suffered, and unlike him, she hadn't had a supportive family to lean on. She'd carried the burden of her parents' deaths for so long Joey's accident must have been too much for her to bear.

In any case, Jake wasn't sure how they could move forward until he was certain she wouldn't abandon him again when things got tough. It didn't help matters that Jillian had acted like they were a couple and hung on him like an itchy scarf.

Approaching a small herd of bison, he slowed. Their mound-shaped silhouettes dotted the landscape as they quietly foraged for grass under the deep snow. The enormous creatures usually rested during the day and did most of their eating at night.

Jake kept a respectful distance as he quietly glided through their territory.

Hearing the sound of a loud pop like a firecracker, he halted, trying to identify the source.

The noise had roused the bison from their grazing, and they began to move in his direction.

Alarmed, he hurried to the safety of the woods. From the edge of the forest, he watched the spooked herd gather momentum.

They soon broke into a sprint. The ground shook and thundered like an earthquake as the stampede headed straight for him.

He ducked behind a large tree. Peering around it, he held his breath and appealed to heaven, bracing for the onslaught.

At the last minute, the herd veered away, toward the open meadow. Their strong musky scent filled the air as they rumbled past him like a runaway train.

He watched them, mesmerized by their speed and power. Waiting until the coast was clear, he silently thanked God he was spared.

Emerging from the woods, he heard the sound of a diesel truck engine from the vicinity of the earlier popping sound. He followed the noise until he spotted a heavy-duty, black truck with big traction tires and a winch in the bed. It drove to where the herd had been, then backed up to something lying on the ground.

Hiding in the shadows, Jake moved closer to see what it was. When he saw the downed bison, outrage burned inside him. *Poachers!* It was illegal to hunt bison in the park.

The driver and another man got out. The driver went to the back of the truck and opened the tailgate, while the other man headed to the fallen animal. The man at the rear of the pickup unloaded a large ramp from the bed and leaned it against the tailgate, next to the bison.

Not wanting to give himself away, Jake craned his neck for

a better look at the men. Both were wearing ski masks, so he couldn't see their faces. The second man harnessed the fallen animal while the driver cranked the winch to hoist it into the truck bed.

Jake had seen enough. He couldn't let them get away with their crime. He skied out from the woods. "Hey, you there! Stop what you're doing!"

The men froze, then shifted in his direction. One of them pointed a rifle at him.

Jake ducked back into the woods.

The hunters quickly retrieved the harness and threw the ramp into the truck before they sped away.

Once they were gone, Jake skied to the lifeless creature on the ground. The sight of the senseless loss triggered a sick, burning sensation in his gut. When he examined the bison and found the bullet hole in its hide, he growled with disgust.

Hunting bison was strictly prohibited in Yellowstone National Park, though it was allowed in other areas outside the park. Whoever did this blatantly violated the law for an easy kill, most likely for sport. The poachers obviously thought they were above the law.

Awakened by the distant howling of wolves, Faith sat up in bed. The eerie noise kept the masked antagonist fresh in her mind, along with Agent Baxter's warning.

The phone on her nightstand rang, startling her. She glanced at the clock. Three a.m.

Cautiously, she lifted the receiver, trying not to disturb Shelly, who stirred when it rang. "Hello," Faith answered in a low voice.

"How was your date?"

The taunting male voice was instantly recognizable. "What are you doing, Tad, spying on me? You've got a lot of nerve calling at this hour."

Ignoring her last remark, he continued provoking her. "He's a lucky guy. I have to admit I'm a little jealous."

"Hey, I'm not discussing my personal life with you, especially at three o'clock in the morning. And who gave you this number anyway?"

"I have a new friend, Jillian Prescott. She has connections at the lodge."

Faith's tight grip on the phone caused her palm to sweat. "I'm not surprised you two would hit it off. You have so much in common."

"In case you didn't know, she has a thing for your midnight ski instructor."

"Do you want something, or are you calling only to harass me?"

"No, actually I'm calling because I saw you talking to the FBI agent tonight. You didn't tell him that I'm here, did you?"

"I didn't have to. He already knows."

"Great," Tad said in a sarcastic tone. "What else does he know about me?"

"It's late and I'm tired. If you want to know more about Agent Baxter's investigation, I suggest you talk to him yourself." With that, she hung up.

Shelly rolled over and opened her eyes. "Who on earth was calling at this hour?"

"No one. Go back to sleep." Faith fluffed her pillow as if it were a punching bag. When she rested her head against it, the wolves' howling grew louder, sounding closer than before.

# CHAPTER TWENTY-TWO

WHEN FAITH AWOKE FRIDAY MORNING, SHE half wondered if Tad's phone call last night had been another bad dream. Then Shelly came out of the bathroom and gave her a dose of reality.

"Are you going to tell me who called at three a.m., or do I have to guess?"

Faith raised up in bed. "It was Tad. He got our number from Jillian."

Shelly slanted her head. "Jillian? How did she get it?"

"Never mind that. I think Tad's freaking out over the investigation into Syngexas."

"Why, is he a suspect?"

"Who knows? My guess is he's more concerned about what may come out of the investigation that will tarnish his reputation. Ready for another bizarre twist? The FBI agent conducting the investigation is here as well. He spoke to me in the lobby late last night. He wanted to know if I'd heard from Monica again. I would have told you about it except you were already asleep when I came in."

Shelly sat on her bed, her mouth gaping. "Wow. Things are getting stranger and stranger."

"I know. It almost feels like I'm the one under investigation. Both Agent Baxter and Tad are keeping tabs on me in case Monica shows up here."

"You don't think she'd do that, do you?"

Faith shrugged. "I just hope she's safe. The FBI agent told me her life may be in danger." She decided not to share that hers might be also.

"Stay clear of Tad, Faith," Shelly said. "He's already burned you once."

And now he was spying on her and conspiring with Jillian. "Don't worry. I intend to."

"By the way, a note was left under our door this morning."

Shelly reached for a slip of paper on her nightstand and handed it to Faith. "It says that our tour schedule has changed. New activities will be planned for this afternoon. It sounds like we're on our own this morning. We can do whatever we want."

Faith scanned the notice with the Wild Adventures bison logo on the letterhead and Chip's signature at the bottom. "I wonder why the change?"

"I don't know, but hurry up and get dressed. We'll discuss it over breakfast downstairs. I'm starving."

After taking a snowcoach shuttle that morning to West Yellowstone, Montana, Jake sat by the window at a diner there, sipping his coffee while he waited for Ned Houston to join him. When Ned entered the diner, Jake stood to greet him. They shook hands and sat across from each other in the booth.

"You must have read my mind, Jake," the friendly, gray-bearded man told him as he removed his cell phone from his pocket and set it on the table. "I was going to give you a call this week. My boss, Dwayne, asked me to review your résumé and job application. I have to say I'm very impressed with your background."

Jake smiled, encouraged by Ned's interest and to learn he was still in the running for the position. "Thanks, that's good to hear. Actually, I called you about another matter."

"Oh?" Ned tilted his head slightly. "I can't stay long. I have a meeting in town."

"I'll make it quick." Jake filled him in on the poaching incident he'd witnessed late last night.

Ned rubbed his beard. "You say the truck was black with snow traction tires and a towing winch."

"That's correct. Whoever is doing the poaching must have connections with the park or know their way around the authorities."

"Thanks for letting me know. I'll look into it."

Jake felt better. He knew Ned and trusted him to follow through. "You said you wanted to call me this week?"

"That's right. About your job application, tell me more about the work you did in Colorado and Alaska."

Jake summarized his job experience in those states, highlighting his specific skills and duties pertinent to the park service position.

"What made you decide to move here to Wyoming?"

"My cousin, Chip Reynolds, offered me a job with his tour company, and I wanted to work in a national park again. With my background and education in geology and wildfire science, Yellowstone is the perfect place for me."

Ned appeared pleased with his answer. "If it were my decision, Jake, I'd offer you the job right now. However, my boss, Dwayne, is the hiring manager."

"I understand."

"What's this I hear about a feud between you and Oscar Prescott? You know, he's hunting buddies with Dwayne."

Jake stiffened. "He blames me for his company's recent park citations."

"Dwayne told me Oscar thinks the violations were trumped up because his tour business is competing with the one you work for."

"That's not true."

"Maybe not, but Oscar has a lot of connections and influence around here."

Jake did his best to stay composed. "Are you saying he could keep me from getting the job with the park service?"

Ned eyed Jake with a look of fatherly concern. "Not if I have anything to say about it. Just watch your back where Oscar is concerned. I can't promise you'll get the job. However, I will recommend you to Dwayne with my own personal endorsement."

Encouraged by the upstanding man's support, Jake felt the tension in his muscles relax. "That means a lot, Ned. Thank you."

The older man's cell phone beeped, and he glanced at the message. "Sorry. That's Dwayne. I've got to go, but I'll be in touch."

Faith was disappointed that Jake wasn't in the lodge restaurant for breakfast. She regretted their evening had ended the way it had. April's attack had been a shock to them both. Then Jillian's kiss and flirting with Jake had sent Faith over the edge. She now realized she had been too hasty in giving him the brush off without the benefit of the doubt. She knew deep down no one was more trustworthy than Jake. Jillian, on the other hand…

"You're not eating your pancakes," Shelly said. "Aren't you hungry?"

Faith played with her fork. "I have a lot on my mind."

"You didn't get much sleep either. I still can't believe the nerve of Tad calling you in the middle of the night."

Faith didn't want to think about Tad. She noticed Alec being seated with Leslie at a table across the room.

He narrowed his eyes at Faith before taking a seat with his back to her.

The snub didn't bother her in the least. After his obnoxious behavior last night, she hoped he never spoke to her again.

Leslie turned in Faith's direction and cast her a shrewd look.

"What do you make of those two hanging out together?" Shelly asked, focusing on the other table.

"I don't know." Faith studied the pair, trying to figure out what game Leslie was playing. "It surprises me, considering she warned me about his bad reputation with women last night."

"Leslie looking out for you? That's a switch."

"I know."

"She probably wanted you out of the way so she could have him all to herself."

Faith laughed at Shelly's remark. "She's welcome to him. More likely she's gathering research for an exposé."

Shelly shifted her attention to Faith. "Enough about them. What have you decided about Chip's job offer?"

"I'm still considering it. However, I've decided to wait on God to show me what to do."

Shelly nodded. "It's an important decision—which reminds me. We still need to figure out what we're going to do today. I noticed a stand of travel brochures in the lobby. Why don't we check it out after breakfast?"

A little while later, having finished their meal, they stopped to browse the brochures.

Shelly grabbed one and showed it to her. "Hey, how about taking a day trip to West Yellowstone? We can do some shopping and grab lunch in town."

Faith lifted a brow. "How would we get there?"

"We'll take a snowcoach shuttle." Shelly pulled another brochure for that. "It'll be fun."

Faith hesitated, remembering the crazy guy in the ski mask was still at large. "I don't know."

"I'll call Chip. I bet he can help us find a ride."

A man's voice responded from behind them. "A ride to where?"

Faith was surprised to see Jake's cousin standing there. "Hi, Chip."

Shelly pointed to the brochure. "We want to go to West Yellowstone this morning. Can you help us?"

"Absolutely," he cheerfully replied.

"By the way, have you seen Jake?" Faith asked. "I've been looking for him all morning."

"He had a meeting in town. I came to coordinate activities for your group. I assume you know about that incident with April last night."

"What incident?" Shelly asked.

Faith filled her in. "A man tried to push April into the Firehole River last night. Jake and I were skiing nearby and chased him off."

Shelly covered her mouth. "Oh, my…"

Concerned about the young college student, Faith turned to Chip. "How is April this morning?"

"She'll be all right, but we thought it would be best to give her the day off. That's why I canceled the events for this morning and I'm re-planning the rest of the day. Until that creep is found, the park is on high alert.

"Regarding your ride to West Yellowstone, how about taking snowmobiles? You'd need a permit to drive one in the park without a guide. However, I can hire a friend of mine to be your guide, if you'd like."

Faith exchanged a quick glance with Shelly. "That's nice of you, Chip, but we want to pay for it."

"No, it's the least I can do for disrupting the tour today. Besides, your tour is free, remember?"

Though she knew she couldn't change his mind, Faith didn't feel right accepting his generosity when his company was having trouble making ends meet. "Thanks. Please let April know we're thinking of her."

"Will do. I'll meet you in the lobby in a few minutes."

After Chip left to see his friend about arranging the snowmobile ride, Rick appeared from down the hall. "Hello, ladies. How are you planning to spend the day now that we're on our own?"

"We're taking snowmobiles to West Yellowstone," Shelly said.

His brows lifted. "Mind if I come along? Alec went cross-country skiing with Leslie this morning, and I didn't want to be a third wheel."

With Alec out of the picture, Faith didn't see any reason why not. "Chip has gone to arrange it with a guide. You'll need to ask him if you can come with us."

The three of them walked to the lobby where they waited for Chip.

"Good news," he told them when he returned. "Dex says he can go with you, as long as you return here by twelve-thirty. He has another tour scheduled for one p.m. I'm afraid that only gives you time for an early lunch in West Yellowstone and maybe a little shopping."

Faith smiled. "That should work fine for us. Thanks."

Chip eyed Rick. "Are you going too?"

"If that's okay."

"I'm sure Dex won't mind. I told Faith and Shelly I would pay for the tour to compensate for inconveniencing everyone with the change in schedule."

"I don't mind paying my own way."

"Nope. It's settled," Chip said. "I'll let Dex know he's got a party of three. He'll meet you here in the lobby in ten minutes. Be sure and bring your driver's license and wear something made of fleece or polyester to keep you warm and dry. Dex will provide your helmets and snowsuits."

The two women left Rick in the lobby and went to their room to change. After Faith had put on the appropriate attire, she grabbed her wallet with her driver's license to take with her.

Walking down the hall toward the lobby with Shelly, Faith started to feel uneasy about going out without Jake as their guide. Dex wasn't aware of the recent incidents and might not be as vigilant. On the other hand, she wouldn't be alone, and Shelly was looking forward to seeing the town. Faith didn't want to disappoint her. Besides, now that the rangers were searching for April's attacker it was only a matter of time before he would be caught. Even so, Faith would have felt better if Jake were going with them.

When she and Shelly arrived in the lobby, a man in his mid-twenties with shoulder-length hair and a scruffy three-day beard came through the main door and spotted the two women. "I'm Dex. Are you Chip's friends?"

"Yes," Faith said, "and there's one more coming."

Rick appeared from the hallway and strode toward them. "Sorry I'm late."

"You're right on time." Dex introduced himself to Rick, then addressed the group. "All right, let's get your gear, then I'll give you a few driving lessons before we head out."

They followed him to the outfitters store in the lodge, where Dex provided them snowsuits to put on over their clothes, along with goggles, helmets, and gloves. Once they had donned their insulated coveralls and collected their things, he led them outside to where several blue snowmobiles were parked. He then gave them a quick course on how to control and maneuver the vehicles and also went over the park snowmobile regulations. Shortly thereafter, the group began test driving their motorized sleds in a vacant area of the lodge parking lot.

It took a few minutes for Faith to get used to the accelerator and brake controls on the handle bars, but she quickly learned and was eager to take it for a spin.

As soon as they were ready to depart, Dex led the three to the snow-covered road, and they went north toward Madison. It didn't take long before they picked up their speed, enjoying the ease and freedom of touring the park on the snowmobiles.

It was a beautiful clear morning, and the white landscape glittered in the sunshine as they rode through the wilderness, stopping at a few pull-offs where they saw elk, bison, and a coyote along the way.

Though Dex was a good guide, Faith missed hearing Jake's interesting anecdotes and history about the park. It was already Friday, and the tour was almost over. They would be heading back to Moose Run tomorrow afternoon. The thought saddened her. Wanting to postpone her departure, she began to consider Chip's job offer more seriously. But now that Jake knew the truth about the past, how would he feel about working with her? And where did things stand with Jillian? Had she convinced him to spend Christmas with her family last night after Faith gave him the brush off?

The foursome traveled about half an hour, then pulled into a rest area near Madison Junction to stretch their legs. Judging by the number of snowmobiles parked near the cabin, it was a popular stop. Dex told them it was a warming hut with restrooms and refreshments inside.

While he took a break and chatted with other guides, Faith, Shelly, and Rick headed to the warming hut. Entering the small building, Faith was struck by the crowd of people gathered there enjoying hot drinks and snacks while thawing out in the heated shelter.

She and Shelly found an empty section of a bench and sat

down.

"I'll be back in a minute." Rick told them. He crossed the room to wait in the fast-moving line at the concessions counter.

"We should have given him our orders before he left," Shelly said to Faith, half-joking.

Faith took out her wallet, removed a ten-dollar bill, and handed it to Shelly. "Here. Tell him to buy us a couple of hot cocoas. I'll save your seat."

Shelly nodded and rose from the bench. "I'll be right back."

After her friend left, Faith scanned the other snowmobilers, hoping Jake might be among them. Chip had said he had an appointment in town that morning. She wondered what kind of appointment it was, and in which town—Moose Run, Mammoth Hot Springs, or West Yellowstone?"

Soon Shelly and Rick returned, carrying three steaming cups. Carefully, Shelly handed Faith hers. "Here you go. Be careful, it's hot."

Faith took the cup and slowly sipped it. The sweet, chocolaty beverage was the perfect pick-me-up on the cold wintry day. "Thanks, this is just what I needed."

Shelly reached in her pocket and handed Faith her money back. "Rick insisted on paying."

He shrugged. "It's the least I could do after you ladies let me tag along this morning."

Shelly gave him a teasing smile. "If you're ever in the Dallas area, we'll treat you to an iced tea."

He chuckled. "I might take you up on that. I've always liked Dallas."

Shelly's brow arched. "You've been there?"

"For work. It's been a while though."

"You should come back for a visit."

A glint of interest lit in his eyes as he gazed at Shelly. "Only if you'll give me a tour."

"Of course," she said in a perky tone.

Watching the two of them flirting, Faith was starting to feel like a third wheel. It occurred to her that possibly she had crossed paths with Rick in Dallas and that's why he looked familiar. Since Alec had done consulting work for Syngexas and knew Tad, maybe Rick had come with his boss on his business trips.

Their guide came into the warming hut and waved. "Are you guys ready?"

Faith swallowed the last of her hot chocolate. "Time to brave the elements again."

Outside, on their way to the snowmobiles, Rick and Shelly chitchatted about the airline she worked for, while Faith discreetly fell back. Rick's interest in her friend appeared to go beyond casual curiosity, and Shelly acted like she enjoyed his attention. It was funny because he didn't seem her type.

Faith tried not to let Rick's close professional ties to Alec cloud her opinion of him. However, Alec's intimidating behavior last night, coupled with Leslie's warning about him, continued to gnaw at Faith. It caused her to wonder how much Rick knew about his boss's shady past.

It also made her realize that Alec could be the one targeting her. Was he there watching her now? Looking around, she didn't see any sign of him, but the bad vibes persisted.

She hurried to catch up with the others. If Alec was behind his wife's boating accident, what else was he capable of?

# CHAPTER TWENTY-THREE

AT TEN O'CLOCK THAT MORNING, Faith arrived in West Yellowstone with her three travel companions. Following Dex, she drove her snowmobile on the main road through the small tourist town comprised of shops, eateries, and hotels. It seemed a stark contrast to the uninhabited wilderness of the park. The guide led them a couple of blocks down and turned into the small parking lot on the left.

When they had all parked, Dex took off his helmet and addressed them. "I'm going to the restaurant down the street for breakfast. You're welcome to join me or explore on your own. We'll meet next door at the coffee shop by eleven-thirty. I need to return to the snow lodge in time for my afternoon tour."

Faith took off her helmet and goggles. "Shelly and I are planning to do some shopping."

Rick gestured down the street. "I think I'll walk around a bit and check out the town."

As the group split up, they left their helmets and goggles behind with their snowmobiles. From the parking lot, Faith and Shelly crossed the plowed street to the shoveled sidewalk lined with stores.

Shelly stopped at the first clothing and gift shop they came to. "Look, there's a sale. Let's go in and see what they've got."

Faith followed her inside and browsed the store with the other tourists looking for souvenirs. She checked a few price tags, then decided she couldn't afford to buy anything right now, even on sale.

Shelly quickly found several items of clothing in her size on the sale rack. When she went into the dressing room to try them on, Faith stepped outside to wait so she wouldn't be tempted to spend money.

She scanned the storefront next door. The window display

had a snowmobile with a life-sized mannequin of Santa in the driver's seat. What struck her was the red and black pattern on the snowmobile body. It matched the one that almost ran her down.

Above the display, the business name, Wolf Pack Tours and Outfitters, was printed on the plate glass.

Faith glanced at her watch. They wouldn't be in West Yellowstone very long. If she popped in the store for a minute, maybe she could find out something about the snowmobile before Shelly finished trying on clothes.

As she opened the door to go in, sleigh bells jingled to announce her entrance, though she didn't see any employees ready to assist her.

While she waited, she looked around and noticed the mounted elk, bison, and deer heads lining the back wall. The head and hide of a giant grizzly bear hung on another wall. Having seen many of the creatures alive in the wild, the sight of the hunting trophies disturbed her. Maybe coming in here was a bad idea.

"May I help you?" A muscular-looking young man was standing behind the register. He had stubble on his face and was wearing a red and black plaid flannel shirt with a name tag that said Travis.

She approached the counter, trying to act casual. "I couldn't help noticing the Christmas display in your front window. That's a very sporty-looking snowmobile Santa is driving. Is the red and black color scheme exclusive to your company or is it pretty common around here?"

He grinned proudly. "You won't find any other snowmobiles like ours. We custom order them straight from the manufacturer."

Her heartrate went up a notch. "The reason I'm asking is because I saw one like it earlier this week… The person riding it almost plowed into me."

Travis's brows pressed together. "I doubt it was one of ours. Maybe you didn't get a good look at it."

"No, I'm sure it was exactly like the one in your window.

Would you mind checking your records to see who rented a snowmobile from you on Wednesday of this week?"

The store employee's eyes grew wary. "You must be the woman the rangers and police told me about. They've been asking about that snowmobile too. We have a strict privacy policy to protect our customers, and like I said, I'm sure it wasn't one of ours."

Disappointed that he wasn't being more cooperative, she kept probing. "Have any of your snowmobiles been stolen recently?"

"No, they're either here and accounted for, or rented to paying customers."

"What about the ones rented out? Could one of them have been stolen without anyone's knowledge?"

He paused and scratched the scraggly whiskers on his chin. "I suppose someone could have stolen one that was parked and then returned it without being caught. We're always telling our customers to take the keys with them when they're not with the snowmobiles."

She mulled over what he'd said. The entire incident hadn't taken more than fifteen minutes. That was a short enough time to return the snowmobile without anyone being the wiser, and it supported the possibility that Alec could have been the culprit.

Travis crossed his arms. "It sounds to me like someone wanted you to think it was one of our snowmobiles—to put us out of business."

His theory sounded ironically similar to Jake's suspicions that someone might be targeting Wild Adventures to ruin Chip's company. Was it a coincidence, or did someone have an ax to grind against tour companies in general? She wanted to question him more about his theory but didn't have time.

"If any of your snowmobiles turn up missing, please give me a call. I'll give you my phone number." She reached in her pocket for her wallet and removed a business card. "Do you mind if I borrow a pen?"

He reluctantly retrieved one from under the counter.

"Here."

She crossed off her old Syngexas contact information and wrote down the Old Faithful Snow Lodge, then handed him the card. "I lost my cell phone, but I noted where I'm staying. I don't know the phone number. I'm sure it's available online. You can leave a message for me with the front desk."

"Are you on a tour or something?"

"Yes, with Wild Adventures."

A slight grimace crossed his face. "Chip Reynolds' company, huh?"

"Yes, that's the one."

The store clerk gave her a smug grin. "Too bad you didn't book with us. Our tours are more exciting."

"Jake Mitchell is our guide. Do you know him?"

Travis snorted. "Know him? He's been trying to shut us down."

Surprised, she hid her reaction behind a casual facade. "Why?"

"I guess they're afraid of a little competition."

That didn't sound like Jake, but she didn't want to probe too much since she wanted the man's cooperation.

Travis was reading her business card. "It says here you're an accountant."

"That's right."

His brow lifted. "Our company has grown so much we've been looking for an accountant to run the business side of things."

She tilted her head, surprised and curious. "Oh?"

"If you have a few minutes, I can go over the job description with you."

Remembering her decision to postpone her job search until after the tour, she thought she'd better leave before she changed her mind. "Maybe another time. I'm supposed to meet up with my tour group shortly."

A thinner, younger man emerged through the door behind the front desk.

Travis introduced him to Faith. "This is Bud, my brother.

As you can see, we're a family-run business."

"I take it you don't have any accountants in the family."

Travis chuckled. "That's right. Only hunters and outdoorsmen, except for my sister who's in the hotel business. If you want to submit your résumé, I'm sure my father would be interested in taking a look. Accountants are hard to come by around here."

"Thanks, I'll keep that in mind." She shook his hand. "Well, I'd better be going."

The men waved as she walked away.

As soon as Faith left the store, she heard a familiar male voice in front of her.

"Faith?"

Lifting her eyes, she was surprised and delighted to see Jake walking toward her. "Hi, I was hoping I would run into you today. I looked for you this morning, and Chip said you had an appointment."

He glanced behind her at the Wolf Pack Tours building where she'd been. "What are you doing here in West Yellowstone?"

"Oh, I came with Shelly and Rick on snowmobiles. It was a lot of fun actually." Noticing Jake's serious expression, she wondered what was up.

"Why didn't you contact me? I would have arranged a tour for you with a different company."

She glanced over her shoulder. "Oh, I didn't come with Wolf Pack Tours. Chip arranged it with Dex."

Jake's frown softened a bit. "Then why were you in there?"

"I was waiting for Shelly and saw their window display." She turned and gestured to it. "That snowmobile with Santa is exactly like the one that tried to plow me down."

Stepping toward the store window, Jake examined the vehicle.

She moved beside him. "I went to inquire about it, but the man I spoke to wasn't all that helpful. I think he wanted to get rid of me—that is, until he discovered I was an accountant. Then he acted like he wanted to hire me."

Jake's jaw tightened. It was obvious what she'd said bothered him. He glanced at her from the corner of his eye. "What about Chip's offer?"

"Oh, I'm still considering it. This other opportunity came totally out of the blue. In any case, I've put my job search on hold until after this week." She sighed. "I sure hope Travis comes up with a lead on that snowmobile that chased me down. I told him to contact me at the snow lodge if he does."

Jake turned in her direction. "I wouldn't hold my breath on that."

"Why not?"

Thrusting his hands deep in his pockets, he grimaced uncomfortably, then stared down at his boots. "Never mind. I've got errands to run." He sent her a stiff wave as he turned to leave. "I'll see you back at the lodge."

Faith watched him cross the street, wondering what that was all about.

Shelly walked out of the shop next door. "There you are. I thought you'd disappeared."

"Didn't you buy anything?" Faith asked.

"No, the clothes looked better on the rack than on me."

After they finished taking a quick walk around town, they arrived at the coffee shop a few minutes early. By then, the weather had changed. Gray clouds now blocked the sun, and it had turned colder and windy.

When they came through the door, Rick was already there. "Looks like a storm is blowing in."

"I know," Faith said. "I hope we can make a quick trip back to the lodge and beat the snow."

He gestured in the direction they had come. "Was that Jake you were talking to a little while ago?"

Faith glanced outside, but he was nowhere in sight. "Yes. I sort of ran into him."

"I noticed you both standing in front of Wolf Pack Tours." Interest resonated in Rick's voice. "I ran into Jillian at the snow lodge yesterday—you know, the woman who helped with our tour orientation at Moose Run? She said Jake would be taking a job at Wolf Pack Tours soon. Her father owns the company."

Faith's heart lurched. *Jillian's father owned Wolf Pack Tours?* All of the sudden, she made the connection and remembered Beth telling her Oscar Prescott was Jillian's father when Faith had dinner with Chip's family. Travis and Bud must be Oscar's sons and Jillian's brothers. That's why the woman acted so uppity. She expected her father to lure Jake away from Wild Adventures.

Chip had said Oscar tried to bribe him to fire Jake as payback for reporting him to the park authorities. What if the real reason Oscar wanted Chip to fire him was so Jake would have to come work for Wolf Pack Tours? That almost made her laugh. She couldn't imagine him ever working for Chip's competitor, especially given how Jake felt about Oscar.

Rick glanced at his watch. "I hope Dex gets here soon. I was hoping to catch him before I have to leave."

Faith slanted her head. "You aren't coming with us?"

"Alec called me. The Wi-Fi is out at the lodge, so he's coming here on a snowcoach shuttle and wants us to work in the library where there's Internet and it's more private than here in the coffee shop. I'll catch the snowcoach shuttle back with him."

He handed Shelly the keys to his snowmobile, and she gave him an amiable smile. "Well, thanks again for the hot cocoa at the warming hut."

"My pleasure," he replied.

Faith studied her friend, trying to figure out if she was really interested in Rick. And what about Phil? Faith had thought there might be a spark between them too. Then again, what did she know about relationships? Hers always ended in disaster.

After Rick left, Faith stared out the window at the Wolf Pack Tours building, recalling her conversation with Jake. No wonder he reacted the way he did when she told him about her discussion with Travis. Jake obviously suspected the Prescotts of trying to sabotage Chip's business, and now he probably thought she was interested in working for them.

Her chest tightened at the thought that Travis could have been the maniac on the snowmobile, and she had even told him where she was staying! But how did the Lone Star file and anonymous note fit in?

CHAPTER TWENTY-FOUR

FAITH WAS EAGER TO RETURN TO the snow lodge at Old Faithful. The gray clouds had become darker and more foreboding, and the weather forecast on Shelly's phone said a snowstorm was on the way.

When Dex showed up, Shelly handed him Rick's keys and said that Rick planned to stay in town to work and would catch a shuttle later.

Their guide did not appear pleased. He released a long sigh. "I guess I'll have to call a friend in West Yellowstone to drive the snowmobile back to the lodge this afternoon."

Faith immediately thought of Jake. "I ran into Jake Mitchell in town. Maybe he could do it."

It turned out Dex knew Jake and gave him a call. After the guide hung up, he turned to the two women. "Good news. Jake is still here and agreed to take the snowmobile back once he's finished his business in town."

Going outside with Shelly and Dex, Faith could feel the weather moving in. She hoped they made it back to the lodge before things got worse. It worried her a little that Jake would be leaving later than them, but he was an experienced wilderness guide and knew how to take care of himself.

As the three drove out of town toward the park, Faith felt more comfortable driving the snowmobile at a faster clip, though she was careful not to exceed the speed limit. The exhilaration of riding through the open country helped free her mind from her job woes and the menace stalking her, and she relished the exciting diversion.

Shelly was riding to her left, with Dex in the lead. It was starting to snow, and her friend turned her head in Faith's direction, gesturing to the flakes coming down. Hopefully, it wouldn't get much worse and affect their visibility.

Faith's insulated coveralls and the heated seat and

handlebars on the snowmobile helped counter the chill, but the wind had started gusting. The falling flakes were also increasing. The road sign ahead said the junction at Madison was still five miles away. With the decreased visibility, Faith made a mental note of that since it was a major milestone near the midway point of their trip and also where she needed to turn south toward Old Faithful.

Peering in her side mirror, she noticed a lone snowmobile in the distance, catching up to them. She thought it might be Jake, driving Rick's snowmobile back, but it wasn't blue like theirs.

As the vehicle drew closer, she recognized the distinct red and black pattern on the body like the one that chased her down and the display model at Wolf Pack Tours.

Her pulse racing, she frantically waved to Shelly and pointed behind her.

Shelly glanced in her mirror. When the danger registered, she returned a wary nod.

Faith gestured for her to speed up toward Dex, then the two split off and accelerated. As they came beside him, the red and black snowmobile wedged between Faith and Dex, forcing her to veer right.

She saw the guide careen in the opposite direction and collide with Shelly into a snowbank.

Faith gasped. She desperately wanted to stop and check on them, but the relentless pest stayed on her tail.

When she sped up, he sped up.

Through her side mirror, she caught a fleeting glimpse of Dex freeing himself from his overturned snowmobile and going to help Shelly. Hopefully, she was okay.

On her own now, Faith had to find a way to lose her red and black shadow. But how?

Glancing in her mirror again, Faith tried to get a good look at the driver, but the helmet and goggles masked his face. At the same moment, she hit a major bump in the road. Gripping the handlebars like a lifeline, she went airborne—and prayed she'd come out of this alive.

When she landed, she was amazed to still be in control of her machine. However, she was on a snow bank off the road. Glancing behind her, she groaned. Her shadow had made the jump as well.

Leaning forward, she accelerated again, skating over the drift and across a white meadow.

The snowsquall shrouded everything. Faith could only see a few feet ahead of her. Suddenly, she made out a stand of trees directly in front. Steering and pitching her body to the left, she careened her vehicle out of harm's way.

It skidded down a slope and landed back on the road. Surprised and impressed by her daring maneuver, she couldn't stop to pat herself on the back. From her mirror, she could see the other driver had mimicked her action and was still on her tail.

Staring at the snow-covered highway ahead of her, Faith remembered the road sign earlier. Estimating the distance she'd traveled based on her speed and the duration of the chase, she knew they were fast approaching the turn at Madison. Straining her eyes, she searched for a landmark. Suddenly, a sign came into view. She threw her body to the right and swerved the snowmobile in that direction.

Her abrupt move launched the left side of her machine into the air. Gripping the handle bars, she held her breath as she tried to regain control of the teetering sled. Shifting her weight again, she landed the airborne side on the ground.

Glancing behind her, she saw her pursuer careen through the turn after her.

She craned her neck, trying to find the side road to the warming hut through the veil of snow. She'd almost passed the turnoff when she spotted snowmobiles parked in the distance and swerved toward them.

From her side mirror, she saw the maniac driver miss her detour and come to an abrupt halt. The pounding of her heart amplified as his head briefly shifted in her direction, then he made a quick U-turn and sped away toward West Yellowstone.

Breathing a huge sigh of relief, she gazed forward and rode

toward the ranger standing in the parking area. She was safe for now.

Riding Dex's snowmobile back to the snow lodge, Jake had time to think about his encounter with Faith in West Yellowstone. He'd been on his way to Wolf Pack Tours to give Oscar a piece of his mind for making false accusations about him to the park service. He'd also planned to quiz Oscar about any involvement he might have had in the incident that happened to Faith at Tower Fall. However, seeing her there changed his plans.

Now that he had cooled off, he felt badly for how he had acted when she told him about the accounting job. He realized she didn't know much about the Prescotts' unethical leanings or his own personal issues with them. How could he blame her for considering a job with them, not knowing the whole truth?

What bothered him the most was that she'd gone to West Yellowstone without him to keep an eye out for danger. If she had discussed it with him, he probably would have advised her to stay put at the snow lodge and not venture out, though he couldn't blame her for wanting to see West Yellowstone.

Farther ahead, Jake spotted two snowmobiles by the side of the road. He pulled over and saw Dex helping Shelly to her feet. "What happened?"

Anger hardened Dex's usual laid-back personality. "Some maniac drove us off the road."

Jake looked at Shelly. "Are you okay?"

"My foot got caught under my snowmobile when it overturned. I don't think anything is broken." Her tone turned distressed. "You have to find Faith. That mad man went after her."

Faith was resting inside the warming hut, waiting for Dex and Shelly. Though she was safe and warm, she couldn't shake the chill from being chased down like a hunted animal, and the frustrating question remained—why was this happening?

After she'd reported the snowmobile incident to the park ranger there, he put out a BOLO for the driver and vehicle, but Faith knew he would be hard to catch. He'd probably ditched the snowmobile by now like she suspected he'd done before. However, she did tell the ranger about the matching snowmobile she saw in the window display at Wolf Pack Tours. She also asked him to call Dex and let him know she was safe at the warming hut.

"Faith!"

At the sound of Shelly's voice, she lifted her gaze.

Her friend hobbled over and gave her a big hug. "I was so relieved when Dex told me you were all right."

"You're hurt," Faith cried.

"Not bad. My foot got caught under my snowmobile. I'll be good as new tomorrow. Did you see his face this time?"

Faith groaned. "No, he was wearing a helmet and goggles. It's got to be the same person though. The snowmobile was exactly like the one at Tower Fall."

"Let's go back to the lodge. What you need is a warm shower and a hot meal. That will cheer you up. By the way, have you seen Jake?"

"No, why?"

"He stopped and talked to us on the side of the road. I told him what had happened, and he went to look for you. He's probably almost to Old Faithful by now."

Faith remembered his disgruntled reaction when she told him about the job opportunity at Wolf Pack Tours. He probably couldn't wait for this week to be over and be done with her. Maybe she should do him a favor and leave early.

Dex stepped into the hut and joined them. "I just spoke to the ranger outside. Good thinking coming here, Faith. That loose-cannon snowmobiler wasn't crazy enough to follow you here with the ranger and other people around."

Faith was just thankful to be safe. "If we hadn't stopped here earlier, I might still be on the run."

"The ranger will give us an escort to the snow lodge whenever you're ready."

Faith stood. "I'm ready now. As far as I'm concerned, the sooner we get back, the better."

After riding straight to the snow lodge with no sign of Faith, Jake parked the snowmobile and hurried inside. He asked the attendant at the front desk to call Faith's room since the person wasn't allowed to give out her room number. When Faith didn't answer, he searched the lodge for her. With no success, he got on his snowmobile again and backtracked. This time he turned off at the warming hut. It was hard to see from the road in the snowy conditions, which was probably why he didn't think to check there earlier.

As soon as he parked, his ranger friend, Noah, appeared from the hut. He informed Jake that Faith, Shelly, and Dex had been escorted to the lodge by another ranger, and an updated BOLO had been issued for her pursuer.

Relieved to hear that, Jake realized he'd probably just missed her at the lodge. He called Chip and asked for Shelly's cell phone number so he could contact her and make sure she and Faith were all right and also get their room number before he headed back there.

A short while later, when he knocked on their door, Shelly answered with an impatient frown.

"Is this a bad time?" he asked.

She urged him inside. "No, please come in. Maybe you can talk some sense into Faith." Gesturing helplessly at her, Shelly sighed. "She won't listen to me."

He strode into the room, where Faith was packing her suitcase.

She stopped long enough to give him a sidelong glance.

"You're leaving," he said.

Looking away, she resumed her task. "It's time I went home. It's too dangerous for me to stay any longer."

After rolling her eyes, Shelly appealed to him. "Please talk her out of it, Jake. Tell her she's safer here with us than at home alone."

His gaze lingered on Faith, while he talked to Shelly. "It's not the danger she's running from. It's *me*."

Faith shot him a look as if he'd pierced her heart.

Shelly wisely headed for the door. "I think I'll leave you two alone for a few minutes."

After she left, Faith's eyes flared in defiance. "I am not running away."

"What do you call it then?

"I'm simply going home a little early. That's all."

He scoffed and crossed his arms. "Well, that figures… Are you taking the job with Alec's firm?"

"No, and I'm not going to pursue the one at Wolf Pack Tours either." She moved to the dresser and began gathering her socks to load in her suitcase. "But I do need to find a job. I have a mountain of bills to pay and gallivanting across Yellowstone is only postponing the inevitable. I need to get my life in order."

"Yes, you've always been good at taking care of yourself, haven't you? Forget about everyone else as long as Faith lands with both feet on the ground."

She spun around. "That's not fair!"

He dropped his arms and stepped toward her. "You want to talk about what's not fair? For once, you've finally leveled with me and the next day you decide to leave—that's not fair! When things get tough, instead of sticking it out and dealing with it, you cut and run. That's your pattern. Now you're about to do it again."

She turned away and covered her face, sobbing.

It pained him to see her cry, and he felt bad for hurting her. Softly stepping toward her, he tenderly turned her around. "Don't leave, Faith."

Lifting her gaze, tears glistened in her eyes. "What about Jillian?"

"What about her?"

"Where do things stand between you two?"

He gently wiped a tear from Faith's face, then rested his hands on her shoulders. "We work together, that's it. Now tell me you'll stay."

Faith peered at him from under her furrowed brow. "It seems all I do is cause you pain and suffering."

"That's not true. We were happy once, remember?"

Closing her eyes, she nodded.

"So you'll stay and finish the tour?"

Opening her eyes again, she responded in a lighter tone. "Only if you promise to take me cross-country skiing again."

He leaned away with a deadpan look. "You're so demanding… Okay, I promise."

A delighted expression graced her pretty face.

Captivated by her sweet smile and the way her blue eyes sparkled like Yellowstone Lake, he would have promised her the world if she'd asked for it.

Her radiance dimmed as worry creased her brow. "Seriously, Jake, I couldn't bear it if anyone got hurt because of me."

He tried to reassure her. "The police already have a BOLO out. After what happened today, I'd be surprised if they don't catch the perpetrator tonight, but if they don't, we'll cancel the activities for tomorrow too and stay close to the lodge."

She slowly moved away from him, twisting a lock of hair around her finger.

"I know that look. What are you thinking?"

"That snowmobile on display at Wolf Pack Tours. It looked exactly like the one that tried to run me down a couple of days ago and again today. When I mentioned the Tower Fall incident to Travis, he said it could be someone trying to frame his company and put them out of business."

Jake's jaw clenched. "Oh, he did, did he? No doubt I'm the one the Prescotts will try to pin the blame on." He pulled out his cell phone.

"What are you doing?"

"I'm going to give Oscar a piece of my mind."

She snatched his phone away from him. "No, you're not."

"Give that back to me!"

"Not until you promise not to call Oscar. If you call him now while you're angry, it will only make things worse."

Frustrated, Jake ran a hand through his hair. "I don't think that's possible."

# CHAPTER TWENTY-FIVE

BECAUSE JAKE NEEDED TO LEAVE TO coordinate plans for the next day, he promised Faith he wouldn't call Oscar, though he was still angry at the Prescotts. After he met with Chip and discussed the tour agenda, Jake stopped by the grill in the lodge to grab a snack and a coffee. Standing at the counter to order, he heard Jillian call his name.

Remembering his promise to Faith about Oscar, Jake decided he could at least set the man's daughter straight about a few things. As he about-faced and marched to her table, he saw her chatting with a man he didn't recognize.

Jillian excitedly jumped up from her chair. "Jake, there's someone I want you to meet."

The smug grin on the man's face already didn't sit well with Jake, and they hadn't even been introduced.

"This is Tad Winters, Faith's old boyfriend."

At first, Jake wondered if she was pulling his leg, but the pair's shrewd, conspiring glances confirmed it was true.

Tad rose from his seat. "Nice to make your acquaintance, Jake. It's funny that Faith never mentioned you."

Instead of shaking his hand, Jake crossed his arms and scrutinized him. "Faith knows you're here?"

"Oh, yes. We met in the restaurant last night. I'm glad I finally tracked her down. This place is amazing."

Jake clenched his jaw. Was the guy merely yanking his chain or was Faith still keeping secrets? "What was so important that you came all this way?"

The cocky man casually sat down again. "I guess you could say I want to make up for past mistakes. By the way, your girlfriend Jillian here has been very helpful."

"She's not—"

"In fact, she was telling me about your new job with her father's company. Congratulations."

Jake glared at Jillian. "I already have a job."

She played coy. "Uh-oh, did I jump the gun? When my father told me about the sweet deal he offered you, I assumed it wasn't a secret."

Something or someone caught Tad's notice. His cunning expression disappeared, and he developed a nervous neck twitch as he quickly rose from the table. "I wish I could stay and talk more, but I've got an urgent call to make. See you around."

Jake watched him exit the café in a hurry. Shifting his gaze, he spotted the FBI agent Faith had spoken with last night. He was ordering something at the counter. Apparently, Tad was avoiding him.

Jillian's voice interrupted his thoughts. "Jake, you're not leaving too, are you? Why don't you stay, and we can discuss our plans for Christmas?"

It was time to put an end to this nonsense. He spun around and pointed his finger at her. "Get this straight, Jillian. I'm not spending Christmas with you or your family, I will not work for your father, and I am not your boyfriend—so quit interfering in my life!"

She opened her mouth and huffed at him. "This is because of Faith, isn't it? Didn't you hear what Tad said? You were persona non grata to her. It's obvious she's moved on. Why can't you?"

Fuming, Jake decided he'd better leave before he said something he might regret.

As he pivoted and started to follow Tad's beeline for the exit, a distinctive baritone voice stopped him. "Jake, may I have a word with you?"

He slowly turned around and saw Agent Baxter, holding a tray of food in his hands. *This day was going from bad to worse.* "Of course." Jake managed to keep his tone respectful, though he wasn't in the mood to talk to anyone else right now.

The investigator inclined his head toward the far corner of the room. "How about that table over there?"

Jake followed him and waited until he had settled there

with his food, then sat down. "What's this about?"

The man across the table from him opened a package of crackers for his soup. "I understand you know the snowcoach driver who was attacked last night."

Jake nodded. "April Brooks."

"She reported to the police that the perp asked her about a certain file...the Lone Star file."

Jake remembered April mentioning that. "Yes, she told me that too."

"Since you and Faith Chandler are old friends, I was wondering if she's mentioned anything to you about that file."

Evidently, the agent had been looking into Faith's past. Curious where he was going with his questions, Jake tilted his head. "No, why?"

"I've been thinking the attack on April last night could have been a case of mistaken identity. April is about the same height and build as Faith and has long brown hair."

Jake hadn't really noticed the similarity before, but Faith had suspected the same thing. "She was also wearing a parka exactly like Faith's. Assuming it is a case of mistaken identity, how does the Lone Star file fit in?"

"We think that could be the smoking gun in the Syngexas scandal. Several of the company executives were being blackmailed, and we believe Faith's friend and coworker, Monica Wallace, may have been the one behind it. In her position with the company she had special access to sensitive financial data, which we think is in that file."

It was finally starting to register. "You suspect Faith was the target because she knows something about it."

Though the astute man didn't say anything, his eyes revealed a shrewd glimmer.

"April said it was a man who attacked her. It couldn't have been Monica."

"It's possible another person is working with her."

"Who?"

The agent sipped a spoonful of soup. "That's what I'm here to find out."

"My understanding is that Faith and Monica had a falling out."

After washing down his food with a drink of water, the man responded. "Because of Tad Winters."

"He's here, you know. In fact, you just missed him. As soon as you showed up, he took off in a hurry."

The agent casually glanced around. "I'm not surprised. Too bad he couldn't join us." Calmly raising his soupspoon back to his lips, the big man peered at Jake. "Tell me about the snowmobile incident that happened today."

When Jake finished sharing what he knew, he caught the ominous frown on the investigator's face. It compelled Jake to speak his mind. "Agent Baxter, I can't just stand by and do nothing while Faith's life is in danger. Please cut to the chase and tell me what I can do to help her and keep her safe."

The agent paused, then slowly nodded. "For now, all you can do is keep an eye out and inform me of anything suspicious. Until her assailant is caught, he won't stop until he gets hold of that file. For Faith's sake, I hope she's telling the truth that she doesn't know where it is. Otherwise, it puts her in even more danger and makes her an accessory after the fact."

A cold, sinking sensation came over Jake, like falling through a frozen lake. *I hope you know what you're doing, Faith.* He also had to think about the safety of the others in his group. "Based on what you've told me, it sounds like we should cancel the rest of the tour."

"Not necessarily. However, it would be a good idea to bring along a law enforcement ranger or two just in case." Once he'd given Jake that advice, the older man turned his attention to his food, signaling their conversation was over.

Jake left him in the grill and started limping down the hall to his room in the lodge. The mounting tension from their serious discussion had triggered a painful cramp in his injured leg. Between Tad's impromptu visit to see Faith and the special agent's suspicions that she was withholding information about the Lone Star file, Jake wrestled with new doubts. *What other secrets are you keeping, Faith?*

# CHAPTER TWENTY-SIX

EARLY THAT EVENING, FAITH USED THE landline phone on her nightstand to call Jake's room in the lodge, but he didn't answer. Since Shelly had made plans to eat with Donna and Mary, Faith searched the lobby for him, hoping they could have dinner together. When she finally found him at a table in the restaurant, he was sipping a hot drink and reading a book.

She greeted him in a cheerful voice. "Here you are. I've been all over the lodge trying to find you."

He peered up from his book. "I didn't know I was lost."

She laughed and sat next to him. "I was hoping we could have dinner together and maybe go skiing tonight."

He laid down his book and gestured toward the large window near his table. "In case you haven't noticed, the snowstorm is shaping up to become a blizzard."

Gazing through the glass, she saw the dense fog of falling flakes and realized skiing was out of the question in the inclement weather. "That's disappointing. How will it affect the tour tomorrow?"

"It depends on how bad it gets. Chip and I have been working on contingency plans because of the weather and other things." A rigid frown gripped his face. Something was disturbing him more than the storm outside.

"By other things, do you mean the bizarre incidents that have happened to April and me?"

He briefly glanced at Faith, then looked away. "That's definitely a concern. It would be safer if everyone stayed close to the lodge until the attacker is caught."

"Is that all that's bothering you?"

"Isn't that enough?" Pausing, he closed his eyes. When he reopened them, he spoke in a calmer tone. "I had an interesting chat with the FBI agent you spoke with last night."

So that's why Jake was upset. "Agent Baxter? What did he

say?"

"He suspects you know more about the Lone Star file than you've told him."

Hearing the name of that baffling file dampened her happy mood. "Well, I don't." She started fidgeting with a lock of hair.

Jake lowered his gaze.

"Don't you believe me?"

He tapped his fingers on the table, then peered at her. "I met Tad earlier today. Why didn't you tell me he was here?"

*Tad.* Now she understood. "I didn't know until yesterday. I saw him in the dining room while I was having dinner with Shelly, and I confronted him."

Jake remained distant. "Why did he come?"

She swallowed hard, regretting now that she hadn't told Jake about Tad earlier. "He's looking for Monica. Agent Baxter knows he's here. In fact, I think he may be a person of interest in the investigation."

From Jake's doubtful frown, her explanation didn't appease him much.

Phil burst into the restaurant. When he saw the two of them, he sprinted to their table. "Have you seen Leslie?"

"No," Jake said, rising from his chair. "What's wrong?"

"She sent me a text that she had a lead on a story. She was trying to find a ride to Moose Run this evening so she could take the airport shuttle to Bozeman and catch the next flight to New York. I urged her to wait until morning, and I would leave with her. But now she's not in her room, and she's not answering her cell phone either. I've searched all over the lodge. She must have gone without me. I'm concerned she may be stranded in the storm."

"I'll help you find her," Jake told him.

Faith jumped to her feet and clutched his arm. "You can't go out in this weather, Jake."

He glanced at her, concern thawing some of the coldness in his expression. "I'll be okay. You stay here in the lodge, where it's safe. Tell the rest in the tour group they need to remain inside and not venture outdoors under any circumstances. Promise me you'll do that?"

She nodded, while her heart begged him to stay. Despite his assurances, the prospect of him going out in the blizzard filled her with trepidation.

As if sensing her worries, he tenderly touched her hand clutching his arm. "Stick close to Shelly and Agent Baxter. I don't want you to be alone while I'm gone."

Nodding, she slowly released his arm.

"I'm going with you, Jake," Phil said. "I've had first-responder training. You shouldn't be out in the storm alone."

"He's right," Faith said.

Jake ceded their points. "Okay. I'll ask Dex if he can loan us a two-seater snowmobile. That way we won't get separated."

A bad feeling came over Faith as she watched Jake leave with Phil. She knew there was no use trying to talk him out of it. He would travel to the ends of the earth in a hurricane to rescue someone in need. It was one of the many things she loved about him. Still, she wouldn't rest easy until he was back safe and sound.

Lowering herself back in her chair, she stared out the window at the snow. Lost in her thoughts, an unwelcome voice addressed her.

"What a coincidence. I was hoping to see you today."

Twisting in Tad's direction, she could barely restrain herself. "Why don't you fly back to Dallas where you belong?"

He chuckled and sat in Jake's empty seat. "You can't get rid of me that easy. Besides, with this snowstorm, I couldn't leave even if I wanted to."

"If it's the Lone Star file you want, you're wasting your time with me."

"I'll take my chances. Besides, this place is beginning to grow on me." He tossed her a taunting grin. "By the way, I met your old flame. I'm surprised you never told me about him."

"It never came up."

Studying his nails, he snickered. "I met his girlfriend Jillian too. She introduced us."

That got Faith's temper flaring. "She's not his girlfriend—

only another opportunist like you."

"Really, Faith, I'm surprised you'd settle for someone like that when you could do so much better."

The man's condescending attitude disgusted her. "I'm not the shallow person you think I am. I've changed."

"No you haven't. It's this frigid air—it's freeze-dried your brain. As soon as you return to Dallas, you'll thaw out and be back to your old self." He switched to a charm offensive. "Look, we had a good thing going. I know I blew it, but why not give me another chance?"

She rolled her eyes. "You're wasting your time, Tad. I'm wise to your ways now. This is all about the Lone Star file. The question is, how far would you go to get it?"

Tad's smooth facade disappeared, revealing a desperate man terrified that his house of cards was about to collapse. "You have as much to gain by finding that file as I do. After all, Agent Baxter didn't come all this way looking for me." Tad checked his phone. "I'd love to stay and chat, however, I'm meeting someone for dinner."

Jillian walked into the restaurant and waved to him.

"Ah, there she is now." He waved back. "Care to join us?"

"No thanks," Faith replied in a clipped tone, ready to be rid of him.

"Suit yourself." He paused before leaving. "Wouldn't it be interesting if we were all snowed in together?" Then he sent her a parting grin and joined Jillian at the other table.

Why did he persist in thinking she knew something about the missing file and Monica, despite her telling him otherwise? Jake had said the special agent suspected she knew about the file too. A distressing thought suddenly crossed her mind. What if Tad was right, and *she* was a person of interest in the investigation?

AFTER SEARCHING THE LODGE AND SURROUNDING area with no sign of Leslie, Jake spent the next couple of hours with Phil, riding north through the park on the two-man snowmobile, keeping an eye out for stranded vehicles. He had also contacted his ranger friend, Noah, to alert him to the situation. When the weather conditions worsened, Jake decided they should return to Old Faithful. Hopefully, Leslie was in Bozeman by now, safe at the airport or a hotel.

Heading south toward the snow lodge, Jake was forced to reduce their speed. The poor visibility and wind gusts made it almost impossible to navigate the road.

Ahead of them, faint red lights came into view.

Gesturing to Phil in the second seat, he shouted over the wind. "We'd better check it out."

He parked the snowmobile on the side of the road, and both men quickly dismounted and hurried to the small beacons.

Realizing they were flares, Jake spotted another one down a side road. He motioned to Phil, and they headed to their snowmobile and hopped on again. Driving a few yards beyond the last flare, Jake came upon a good-sized truck, covered in snow.

He dismounted the snowmobile and approached the pickup. Peering over the tailgate, he saw a huge hairy mound, partially shrouded in snow, and a hand-crank winch. Bison poachers! He brushed the snow off the tailgate. Its black exterior was like the one used by the two men he'd caught hunting bison last night.

Now that he knew who he was dealing with, Jake didn't feel good about the situation, but he couldn't turn back now. If someone needed help, he was obligated to provide it. He cautiously walked to the driver's side and called out in the howling wind. "Hello, is anyone in there?" As he came around to the window, he rapped on it with his knuckles.

A moment later, the door opened, and Bud Prescott jumped out.

At first, he appeared as shocked as Jake. Immediately, his surprised expression changed to an urgent plea. "It's Travis. He's injured and our truck engine froze up. We need to get him to the hospital in Bozeman right away."

Four hours had passed since Jake left, and Faith was antsy. The storm had intensified, and now it was dark outside. As the wind beat against the windows of the lodge like an angry monster trying to get in, the lights flickered off and on. The thought of him out there in the dangerous conditions reminded her of Joey's accident on the icy bridge. She couldn't bear it if anything happened to Jake.

Earlier, Shelly had tried to talk her into eating dinner, but she wasn't hungry. Eventually, her friend persuaded her to help work a jigsaw puzzle in the lobby area while she waited for Jake's return. Ruth and Norman, along with Mary and Donna, had gathered around the table too, and the group busied themselves filling in the picture of the Old Faithful geyser.

As Faith completed the outer edge, her mind tried to solve another puzzle—the mystery behind the Lone Star file and why everyone seemed to think she had it or knew where it was when she didn't have a clue.

A little ways down the hall, Agent Baxter was reading a newspaper in a large stuffed chair.

Since he was the only one who might have answers, she excused herself from her friends to go over and have a word with him. Not wanting to surprise a man wearing a concealed weapon, she cleared her throat as she approached. "Hello, Agent Baxter, how's the investigation going?"

He lowered his paper. After he peered at her, he quickly folded it. "About the same."

She pulled a chair close to him and sat down. "I thought of something else that might be helpful."

The investigator tilted his head. "Yes?"

"I told you last night that I lost my phone. Now I'm starting to think it may have been stolen. You see, I didn't discover it was missing until after we arrived here at the snow lodge yesterday."

"Do you suspect anyone in particular?"

"No, but the last time I saw it was right before we boarded the shuttle in Moose Run to come here. I'm pretty sure I put my phone in my backpack, which I never left unattended except once when we stopped for a short hike at Norris Geyser Basin. I thought it would be safe in the snowcoach until we returned."

"Who was with you?"

"Only the members of my tour group, plus Jake, and April Brooks, who was our snowcoach driver."

The agent stared into the distance as he processed the new information.

"By the way, I saw Tad in the dining room again this evening. It bothers me that he's still here."

Agent Baxter shifted his gaze to her. "Maybe he thinks you know where the Lone Star file is."

She laughed uncomfortably. "That's ridiculous."

"Why?" he asked with the same doubtful expression Jake had when he'd questioned her about the file. Why didn't anyone believe her?

"I told you I don't know anything about that file. Maybe it's back in Dallas." The memory of her stolen computer suddenly popped in her mind. "I just thought of something else."

"Yes?"

"Before I came here, my car was broken into and my laptop stolen." She covered her mouth. What if it was all connected to Syngexas and the missing file? The only person she could think of who'd made it clear he wanted that file was her ex-boyfriend.

"Ms. Chandler, are you all right?"

"Do you think Tad attacked April because of me?"

The FBI agent calmly responded. "My room is next door to his. I've been keeping close tabs on him, and he was here when it happened."

"Then if he couldn't have done it, you must suspect someone else."

An amused grin cracked the investigator's poker face. "You know, Ms. Chandler, you'd make a pretty good special agent."

His compliment drew a reluctant smile. "Could the Bureau use an accountant? I'm looking for a job."

He chuckled. "You don't want to work for Wild Adventures or Wolf Pack Tours?"

Amazed and intrigued, she slanted her head. "How did you know about that?"

"I have my ways."

The man seemed to know everything about everyone. "Wild Adventures is a strong possibility. I decided not to pursue the one at Wolf Pack Tours."

"Smart decision. I've done a little digging and that company has enough baggage to bring down a 787. You can do much better."

His comment amused her. "Thanks. Do you have any other career advice for me?"

"I have some advice, but not about your career." He scanned the area, then lowered his voice. "Until Monica and the missing file are found, watch your back and never go anywhere alone. Understand?"

Faith nodded, shuddering slightly from his sober warning.

Shelly walked toward them and stopped to check on her. "Sorry to interrupt. Are you ready to head to the room, Faith?"

When Faith stood to leave, the agent's parting words followed her down the hall. "Remember what I said."

Jake sat in a chair at the hospital, waiting for word on Travis's condition. He'd driven him by snowmobile to the clinic at Mammoth Hot Springs. From there an ambulance took them to the hospital in Bozeman, Montana, where Travis was now undergoing surgery for a ruptured spleen.

Since Jake was unable to take both Phil and Travis with him on the snowmobile, he left Phil behind with Bud and radioed the ranger station that the two were stranded and where they were located. He mentioned the dead bison in the bed of the truck as well. No doubt a ranger had rescued them by now. While in Mammoth Hot Springs, Jake had contacted Oscar and Jillian to let them know what had happened and the hospital where the ambulance would be taking Travis.

Now that he had some time on his hands, Jake started to type a text to let Faith know he was safe in Bozeman, then he remembered that she'd lost her cell phone.

He tried calling her room at the lodge.

A busy signal.

It was strange that it didn't roll over to the voice mail. That probably meant the phones were out at Old Faithful. Nothing was reliable in this weather.

Staring through the window at the blowing snow and mounting drifts, he knew it wasn't safe to head back tonight, yet he couldn't stand being so far away from Faith. With a potential killer on the loose, he didn't want to leave her out of his sight for one second, much less overnight.

Tomorrow was Saturday, the last day of the tour. In the afternoon, his group would take a snowcoach to Moose Run and go home from there. The fact that the tour was almost over triggered a bad case of the blues. He should be looking forward to having the next week off for Christmas, but he dreaded the thought of Faith leaving. Everything within him wanted her to stay—but what kind of future could they have if she was still keeping secrets from him?

A familiar woman's voice intruded on his thoughts. "Jake."

He glanced up. Seeing Jillian's worried expression, he rose from his chair.

She ran up and hugged him. "Thank you for letting me know about Travis. I'm glad I returned to Moose Run right after dinner before the storm got any worse. Dad texted me. He's on his way here now."

Jake gently pulled away from her, trying to maintain distance between them. "Travis is in surgery. I expect an update any minute. The doctor at the Mammoth Hot Springs clinic told me he should make a full recovery."

"Do you know what happened?"

"He was gored by a bison." Jake quickly filled her in on the details of how he and Phil had found her brothers.

She covered her mouth in shock. "What on earth were they doing in the park tonight, of all nights?"

Jake decided he shouldn't be the one to tell her that they were poaching. "You'll have to ask them that."

"I don't know how to thank you." She moved toward him.

Raising his hand, he stopped her. "Jillian, I'm sorry about your brother, but it doesn't change what I said earlier."

Her eyes narrowed and she stepped away. "Because of Faith."

"It would never have worked out between us anyway. Deep down you know it too. You and I want different things out of life."

She crossed her arms. "If you think Faith will leave her career and the big city to move out here, then you're more naive than I thought." Anger rose in her voice as she pivoted to leave. "You'll regret this. No one rejects me and gets away with it."

"Jillian!" a man shouted from the other direction.

Jake looked that way and saw Oscar.

Either his daughter didn't hear or was too angry to respond because she proceeded to storm down the hall.

Oscar blew out a heavy breath and staggered wearily toward Jake, dropping into the plastic chair closest to him, which was much too small for the man's overweight body. "I'm sorry about my daughter's behavior," he said. "She's not used to getting no for an answer. I guess I'm to blame for that."

Jake sat beside him, surprised by Oscar's candor. "I want you to know, I never encouraged her or led her on."

Oscar gave him a sideways look and nodded. "Truth is, I've always respected you, Jake, despite our differences. I actually thought you might be good for Jillian, a stabilizing influence on her, but I should have set her straight earlier that you weren't coming to work for my company. I didn't want to disappoint her, and I guess deep down I was hoping you might change your mind."

Jake appreciated Oscar's openness and the unexpected compliment. It gave him hope the man might be willing to drop his unfair vendetta against him.

Oscar glanced at Jake again. "By the way, thank you for helping my son… I can't imagine what possessed him and Bud to be in the park on a night like this."

After thinking it over, Jake decided he'd better tell him. It was only a matter of time before the park service would charge the two young men with poaching, and he didn't want their father to be blindsided. Jake rubbed his hands together, mustering his courage. "There was a dead bison in the bed of Travis's pickup, and I'm pretty sure it was them I saw last night poaching another bison in the park."

Oscar raised his head and squinted at him. For a moment, Jake thought he might haul off and hit him. Instead, he brought his hands to his forehead and lamented. "Sometimes I think those crazy sons of mine are going to be the death of me."

Despite his past history with Oscar, Jake felt bad for him now. "If they turn themselves in and agree to pay the fine up front, the authorities will probably go easier on them."

The older man nodded and seemed to take some consolation from that.

"Do you know what made them start poaching in the first place? If they wanted to hunt bison, there are other places outside of the park."

Oscar blew out another breath. "Travis got in trouble with the law a few months ago. He had too much to drink and was in an argument with his girlfriend when he pulled a gun. Fortunately, his friends managed to get it away from him, but he was arrested. As a result, he lost his gun rights and can't get a hunting license." Oscar paused and glanced at Jake from the corner of his eye. "I suspect he and his brother thought no one would notice if there were a few less bison in the park, especially since it's the dead of winter." Oscar hung his head despondently. "Now Travis is in the hospital…"

"He should make a full recovery," Jake said to encourage him.

"Thanks to you." A sincere glimmer shone in the man's eye. "But I'm not going to bail him out anymore. It's time my sons faced the consequences for their actions."

Jake respected that. At least something good might come out of all of this. That was more than he could say for the attacks on Faith and April. Considering all the bizarre incidents in light of what Agent Baxter had told him, Jake was convinced that Faith had been the target all along. Fearing for her safety, he made up his mind to return to Old Faithful as soon as possible, before the madman struck again.

Faith sat on her bed, opening a few pieces of the mail she'd brought from home, then decided it was a waste of time. Until Jake came back, she wouldn't be able to focus on anything else. After stuffing her unopened mail in the bag, she looked at Shelly. "Can I borrow your phone? The one in the room is still out. I need to text Jake and make sure he's all right."

Shelly sighed. "Mine's out also. I tried to send a text a few minutes ago, but there's no service. I checked the front desk, and they said the storm may have damaged the cell tower. I hope nothing's happened to the guys. Phil and I were supposed to go ice skating tonight."

"Phil? But I thought you liked Rick."

"What gave you that idea?"

"During the snowmobile trip to West Yellowstone he seemed interested in you."

"I think you were reading too much into it. He's not my type."

"Oh, and Phil is, huh?"

Shelly grinned.

Faith lowered her voice. "Okay, out with it. What's going

on with you two?"

Her friend's eyes glimmered with a secret. "Last night when you left the dominoes game for your date with Jake, Phil took your place. After we finished the game, we walked to Old Faithful in the moonlight. We talked for a while, then we went inside and had a late dessert in the restaurant."

The two friends giggled like college co-eds.

"This is crazy," Faith said. "We'll be going home soon, you know."

The light in their room suddenly flickered, then went out.

"Uh-oh!" Faith fumbled in the dark and found the flashlight on the nightstand. As soon as she turned it on, the sound of footsteps paused outside in the hallway, followed by a clicking noise at their door.

"Stop what you're doing!" It was a woman's voice, coming from outside their room.

Shelly spoke to Faith in a loud whisper. "Someone's trying to break in!"

When they heard a high-pitched scream, Faith jumped out of bed with the flashlight and grabbed her robe. "Come on!" She hurried to the door and jerked it open.

The emergency exit lights at the end of the hall illuminated the corridor just enough to see a figure in the shadows struggling to get up. As Faith knelt to help, she recognized her. "Mary! Are you okay?"

"I-I think so," the older lady's voice quivered as Faith assisted her until she could stand on her own. "A woman was trying to break into your room. When I told her to stop, she knocked me down and ran off."

"A woman?" Faith said.

Mary nodded. "It was hard to see her face in the shadows, but she had long dark hair that fell in ringlets down her back."

*Monica!* Like a broken faucet, Faith felt the blood drain from her face. She exchanged a troubled glance with Shelly. Then the lights came back on.

Faith and Shelly helped Mary inside their room. Once the frightened woman was resting comfortably on Faith's bed, there was a knock on the door.

Answering it, Faith saw Agent Baxter standing in the hallway.

"Is everything okay?" he asked.

She stepped into the corridor with him and closed the door behind her. "Our friend, Mary, stopped someone from breaking into our room. From her description, it sounds like Monica."

A grim expression hardened the investigator's face.

The burden of it all brought Faith to tears. "First April, now Mary. People are being hurt because of me, and there's nothing I can do to stop it. This can't continue any longer. I'm going back to Dallas tomorrow."

"No," he said in an adamant voice. "You should stay, and Jake should proceed with his plans for the tour in the morning. I'm coming with you."

# CHAPTER TWENTY-EIGHT

Early Saturday morning, Faith stared out the window in her room, admiring the new-fallen snow glittering in the sunlight. It helped brighten her outlook after the assault on Mary last night. Thankfully, the extent of her injuries only amounted to a few bruises.

Following the ordeal, Shelly wanted answers, so Faith had stayed up late telling her about the investigator's suspicions that the attacks might be connected to the mysterious Lone Star file, and that she was most likely the target.

Jake also weighed heavily on Faith's mind. Because the phones and Wi-Fi were still out, she hadn't heard from him since he left with Phil to find Leslie last night. Faith hoped to run into him before breakfast.

After Faith and Shelly had left their room and were on their way to the restaurant, Faith stopped and spoke to her friend. "Go ahead and find us a table while I look for Jake."

Shelly hesitated. "Don't be long. After what happened to Mary, I don't think you should be alone."

Faith pointed to the cluster of people hanging out in the spacious corridor. "There are plenty of others around. Besides, it's seven in the morning. Nothing is going to happen to me at this hour."

Shelly's worried expression eased a bit. "I guess you have a point. Oh, if you see Phil, invite him to join us as well."

"Got it," Faith replied with a sly wink.

While Shelly headed for the restaurant, Faith quickly backtracked to the lobby. Still no sign of Jake. She would have asked for his room number at the front desk, but they usually didn't give that out. Then she glimpsed a dark-haired woman exiting the main door of the lodge. *Monica?*

"Looking for me?" a man said from behind Faith.

The voice didn't sound like Jake's, but she eagerly spun

around, wanting to believe it was him anyway. The sight of Tad instantly dashed her hopes. "You're still here."

"Well, nice to see you too. I stopped to say goodbye. I'm leaving today."

"Adios—now get out of here." She pointed him toward the door where she'd seen the woman leave.

He lingered, a smug spark flaring in his eyes. "You know, I used to think you were a smart, savvy business woman. Now it's obvious that you were only a small-town hick with a fancy condo and car, pretending to be something you're not."

She stared at him, unfazed. "A week ago, that would have offended me, but now I take it as a compliment. You see, I've finally come to terms with who I am and what I want. I've also owned up to my past mistakes—you should try it sometime."

He gave a derisive laugh. "Who are you to lecture me? As soon as you get off your high horse, you'll come running back to Dallas begging for a job, but don't expect any help from me. You've burned that bridge."

As he disappeared down the hall, the tension in her body relaxed. She pitied him in a way. Until this trip, she was headed down the same crooked road he was on. Thankfully, she'd gotten back on the straight and narrow one.

Pivoting to join Shelly for breakfast, Faith saw Jake coming in from the cold. The sight of him sprung her heart to life like a blooming crocus in snow. As she strode to the door, she wanted to wrap her arms around him and give him a big kiss— then the memory of his coolness toward her last evening caused her to use more restraint. "Jake, I'm so glad you're back. I was worried."

His tired, troubled expression brightened when she greeted him. "I wasn't sure I would make it. I spent most of the night in the hospital waiting room in Bozeman."

She pressed her palm to her chest. "Oh, no. What happened? Is Leslie all right?"

He shrugged. "Phil and I never found her. I notified the rangers last night that she was missing. You still haven't heard from her?"

"No, the phones and Wi-Fi have been out since the storm. It knocked out the cell tower as well. Hopefully, Leslie is safe in New York by now." Still curious and concerned, Faith wanted to hear more of Jake's story. "So why were you at the hospital?"

"We found Travis Prescott and his brother, Bud, stranded in the storm. Travis needed urgent medical attention—it's a long story."

Since it was obvious he didn't want to talk about it, she filled him in on what had happened at the lodge while he was away. After she told him about the incident with Mary and assured him that she was okay, a look of concern mixed with disbelief hit his face. "Monica's here?"

Faith sighed. "It appears so. A few minutes ago, I thought I saw her in the lobby." She realized that in addition to being up most of the night, Jake probably hadn't had much of anything to eat. "You must be starving. Shelly's saving us a table in the restaurant." Faith started to escort him in that direction.

He paused. "Thanks, but I'm going to grab something quick. I need to inform the group that our plans for this morning are canceled in case they want to catch an earlier shuttle to Moose Run."

A lump lodged in Faith's throat as she tried to hide her disappointment that he'd declined her breakfast invitation. She wondered if it was an excuse to avoid her because she hadn't told him about Tad being there. "Actually, Agent Baxter wants you to proceed as planned. He intends to go with us."

Jake squinted at her. "What? Are you kidding me?"

A bass voice surprised them. "Good morning, you two."

The FBI agent had come from the hall off the lobby.

Faith stared at his knit cap and the supersized ski jacket covering his big frame and concealing his weapon.

The agent grinned. "I hope you've got room for one more this morning. I spent a fortune on this winter gear."

After breakfast, Faith gathered with the remaining members of the Elk group in the lobby of the lodge for an impromptu meeting Jake had called. Agent Baxter and Jake's ranger friend, Noah Fulton, were standing beside him.

Before the meeting, Agent Baxter had shared his plan and special instructions with only the Wild Adventures staff, the park ranger, and Faith and Shelly. He told them he didn't want the rest of the group to know he worked for the FBI, so Jake introduced him simply as Gordon Baxter. "Gordon will be our guest today since we have an extra seat due to Leslie leaving early."

Jake then gestured to his friend. "This is Ranger Noah Fulton. He will also be joining us this morning and giving a special ranger talk."

The introductions over, Jake calmly informed the group about the incident with Mary last night as well as April's attack the night before. "Of course, we're not expecting anything bad to happen today, but having Ranger Fulton onboard will also provide an extra level of security and protection. However, if anyone wishes to stay behind at the lodge, you will be fully compensated for today's tour cost by Chip."

Most of the group were delighted to have a ranger with them. The only person who bowed out was Mary. Still shaken by what happened last night, she decided to stay at the lodge and take it easy.

Faith wished Alec had bowed out too. Now and then she'd catch him glaring at her and it gave her the creeps.

Agent Baxter had tried to assure her earlier that as long as she was with the group, and under his and the ranger's protection, no one would harm her. She wasn't completely convinced, and this cross-country ski excursion seemed a bit risky given the situation. It was only because she wanted the nightmare behind her that she went along with the plan, hoping it would draw her enemy out of hiding so the officers could catch him and put him away for good.

Jake had expressed misgivings as well. Same with Chip, who finally agreed to it only after Agent Baxter told him that until the troublemaker was caught and the mystery solved, Wild

Adventures might continue to be targeted, putting Chip's customers at risk.

When Jake finished addressing the tour group, they mustered outside in front of the snowcoach for their final outing together. Per Agent Baxter's plan, Faith positioned herself on the first row, directly behind Jake and April. Shelly and the ranger sat on either side of her. That way Noah would be able to give his ranger talk from the front, while being close to Faith as an extra safeguard, and Gordon could keep an eye on things from the back row.

As the rest of the group boarded, Faith stared out the window at the pristine snowdrifts glistening under the clear, blue sky. She wished her life was as simple and serene.

Shelly cheerfully spoke in her ear. "I hope you dressed warm. It's only five degrees."

For her friend's sake, Faith managed to smile. "If I wear any more layers, I won't be able to move." The cold was the last thing on her mind this morning. With her attacker still at large, it was hard for her to take things in stride, though having two law enforcement officers aboard did make her feel a little more secure.

She glanced over her shoulder past Alec, Rick, Phil, and Donna sitting directly behind her and saw the agent staring out the window on the back row. With Leslie and Mary missing from their party, it helped free up space for the two lawmen. Even so, the big FBI agent appeared pretty miserable in the cramped seat beside Ruth and Norman.

Faith recalled his dislike for the cold and snow. No doubt he wished he was at home in Dallas decorating his tree with his family. Faith had to keep reminding herself to use his first name, Gordon, instead of calling him 'Agent', which would blow his cover.

As she turned her head forward, she caught Alec glaring at her from the second row. He obviously still carried a grudge. One more reason to be thankful the FBI agent was there and had her back.

Behind the steering wheel, April appeared to be in her

usual good spirits as she drove the group to their destination. Jake, on the other hand, was quiet and preoccupied. He'd relinquished his microphone and park education responsibilities to the ranger.

Faith wanted to believe Jake's somber mood was due to his long night searching for Leslie and taking Travis to the hospital, and not because of her past mistakes or as a result of Tad following her to Yellowstone. Otherwise, she might as well kiss any hope of a second chance for them goodbye.

The snowcoach slowed as it reached their destination—the trailhead for Lone Star Geyser. It was a strange irony that on the last day of their tour, they should visit a geyser bearing the same name as the mysterious file that had caused so much angst and mayhem. It didn't seem likely that there was a connection, other than they were both associated with the state of Texas.

As soon as April parked the vehicle, Jake got out to lower the steps for people to exit. When it was Faith's turn, he extended a hand to her.

Not wanting to slip again, she gladly took it and tried to ease the tension between them with an appealing smile. It seemed to barely register as he quickly moved on to assist the person behind her.

Once everyone had exited the snowcoach and put on their skis, Jake summoned them all together. "In this cold, it's imperative that we all stick together. I don't want anyone trailblazing or going off on their own."

Everyone nodded except Alec. He crossed his arms and scowled like a defiant teen in need of a serious attitude adjustment.

However, Jake's serious expression told them it wasn't up for debate. "It may look like a winter wonderland out here, but these extreme temperatures are deadly. That's why we're going to stay together. Any questions?"

The group was silent as they huddled close to stay warm.

Jake waved them forward. "We need to start moving to get our blood flowing. When we reach Lone Star Geyser, we'll break for a mid-morning snack."

As the group followed him, Faith stuck with Shelly.

"Not quite as romantic as skiing in the moonlight, is it?" Shelly said to her.

Faith glanced over her shoulder at Noah, Gordon, and Phil, who were behind them and heard Phil ask Gordon a question about the FBI. She cast Shelly a suspicious glance, lowering her voice. "You didn't tell Phil that Gordon is with the FBI, did you?"

Shelly hesitated. "I might have mentioned it to him. Why? What's the big deal? Everyone already knows the ranger is here for our protection."

Faith responded in a harsh whisper. "He's undercover. If Phil knows, he may get word to Leslie, and it'll be on the nightly news."

"Phil isn't a reporter. He knows it's strictly off the record and won't tell anyone." Shelly peered behind her. "Speaking of Gordon, he's having a hard time on those skis."

Faith looked back at the agent struggling to keep up as Noah and Phil coached him. She spotted Alec and Rick lagging even farther behind them, which was strange because they were excellent skiers. She expected them to be in front of the pack.

The group passed through a beautiful wooded area and came to a bridge that crossed the Firehole River. Gliding over the bridge, Faith admired the graceful trumpeter swans floating in the waters that never froze due to the warmth of the geothermal features. Still, it was a wonder the birds didn't catch their death from the frigid air. The image of the masked man who tried to push April into the same river at Upper Geyser Basin flashed through her mind and elicited a shudder.

Faith had to remind herself that two law enforcement officers were watching over her. She wished she could forget about the whole Syngexas scandal and the havoc on this trip. Until the person or persons were found, she was like those swans in the river—a sitting duck.

The vigorous physical activity soon generated enough body heat under Faith's insulated layers to cause her to perspire. The occasional sighting of a fox, rabbit, or grouse helped take her mind off of the missing file and her troubles. However, she couldn't ignore what felt like a growing rift between her and Jake—or was it only her imagination?

Since it was her last day with her tour group, she decided to focus on enjoying the scenery and the company of her new friends, instead of trying to figure out where things stood with her and Jake. The extreme cold and exertion also fueled her appetite. By the time she and the others arrived at the remote Lone Star Geyser, three and a half miles later, she was eager to devour her snack.

The rest of her group appeared ready for a break too and quickly removed their skis and unrolled their pads and blankets on the snow for a place to sit before they broke out their food and drinks.

Seated on the small foam pad she'd carried in her backpack, Faith retrieved one of her energy bars which had stayed warm in her backpack from her body heat. As she took a bite, savoring the satisfying carbs and protein, she heard Norman complain that his canned soda had frozen. Ruth sweetly shared her thermos with him, which stopped his grumbling.

Faith removed her own thermos from her pack and checked it. She was relieved to see the water inside was still liquid.

When she'd finished her energy bar, Jake found her and whispered to her privately. "Have you seen Alec or Rick?"

His serious expression grabbed her attention. "Not lately. The last time I saw them they were behind Gordon, Noah, and Phil."

Moving on to ask the others, Jake soon addressed the whole group. "Has anyone seen Alec or Rick?"

Everyone looked around, muttering among themselves.

Phil spoke up. "They were behind us until we crossed the river."

"Was that the last place you saw them?"

"Yeah. I noticed they were headed toward the woods. I

thought they were going to take a bathroom break. I assumed they would catch up."

Jake pointed to Noah. "You're in charge while I go find them."

April stood. "I'll radio Chip and give him a heads-up."

Faith's instincts urged her to follow Jake. When she rose to her feet, Shelly grabbed her arm. "What are you doing?"

"I don't want him out there alone."

Norman pushed himself to his feet and called to Jake. "I'm going with you."

Phil followed him. "Me too."

Gordon and Noah frowned at the chaos.

Jake stopped to address the group. "Listen, everyone, it'll be safer if you all stay together. Phil can go with me because he's a trained first responder. The rest of you, please finish your snacks and then head back the way we came. I'll meet you at the bridge."

"Don't worry," Norman assured him. "We've got things covered here."

Faith leapt to her feet and caught Jake by the arm as he was leaving. "Don't go, Jake. Something about this doesn't feel right."

His gaze softened as he gently released her grip on him. "I'll be okay, and Noah and Gordon are here to keep an eye on things with you and the others. I'll radio April and keep her updated." He gave Faith a parting wink. "Don't worry about me."

She sighed and relented. Watching him and Phil quickly glide away until they disappeared down the trail, she uttered a silent prayer. *Lord, please watch over them.*

Shelly stepped next to her and patted her shoulder. "It'll be okay. Jake knows what he's doing, and Phil is with him."

Faith noticed the pensive frown on Gordon's face when she and Shelly rejoined the others. Knowing Alec's cunning ways, Jake might need the agent's protection more than she did. She resumed sitting on her foam pad and started eating her second energy bar, but it was already cold and hard.

A sudden loud rumble and shaking under the earth launched her and the others to their feet again. They all pivoted toward the giant column of water spewing from Lone Star Geyser.

Focusing her camera for a picture, Shelly glanced at Faith. "The ranger said it only erupts every three hours. Too bad Jake and Phil aren't here to see it with us."

The others also captured snapshots, taking turns posing in front of it. They were so consumed and awed by it, the thirty-minute eruption passed too quickly. When the gushing subsided, the water vanished into the large mound as mysteriously as it had appeared.

Their stomachs satisfied and the show over, the group gathered their things for the journey back to the snowcoach. April had been keeping them informed of Jake's status. From his last report, they still hadn't found Alec and Rick.

Retracing the ski trail, Faith started at the front of the pack with April, while Noah lagged behind to assist Gordon. Fears about Jake propelled Faith beyond her group as she scanned the woods, looking for him. Finally, the bridge came into view. Racing toward it, she searched the area, but Jake and Phil weren't there. And it had been at least ten minutes since Jake had radioed his status.

April joined her there and paused to check her radio. "It doesn't seem to be working. Maybe the cold drained the batteries."

The silence of the snowy landscape was disrupted by a loud whirring noise.

Faith gazed at the sky and saw a helicopter hovering above. It appeared to be landing on the other side of the woods.

"It's a medevac chopper," April said. "Someone must be hurt."

## CHAPTER TWENTY-NINE

A LUMP CAUGHT IN FAITH'S THROAT as April's words echoed in her mind over and over. *Someone must be hurt.* What if it was Jake?

Shelly had arrived with some of the others and softly touched Faith's arm as if reading her thoughts. "Let's not jump to conclusions, Faith. There could be a million explanations for why that chopper is here."

Knowing her friend was concerned about Phil as well, Faith did her best to put aside her fears and gave Shelly a consoling smile. With both Jake and Phil's lives at stake, they needed to keep each other's spirits up.

Faith spotted tracks in the snow and pointed. "Look, they left a trail. I'm going to follow it."

April stopped her. "You heard Jake. He wants us to stay together."

"He also said he'd be here waiting for us by the time we arrived, and he's not. He hasn't been able to communicate by radio either. I've got to find out what's going on."

"She's right," Shelly said, taking Faith's side. "I'll go with her so she's not alone."

When Gordon caught up to them with Noah, he bent over to catch his breath. "What's going on?"

"Faith and Shelly want to find Jake," April told him.

The big man adamantly shook his head. "That's not a good idea. It could be a trap."

Faith faced him, determined. "You can come with us if you want, but I can't stay here wondering if he's all right."

Gordon uttered a low groan and relented. He told Noah to stay with the group while he accompanied Faith and Shelly on the trail.

Following the sound of the chopper, the three set out to find the missing men. The deep, uneven layers of snow in the woods was difficult to traverse on skis, but Faith wasn't deterred. After surviving a rock slide, almost being hit by a truck, and two snowmobile chases, she figured this couldn't be much worse.

Quickly, she learned how to combine her downhill skills with cross country and began conquering the challenging terrain like an Olympic slalom course champion as she pivoted around trees and low-hanging branches.

Clearing the woods, she could see the helicopter hovering over a snowfield. As she hurried toward it, four people came into view. One was lying on the snow, two appeared to be kneeling beside him, and one was standing.

Sprinting toward the injured one, she recognized Jake and Phil assisting him. Overjoyed at seeing they were okay, she glided toward them while catching her breath.

Recognizing Rick standing near them, she realized Alec was the one hurt.

The loud vibration of the rotor blades made them cover their ears while snow blew in all directions as the chopper landed in the open field.

Two medics jumped out, carrying a board.

The windstorm generated by the blades stopped Faith's progress. As the medics secured Alec to the platform, she yelled from a distance. "Jake!"

The deafening propeller noise drowned out her voice.

After the medics carried Alec to the chopper, Jake turned his head and saw her. He grabbed Phil to come with him. Ducking from the gusts, they hurried in her direction.

Watching the helicopter take off, Faith heard Gordon's raspy voice behind her. "What happened?"

She glanced at the agent and Shelly, who was wheezing with him. "I'm not sure, but I think they're about to tell us."

Jake and Phil jogged up to them while Rick followed at a slower pace. The grim expressions on their faces prepared Faith for a bad report.

When Jake spoke, his voice sounded hoarse and somber. "Alec skied into a tree and it knocked him unconscious. They're taking him to the hospital in Bozeman." He paused and released a heavy breath. "It doesn't look good. We need to pray for him."

The news settled over Faith and her companions like a dark cloud before a storm. When the rest of their party heard, a somber silence accompanied them all the way back to the snowcoach.

Jake was taking Alec's accident especially hard. Faith knew he probably felt partly responsible, though Alec had signed a waiver like the rest of them on the tour, and he and Rick had gone off on their own instead of staying with the group as Jake had instructed.

After the snowcoach finally delivered them to the lodge at eleven-thirty that morning, Faith and Shelly stopped by the front desk to request a late checkout before they went to their room to start packing for their return trip to Moose Run at three that afternoon. From there, they would drive home first thing in the morning.

While Shelly was in the bathroom taking a shower, Faith sorted through the remaining items in her drawer. She tried to focus on the bright side—that everyone else in the tour group was okay. The fact that Gordon's scheme to flush out and catch her stalker hadn't worked caused her to suspect that Alec might have been the culprit all along. If so, she was safe now with him in the hospital. If only she could find a way to patch things up with Jake, then at least she could end this tour on a higher note.

Among her things to pack, she found Jake's Swiss Army knife he'd loaned her. Recalling the happier times when she gave the knife to him for his birthday eight years ago helped to cheer her a little. She wanted to believe that part of the reason he'd held on to it all this time was because it reminded him of her.

Shelly's cell phone rang from the nightstand.

Realizing the cell service was working again, Faith called to Shelly through the bathroom door. "Your phone is ringing."

"Please answer it for me," Shelly said. "If it's Phil, tell him I'll call him back."

When Faith said hello, it was Chip calling to speak to her instead of Shelly. "Jake wanted me to let you know that a ranger found a lead on the snowmobile driver who chased you down. The Wolf Pack Tours business transactions show a rental for yesterday under Alec Underwood's name. Also, one of their other clients reported his snowmobile was parked in a different location when he returned from sightseeing near Tower Fall on Wednesday."

The news, which appeared to confirm her suspicions about Alec, brought Faith welcome closure to the mayhem that had plagued her all week. Yet what did Alec have to do with the Lone Star file and Monica? Faith responded to Chip with another question that was bothering her. "Assuming it was Alec who tried to run me down, why would he rent the snowmobile under his own name?"

"Hmm. Good question. Jake is at the ranger station at Old Faithful right now, getting the full report. Hopefully, he'll have an answer to that. I'll keep you posted. By the way, we finally located Leslie—she's safe in the Big Apple."

Glad to hear the reporter was all right, Faith pictured her happily at work on her latest story, when she wasn't bossing everyone around.

After they ended the call, Shelly walked out of the bathroom dressed warmly in a fleece top and pants. "Who was on the phone?"

Faith filled her in on Chip's news.

"I knew there was something fishy about Alec. It's a good thing you didn't take his job offer," Shelly said. "But why was Chip calling you on my phone?"

"Because mine is still missing, remember? I was hoping it would be found before we had to leave."

Shelly chuckled. "You know, when you lost it, I thought you'd have a meltdown. Instead, you act like you don't even miss it. You've come a long way in a week."

Faith shrugged. "I guess my perspective has changed. Take this tour, for instance. When I first learned that Jake would be our guide, I couldn't wait for it to be over. Now I wish it didn't have to end."

Shelly put a sisterly arm around her. "There's always Chip's job offer."

Faith was willing to take the lower salary if she could live closer to Jake. However, given his cool behavior toward her lately, he was probably ready for her to hightail it home to Dallas. The problem was, she belonged here, not in Texas.

# CHAPTER THIRTY

IN THE LODGE RESTAURANT, FAITH STARED out the window as she waited for Shelly to arrive for a late lunch. Afterward, they would finish packing and leave for Moose Run.

Despite the extreme cold outside, the idea of going home to her empty condo seemed even bleaker. Christmas was only a few days away, and she didn't want to spend the holiday apart from Jake. Assuming he could bring himself to trust her again, it would take time to rebuild their relationship. She'd wait an eternity if it meant she could finally be with him.

Once she returned to Dallas, she'd also need to resume her job search. The idea of changing careers was becoming more appealing to her. Donna's story about her transition from stock broker to philanthropist had inspired Faith. She wondered what type of job she could find where she could use her skills and experience to make a real difference in people's lives.

"What's so interesting out there?"

Surprised to hear Gordon's bass voice instead of Shelly's, Faith shifted in his direction.

The FBI agent was wearing his new winter togs and appeared unusually chipper. He was probably excited about going home to his family in Dallas and decorating that tree.

"I've been admiring the snow. It looks so Christmassy. All it needs is reindeer and a sleigh."

He glanced outside. "It may be pretty, but I'll take Texas weather any day over this." His brown eyes twinkled at her. "I thought you'd want to know that Alec Underwood is now a person of interest in the Syngexas investigation. I've been in touch with the local rangers and police, and it appears he may have been the one who chased you with the snowmobile. He also has a connection with Tad and Syngexas through work his firm did in the past."

"Thanks for telling me. Chip called earlier and said that

Alec had rented a snowmobile from Wolf Pack Tours. Jake is at the ranger station being debriefed."

"That's where I'm headed now."

After the agent said goodbye and strode away, Faith considered what he'd said about Alec's alleged involvement in the Syngexas scandal. It seemed so bizarre. It still didn't add up in her mind. Then again, maybe she didn't have all the facts. In any case, she wasn't going to dwell on it. It was time to move on.

"Sorry, we're late."

At the sound of Shelly's voice, Faith lifted her gaze and saw Phil with her. "Will you be joining us for lunch, Phil?"

Shelly interjected. "Actually, I have another suggestion. Why don't we postpone lunch and take a short walk to the geyser basin and see Old Faithful erupt one last time?"

Catching the couple's coy glances, Faith didn't want to be a third wheel on their last day together. Besides, now that Alec was in the hospital, she didn't need Shelly to be her security detail. "Thanks, but I think I'll grab a bite now and finish packing. I still need to figure out how to fit everything back in my luggage."

Shelly's brows pressed together. "Then we'll stay and eat with you."

Faith flicked her wrist. "Go. I'll be fine. Agent Baxter was just here. He told me that Alec is a person of interest in the Syngexas investigation. And since he's stuck in the hospital, he can't bother me anymore—so go and have a good time."

Her friend finally acquiesced. "Well, maybe for a little while, as long as you stay in the lodge. By the way, since you're going to the room, could you stop by the front desk and ask for another box of tissues? I finished the last one."

"Yes, now go before it gets any later," Faith said, shooing them away. After the two departed, she ate a quick meal of soup and a sandwich. Then she left the restaurant and walked to the lobby. Spotting Rick leaving the front desk, she called to him. "Rick, how is Alec doing?"

Rick paused and turned around. "Not good," he said in a

somber tone. "I just called the hospital in Bozeman for an update. He's unconscious but lucky to be alive. I've made arrangements to have him transported to another hospital in Atlanta as soon as he's stable. I've got a few things to take care of here, and then I plan to catch the next shuttle to Bozeman to see him." His eyes searched the lobby. "Where's Shelly? I was hoping to say goodbye to her."

"She's out watching Old Faithful for the last time. Too bad you missed her." Faith omitted the fact that Phil had gone with her since Rick still seemed interested in her friend.

"The next time I'm in Dallas maybe I'll look you two up."

"That would be nice."

After they said goodbye, Rick headed down the hall to his room.

Faith moved to the front desk. Waiting for someone to help her, she glanced at the clock on the wall. One-thirty already and still no sign of Jake.

An attendant appeared from the back, wearing a badge with the name Myra. "Hello, what can I do for you?"

"I'd like a box of tissues, please. We're completely out."

"Certainly. I'll have housekeeping deliver one to your room right away. What is your name and room number?" When Faith told her, the woman typed it in her computer. Once she'd finished, she reached under the desk. "By the way, someone left this for you." She handed Faith a small white envelope.

Faith examined it, hoping it might be from Jake. There was no return address, only her name was printed on it.

"Is there anything else I can help you with, Ms. Chandler?"

"Yes…please leave a message for Jake Mitchell that I want to see him. It's very important."

The woman politely responded. "I'll see that he gets it."

Faith turned around and saw Ruth and Norman standing in the lobby with their luggage, waiting to talk to her. "Don't tell me you two are leaving already?"

They smiled excitedly. "Our granddaughter called. She's about to give birth to our third great grandchild, so we decided to catch a flight out of Bozeman this evening. We wanted to say goodbye to you and Jake." Ruth looked around. "Where is he?"

"I'm afraid he had business to take care of and isn't back yet."

Ruth's face wrinkled with disappointment. "Oh, dear, we wanted to thank him in person for being such a good guide."

"I'll be sure and tell him when I see him."

"Thank you, dear. It was such a joy getting to know you this week. If you're ever in Idaho, please come visit us." Ruth took out a pen and notepad from her purse and jotted something down. "Here is our email address and phone number," she said, handing the piece of paper to Faith.

After skimming it, Faith put it and the envelope from the front desk in the pocket of her fleece pants. "Great. I'd love to stay in touch." She gave them both a warm hug, then walked outside with them, where their shuttle was waiting.

When they boarded with their luggage, Faith waved goodbye. As the shuttle departed, she saw the outdoor thermometer. It had only warmed up to ten degrees. Brr.

Retreating to the warmth of the lobby, she hurried to the fireplace to warm up. While standing beside the cozy hearth, she remembered the sweet way Jake had pulled her hood and coat snug around her when they were at the Old Faithful Geyser. It filled her with longing to see him and tell him how much he meant to her before she left for Moose Run. She searched the lobby for him once more, but still no sign. Then she remembered the note in her pocket—maybe it was from him!

She settled in a chair by the fireplace to read it. As she scanned the words, her high hopes plummeted into a steaming caldron of anger and trepidation.

*Hello, Faith,*

*In case you're wondering where your phone is, I have it. In exchange, I want the Lone Star file. Come alone and bring it to the Sapphire Pool at Biscuit Basin by two-thirty this afternoon. If you follow my instructions, I'll see that Jake returns safely. Otherwise, your precious tour guide is history.*

*Happy Holidays from You-Know-Who*

Faith's heart pounded in her chest like a ticking bomb. Alec couldn't have written it. He was in the hospital unconscious—unless he did it before his accident. Regardless, she couldn't take any chances.

Resisting the onslaught of panic and outrage, she fought to stay strong. This wasn't the time for a meltdown. She had to find the file. Jake's life depended on it. But how?

Her suitcases were in her room. She knew the exact contents of each one and there was no file.

She strode back to the front desk. A different woman was there now. "Is Myra still around?"

The woman responded in a cheerful voice. "No, she took a break. May I help you?"

"A note was left for me earlier, but there wasn't a name. I was wondering if someone might have seen who dropped it off."

"I'm sorry, I just started my shift. Myra will be back in an hour."

*Too late.* Faith glanced at the clock on the wall behind the desk. It was a quarter of two already. She remembered from a map that Biscuit Basin wasn't far from the snow lodge. She'd have to leave by two to make it there by two-thirty on skis.

Faith stashed the threatening note in her pocket. Anxiously glancing around the lobby, she wondered if she was being watched. Not wanting to lose another second, she ran to her room, pivoting around the housekeeping cart in the hall before she got there. Quickly, she unlocked the door and thrust it open.

Shelly's compact luggage and backpack were neatly resting on her bed—while she was outside with Phil. Faith despised herself for doing what she was about to do, though she had no choice. Hurriedly, she unzipped one of Shelly's bags and carefully ran her hand over her clothes and around all the corners and pockets. Nothing that felt like a file. Faith opened the other piece of luggage. Shelly's laptop case was inside. Faith set it on the bed so she could search the rest of the contents.

Not there either.

*Think, Faith, think.* Maybe the file was at home in Dallas. It could be sitting in her mailbox right now—*her mail!* She'd brought it with her. She pivoted to the canvas bag resting on top of her luggage stacked on the floor. Quickly, she grabbed it and dumped the contents on the bed.

As she frantically sorted through it, the small padded envelope with the Syngexas business label caught her eye. She had assumed it was about her unemployment paperwork. Tempted to rip it open, she decided she should slit the fold at the end instead. What could she use without damaging the contents? Jake's knife! She'd planned to give it to him when she saw him today.

She found it in the pocket of her backpack and released the small blade. After carefully cutting open the end of the envelope, she closed the knife and slipped it into the pocket of her pants.

When she dumped the contents of the pouch on the bed, a smaller sealed package fell out. She snatched it and read the attached note.

*I need a huge favor. Please keep this package unopened in a safe place until I return or contact you. It's very important. My life depends on it.*
*Monica*

Could this tiny package contain the Lone Star file? There was only one way to find out. Faith carefully broke the seal and found a single flash drive inside. How could she read it? Her computer had been stolen before she left Dallas.

*But Shelly had brought her laptop!* Faith moved to her friend's computer case on the bed. Again, she had to brush away her qualms about violating her friend's private things. She'd apologize to her later—after Jake was back safe and sound.

She quickly unzipped the case and removed the laptop. As soon as it booted up, she plugged in the flash drive and began searching the contents. A folder named Syngexas immediately caught her notice. She opened it. A subdirectory simply named

CA stood out. Corporate Accounting? She skimmed the listing under it—and stopped at the file named *Texas Accounts* and selected it.

Detailed financial records suddenly appeared on the screen. Numbers that didn't add up were highlighted in red with notes identifying discrepancies and the names of people and companies involved—*the Lone Star file!*

She studied the incriminating evidence against her former employer and its executives. Instead of the millions in profits the company had claimed, they were millions of dollars in debt. Money had been taken out of the employee retirement accounts to cover the debt without the employees' knowledge. If she handed it over to her blackmailer, the crimes would never be prosecuted, yet she couldn't risk Jake's life.

All at once she understood. Monica's messages pleading for Faith to contact her. The relentless snowmobiler and masked stalker. Maybe even the rock slide too? All because of this document.

Faith reeled from the revelation. One thing was certain, whoever was blackmailing her would stop at nothing until he or she had this file. She quickly copied it to Shelly's computer drive. Noticing the Wi-Fi service was now operational on the laptop, Faith got an idea. She opened Shelly's email application and found an old message from Chip with the tour information. She wrote an urgent reply to him with a brief explanation and specific instructions for who to notify, then she attached the Lone Star file.

As soon as she had sent the email, she grabbed a pen and notepad next to the new box of tissues on the nightstand and scribbled the name of the laptop directory where she had copied the incriminating document. Hopefully, Shelly would find it when she returned. Faith decided to leave the threatening note with it. That way her friend would know where to find her if she didn't return.

Rummaging through Shelly's backpack, she retrieved her Yellowstone guidebook to see exactly where the Sapphire Pool was located. Studying the map, Faith realized it was about two miles from the snow lodge. She could still get there in time but had to make one more stop.

As soon as she'd ejected the flash drive, she grabbed her parka and scarf hanging on a coat hook and threw them on.

Satisfied that she'd done all she could, she deposited the flash drive in the pocket of her parka and zipped it, then left the room to rent a pair of cross-country skis from the store in the lodge.

Ten minutes later, she had changed into her ski boots and was carrying her skis and poles down the hall to go outside. Hurrying around the corner, she nearly bumped into a dark-haired woman—and halted when she recognized her.

"Monica! You've got a lot of nerve showing up here after the trouble you've caused me."

Her former friend and coworker responded in an urgent voice. "The flash drive. What did you do with it? I need it back."

"Are you kidding me? You put my life and everyone on my tour in danger by sending that thing to me, and now you want it back?"

"I didn't want to involve you, but I had no choice."

"Sure you did. You could have gone to the police instead of using it for blackmail."

"I figured you of all people would understand since Syngexas double-crossed me like they did you. They had it coming."

"So you blackmailed them because they let you go? That's insane."

"That's why I need that file back, so I can destroy it. The Feds are on my tail, but they have no other evidence against me."

Faith brushed her aside. "That's your problem, not mine."

Monica grabbed her by the arm. "Give me that file!"

"Let go!" After pushing her away, Faith bolted with her gear out the door. Quickly locking her skis in place, she glanced over her shoulder and saw Monica follow her outside. In her haste, the desperate woman slipped on the snow.

"Give me that file, Faith!" she yelled, struggling to get back on her feet.

Faith didn't have time to lose. She unclipped her gloves from the hook on her parka and pulled them on, then wrapped her scarf around her face. Using her poles to push off, she raced across the Upper Basin on a groomed path. A little to the north was the popular geyser trail, where a smattering of tourists were walking. Shelly and Phil were probably among them, but Faith didn't have time to find them, plus the note said she couldn't bring anyone with her—a violation of Jake's third rule of survival: *never go it alone.*

The cold air stung the exposed areas of her face as she recalled her moonlit skiing adventure with him two nights ago. The thought that she might never see him again spurred her even faster. As she stretched her body to the max, she was reminded of his first rule of survival: *know your limits.* She knew hers now and had well exceeded them.

Faith soon became aware that she was being followed. Skiing as fast as her legs would take her, she couldn't lose her shadow. Glancing over her shoulder, she spotted a man wearing a black ski mask—her personal escort.

Jake's second rule of survival echoed in her mind. *Prepare for the unexpected.* She knew she was walking into a trap, but if she could buy Jake more time, it was worth it. Assuming her shadow was working alone.

When Jake skied back to the lodge from the ranger station, thoughts of Faith's soon departure urged him to do something to convince her to stay, yet he still needed to know for sure he could trust her. By keeping secrets, she could have endangered not only herself but also the entire tour group.

Reaching the entrance of the snow lodge, he disengaged his skis and carried them into the lobby.

Shelly frantically rushed to him, holding a small slip of paper. "Jake, Faith is in trouble! She left this in our room."

Confused, he took the note from her and read. Fear

gripped his heart when he realized that Faith, thinking he was in danger, had gone to save him.

Continuing across the winter wilderness, Faith finally arrived at the snow-covered road she remembered from the map. On the other side was Biscuit Basin. Racing against the clock, she quickly crossed the empty road toward her destination, the Sapphire Pool.

With the exception of her shadow, who continued to follow from a distance, Biscuit Basin was devoid of people after the snowstorm last night. Under normal conditions, skiing through the area would be delightful in the fresh powder. Now, however, the snow seemed to shroud the atmosphere in eerie silence.

Crossing the small bridge over the Firehole River, she searched for the thermal pools and geysers she recalled from the map. The trail was covered in deep snow. However, rising steam clouds in the distance should lead her right to her destination, Sapphire Pool.

After a short sprint, she found the strikingly blue body of steaming water. As she quickly released the skis from her boots, Jake's fourth rule of survival came to mind—*always keep an eye out for danger.*

Glimpsing sudden movement to her right, she shifted and saw the masked skier next to her.

He grasped her arm. "Where is it?"

His voice sounded familiar, yet she couldn't quite place it. Now that she'd seen the contents of the file, she knew he'd never let her leave there alive. He probably planned to dispose of her in the thermal pool or in the river. Recalling Jake's fifth rule of survival—*never let a predator know you're afraid*—she put on a brave front and stalled for time while she fingered Jake's knife to extract the blade. "Didn't you learn to say please? I thought this was an exchange. Give me my phone first."

He gripped her arm tighter until it hurt. "I'm done playing games. Hand the file over. Now!"

"Okay, okay. Let go of my arm so I can reach in my pocket."

Reluctantly, he released her. "Don't try anything cute."

The longer she stalled the more time it bought for Shelly and Chip to read her note and email, which increased Jake's odds of survival. Once she handed over the drive, she'd lose all leverage and the clock would stop ticking. Slowly, she lowered her bent arm toward her pocket—in a split-second decision, she thrust her elbow at the man's hovering face.

While he howled in pain, she raced on foot toward the road.

As she lunged for the bridge, a hand grabbed her foot, causing her to tumble and land in a heap of white powder.

Her assailant tried to pin her ankles down, but she kept jerking her legs.

"Coward! Why don't you take off that mask?" Scooping snow in her palm, she hurled it toward his eyes.

Swearing, he relaxed his grip, and she threw more snow in his face. Before he could wipe it away, she jumped to her feet and bolted the rest of the way over the bridge.

At the edge of the road, she spotted a distant snowmobile approaching and waved the driver down.

"Not so fast!" An arm lassoed her around the chest and began pulling her back toward the bridge.

She grabbed a low-hanging branch and clung to it, resisting.

A woman's voice broke in. "That's enough, Rick. I'll take it from here."

*Rick?* Hearing the name dealt Faith a stunning blow, even as she had rallied from the snowmobiler's intervention. When the restraining arm let go, outrage incited her to spin around and snatch the man's mask.

She stared in disbelief at the familiar face glowering at her with a bloody nose.

"Good job, Faith," the female said from behind her. "I knew you'd lead me to him."

Faith slowly turned her head.

Monica was standing beside the snowmobile on the side of the road. She'd taken off her goggles and helmet, releasing her dark hair to fall in ringlets, and was pointing a pistol at Faith and Rick.

"Now hand me the flash drive," she said.

Staring at her betrayer, Faith's hopes for a rescue were cruelly dashed. Jake's Swiss Army knife was no match for a gun. She prayed that Chip and Shelly received her messages in time and were on their way. "I will, but first you owe me an explanation."

Monica snickered. "All right. I'll fill you in while we all take a walk to Biscuit Basin. After coming this far, I'd like to do a little sight-seeing." She motioned with her pistol for Faith and Rick to about-face and start marching.

Grudgingly, Faith turned and plodded in the snow beside her unmasked assailant.

Monica's voice followed them. "You see, it all began when Rick worked for the corporate IT department at Syngexas."

Faith eyed him scowling beside her. She vaguely recalled a long-haired, younger version of the man wearing glasses and roaming the halls of the company, though she didn't have much interaction with that department. Monica, on the other hand, worked in corporate accounting. They must have been assigned to the same projects. The pieces were beginning to fit together into a dark picture. "So you two have been plotting this for years?"

Rick scoffed. "No, it was all my idea. When I discovered what the executives were doing, I created a back door into the financial system. That way I could keep tabs on them, and no one else would know."

"Until I found out," Monica added.

Faith realized Tad must have told Monica he was being blackmailed, and she put two and two together, then wanted a piece of the action after she was laid off. Faith also remembered that Rick had access to Alec's wallet. The cunning man must have rented the snowmobile from Wolf Pack Tours under Alec's name, using his credit card and driver's license.

Travis probably didn't pay close enough attention to the picture. The two resembled each other enough to pass for brothers.

Faith arched a brow at Rick. "Alec didn't hit a tree, did he? You wanted it to appear that way. If Jake and Phil hadn't shown up, you would have killed him."

Rick gave a derisive snort. "As far as I'm concerned, Alec had it coming. He doesn't even know how many times I've bailed him out. If he did, I'd be a partner by now."

Did that include taking care of Alec's estranged wife? No doubt part of Rick's plan was to eliminate his boss so he could take control of the firm. In order to tie up the loose ends from his Syngexas blackmail scheme, he needed to destroy the copy of the Lone Star file and the two people who could connect him to Syngexas—Monica and herself.

It was clear that her scheming companions were more adversaries than partners. As the three trudged across the snow-covered bridge toward the thermal pools, Faith decided to stir the hornet's nest by goading Rick. "So Monica must have figured out I was coming to Yellowstone and told you."

He scoffed, aiming a glare at the woman behind him holding the gun. "No, she followed me here." Then he smirked in Faith's direction. "You should have been more careful with your laptop and cell phone. I'm a computer security expert. I know all the hackers' tricks. All I had to do was read your messages."

*Her laptop?* Rick had stolen it as well as her cell phone, not that she needed either if they succeeded in their plans. He must have seen her email with the trip itinerary. That was how he found out about the tour.

Rick kept boasting to Faith. "If you hadn't blabbed to her where I was meeting you today, my plan to get the file would have worked."

"She didn't," Monica said from behind them. "I have my own ways of tracking people."

Remembering that she'd grabbed her arm in the lodge, Faith felt her sleeve—a tracking device had been planted there!

"Stop!" Monica's voice called.

Faith flinched and halted next to Rick. Shifting her eyes toward the Sapphire Pool, only three feet away, her hopes sank to the bottomless depths of its deadly waters. At least Monica's appearance had disrupted Rick's plans and hopefully bought Jake more time. As long as he was safe, she could face anything, even death.

"Beautiful, isn't it?" Monica taunted. "Like an inviting blue hot tub. What a lovely way to go."

Faith attempted to stall her. "I thought you wanted the file."

"No, I want the file destroyed. I think 200 degrees Fahrenheit should do the trick." The hard tip of her pistol prodded Faith forward.

Refusing to comply, Faith dug her heels deeper in the snow. Monica would have to shoot her because she was not going in. Strengthened and encouraged by an inexplicable peace, she was reminded that as bad as things seemed, she was not alone. Earlier that week she had turned her future over to God. This wasn't the future she had in mind, but if this was His plan, who was she to argue?

Clamping her moist eyelids shut, she uttered a silent prayer and prepared for the flight home to heaven.

The sudden hum of small engines pricked her ear, followed by the sound of men's voices.

Peering over her shoulder, she saw Monica jerk her head. At the same moment, Rick reached for her gun. While the two wrestled for it, Faith sprinted for the bridge.

The sight of Jake crossing it with Gordon, Noah, and two more rangers induced fresh tears to melt the frost on her lashes as her heart rallied with joy.

Gordon shouted to the two schemers. "Police! Drop your weapon!"

With their guns held at the ready, the four lawmen carefully proceeded past Faith. Keeping his eyes fixed forward, the FBI agent spoke to her. "You did good, Faith. We got this."

She gladly left it in their capable hands and hiked in the

snow toward Jake.

Elated to see him, she waited for him to make the first move. After their recent rift, she needed to know where they stood.

Remorse shadowed his eyes, darkening them to a deep sapphire, like the color of the thermal pool. "I read the note you left at the lodge." He paused, his long exhale forming a misty cloud that hovered between them. "I was completely wrong about you. Can you forgive me?"

Love overflowed her heart like an overdue geyser. "For what?" she asked as if it were already forgotten. "However, if you really want to make it up to me, you did promise to take me skiing again…"

His cheeks dimpled as his eyes glimmered in the sun. "In that case, I'd better make good on my promise—but first things first." Stepping toward her, he swiftly took her in his arms.

Yielding to his kiss, she welcomed the stimulating warmth of his lips on hers like a cozy fire in the cold.

Moments later, he tenderly gazed at her, lifting a brow. "Now, about that promise, what would you say to skiing with me tonight?"

She grinned eagerly. "I'd say, it's a date."

## CHAPTER THIRTY-ONE

Sitting on Jake's couch, Faith snuggled next to him while they finished watching the news on television. Leslie was on the screen, standing in front of the Dallas FBI building as she summarized her special feature on Yellowstone. "…And so, in a strange twist, what had started out as a vacation in a winter wonderland ended in a bizarre tale of corporate corruption, blackmail, and greed—and also remarkable courage on the part of an unlikely hero from Dallas, Texas, named Faith Chandler. Now that the Lone Star file has been recovered and is in the custody of the FBI, it looks like two Christmas Humbugs will finally be brought to justice. This is Leslie Turner, reporting for News First Network."

Jake grabbed his remote and switched to a channel that played Christmas music. "Well, that was certainly an interesting spin on our tour last week. I doubt it's the kind of publicity Chip was hoping for when he invited Leslie and Phil to come with us. At least she had some nice things to say about you."

"I'm just glad it's all over, and Rick and Monica are in police custody." Faith smiled, thinking of her best friend at home in Dallas. "I hope Shelly watched it. She'll get a kick out of it."

As Bing Crosby sang White Christmas in the background, Jake rose from the couch. "Come on. You talked me into getting a tree. Now help me finish decorating it before it's time to leave for the candlelight service at church tonight."

Taking his hand, she rose to her feet. After inspecting the lighted branches, she pointed to the top. "It needs a star."

He moved to the small stack of his mother's Christmas ornaments and searched until he found a beautiful, shiny tree topper. "Voilà!" Reaching up, he carefully placed it high on the evergreen, then gazed at Faith. "Well?"

Admiring his handiwork, she clasped her hands together.

"It's perfect."

"Yeah, but my energy bill will go through the roof with all these lights."

She grinned at his teasing. "It's Chip's fault, you know. He's the one who assigned me to your tour group."

Jake rolled his eyes. "Whatever you do, don't remind him of that or he'll come up with a promotion for Valentine's Day."

She burst out laughing.

Amusement twinkled in Jake's eyes. "I'm serious."

"I wish he would give away a Valentine's tour," she said, feeling wistful. "Then if I won, I could come back and visit you."

Jake tilted his head, regarding her intently. "What if you didn't have to leave?"

She sent him a sweet smile. "That would be wonderful, but I wouldn't want to wear out my welcome at Chip and Beth's. It was especially nice of them to invite me to stay at their house this week so I could spend Christmas with you. As much as I'd love to stay longer, come January, I've got to find a job and a place to live."

"I take it you've decided not to accept Chip's job offer?"

"Actually, I'm thinking of changing careers," she said, waiting to see Jake's reaction.

An intrigued grin crossed his face. "Really? To what?"

"I'd like to teach math, once I'm certified."

"That's great. In fact, we need math teachers right here in Moose Run. Meanwhile, you could work for Chip." Jake paused and gave her a significant look. "I also have an offer for you."

His change in tone drew her curiosity. "It doesn't involve driving a snowcoach or giving tours, does it?"

"No, it's nothing like that, but first I have something to show you." He moved to his desk in the corner to retrieve a photo and then handed it to her.

She stared at the picture of the attractive cabin-style house.

"A friend of mine wants to put it on the market. Now that I can afford to buy my own place, I'm planning to make him an offer." He paused, beaming at her. "It turns out you're not the only one making a career change."

She could barely contain her excitement. "You got the park service job?"

His wide smile gave it away. "My new boss called and told me yesterday."

Slanting her head, she waggled her brows. "What other surprises are you keeping, Jake Mitchell?"

"Only one more." He strode to his desk again and opened a drawer. He returned with a small wrapped package.

When he gave it to her, she shook it lightly, intrigued. "A Christmas present?"

He gestured for her to sit on the couch by the tree, and he sat beside her. "Open it and find out."

She studied him for a moment, then eagerly ripped the paper. Inside was a jewelry box. As she stared at it, her heart quickened with anticipation.

After she paused, he reached over and opened it for her.

The gorgeous diamond ring inside glittered under the Christmas lights, dazzling her. "Oh, Jake…it's beautiful."

"It was Mom's. She would want you to have it."

Deeply moved, Faith placed a hand over her heart. "I don't know what to say…"

"You know, back when we became engaged, I planned to give you a ring for Christmas but never got the chance. I'm hoping things will work out differently this time since I'm giving you the ring first."

Her heart fluttered like hummingbird wings. "This time?"

Bending down on one knee, he appealed to her in a tender voice. "You've always been the only one for me, Faith. And now that we're together again, I want you to be with me forever as my wife."

Warmth radiated through her from head to toe as tears of joy moistened her eyes. "Remember that shooting star, when you said prayer works better than wishes? Well, this is what I prayed for."

Suddenly, they were love-struck teens again, their lips melding in an exuberant kiss as *I'll be Home for Christmas* played in the background.

When the song ended, a distant howling echoed from outside.

Faith paused to listen. "Did you hear that? I think it's our lone wolf."

Jake sat beside her on the sofa and held her close, waiting as another wolf responded. Soon both wolves howled in unison.

She smiled. "Sounds like he's finally found his mate."

Jake nuzzled his nose to hers. "And I'll never let her go again."

# Author Note

Yellowstone is one of my favorite national parks. No matter how many times I go there, the grandeur of the landscape and the awesome thermal features never fail to amaze me. In winter, however, Yellowstone becomes a different park altogether.

Years ago, I took a winter tour with my husband and was struck by the park's transformation from the popular summer attraction most people are familiar with to a quiet winter wonderland. Instead of the usual cars, motorcycles and RVs lining the roads during the peak season, only snowcoaches and snowmobiles were allowed in most areas of the park, including Old Faithful. Exploring the pristine wilderness with a small group of people made the trip even more interesting and enjoyable and created a unique, unforgettable experience.

Among my winter tour adventures, I went snowshoeing for the first time, and like Faith, I developed blisters from my brand-new snow boots. To my relief, I was able to patch up my sore feet enough to go on cross country ski trips to Tower Fall and Lone Star Geyser later that week.

I distinctly remember the day we skied to Lone Star Geyser. It was minus twenty degrees Fahrenheit. In fact, our guide actually demonstrated how cold it was by tossing a cup of boiling hot coffee in the air so we could watch it freeze before it hit the ground. I'd never been anywhere that cold before and didn't know how I would survive. However, once I started moving, the exertion from skiing did a remarkable job of keeping me warm under my layers. Despite the bitter cold, it turned out to be a fun day, and we were rewarded with a front-row seat when the solitary geyser erupted. We also saw lots of wildlife on the tour, including bison, foxes, and trumpeter swans. Though we didn't see any wolves, the elusive creatures captured my imagination and still do today.

Recently, we went back to Yellowstone to revisit some of the places from our tour. In creating the fictional town of Moose Run for this story, I tried to capture the frontier charm of towns like West Yellowstone and Gardiner, Montana. During our winter tour, we actually stayed in the historic Mammoth Hot Springs Hotel and the Old Faithful Snow Lodge. On our return visit, we discovered that the hotel was in the process of a major upgrade. However, the park was essentially the same as it's always been, which is refreshing, given our culture of constant change. It reminds me of the importance of preserving our national parks so we can enjoy the beauty and awesome wonder of God's creation for generations to come.

And while I'm on the subject of our national parks, I'm reminded that this is the fourth and final book in my Peril in the Park series. What an amazing adventure it's been! I couldn't have done it without readers like you, as well as my publisher, Miralee Ferrell. Thank you all! In addition, I want to thank my husband, Jeff, for his support and encouragement of my writing and also for taking me on all the trips to Yellowstone, which sparked the idea for this book.

It's been such a pleasure to share these stories with you. I hope they have inspired you to visit and support our national parks—and most importantly, to give praise to the One who created it all.

Happy Adventures!
Gayla


You can connect with Gayla at any of the following places:

Website: www.gaylakhiss.com
Facebook: https://goo.gl/BrIW6P
Goodreads: https://goo.gl/ywcRaL
BookBub: www.bookbub.com/profile/gayla-k-hiss
Amazon Author Page: https://goo.gl/WrzGcD


If you enjoyed this book, please consider posting a review.

# Book Club Questions

1. When things go badly for Faith, she starts to reexamine her life and priorities. How can going through hard times turn out to be a blessing in disguise? When have you experienced this?

2. A secret from Faith's past threatens her future with Jake. Why is it important to be honest with those we care about? What could happen when we're not honest with them?

3. In the past, Faith has run away from painful circumstances. How do you cope with difficult situations in both destructive and constructive ways?

4. Faith and Jake play a game of 'starting over' without the history of their past mistakes. How has God given you a 'fresh start' in life? (See Bible verses: Psalm 103:12; Isaiah 43:19, 25; Lamentations 3:22-23; John 1:12, 5:24; Romans 6:4; 2 Corinthians 5:17; Colossians 1:13-14; Revelation 21:5)

5. In her desire for material wealth and financial security Faith has lost sight of the importance of spiritual riches. What challenges do you have in balancing the material with the spiritual?

6. Faith believes in God but has difficulty trusting Him with practical things like finding a job. In which areas of your life do you need to trust God more?

7. An inner voice prompts Faith to do the right thing. Have you heard this voice? If so, what did it tell you to do? What is it saying to you now?